Dear Reader,

The editors at Harlequin and Silh
bring you a brand-new featured a
Signature Select aims to single c
themes and oft-requested classic
authors and present them to you
truly striking covers.

You may notice a number of different colored bands on the spine
of this book. Each color corresponds to a different type of reading
experience in the new Signature Select program. The Spotlight books
will offer a single "big read" by a talented series author, the Collections
will present three novellas on a selected theme in one volume, the
Sagas will contain sprawling, sometimes multi-generational family tales
(often related to a favorite family first introduced in series) and the
Miniseries will feature requested, previously published books, with two
or, occasionally, three complete stories in one volume. The Signature
Select program will offer one book in each of these categories per
month, and fans of limited continuity series will also find these
continuing stories under the Signature Select umbrella.

In addition, these volumes will bring you bonus features...different
in every single book! You may learn more about the author in an
extended interview, more about the setting or inspiration for the book,
more about subjects related to the theme and, often, a bonus short read
will be included.

Watch for new stories from Vicki Lewis Thompson, Lori Foster,
Donna Kauffman, Marie Ferrarella, Merline Lovelace, Roberta Gellis,
Suzanne Forster, Stephanie Bond and scores more of the brightest
talents in romance fiction!

We have an exciting year ahead!

Warm wishes for happy reading,

Marsha Zinberg

Marsha Zinberg
Executive Editor
The Signature Select Program

Signature Select™

SAGA

MacAllister's Return

JOAN ELLIOTT PICKART

Silhouette® Books

Published by Silhouette Books

America's Publisher of Contemporary Romance

SILHOUETTE BOOKS

ISBN 0-373-28506-X

MacALLISTER'S RETURN

Copyright © 2005 by Joan Elliott Pickart.

This edition published by arrangement with Harlequin Books S.A.

® and TM are trademarks of Harlequin Books S.A., used under license.
Trademarks indicated with ® are registered in the United States Patent
and Trademark Office, the Canadian Trade Marks Office and in other
countries.

Visit Silhouette Books at www.eHarlequin.com

Printed in U.S.A.

Dear Reader,

When we bid the MacAllister family farewell last summer, I told you I didn't really know if they would return sometime in the future. I later received an exciting invitation to take part in the new Signature Select Series and bring the MacAllisters back one more time. Therefore, the title *MacAllister's Return* fits this novel twofold.

Writing this book not only gave me a chance to tell Jesse's story, but also allowed me to say a final and proper goodbye to the wise and wonderful Robert MacAllister. I'll miss him. In fact, I have a feeling that I will miss the entire MacAllister family, so don't be surprised if yet another generation of MacAllisters demands to be heard.

Again, I thank all of you for your support and loyalty as you continue to read my books, and for the terrific letters you take the time to write to me. Without you, I would not be able to tell my stories.

I sincerely hope you enjoy *MacAllister's Return*.

Warmest regards.

Joan Elliott Pickart

For all that was
For all that is
For all that might have been

Chapter 1

A chill wind whipped across the small cemetery, shredding wilted flowers and scattering scraps of paper dropped by careless hands. Ominously dark clouds rolled across the gray sky with the threat of rain, and thunder rumbled in the distance.

Jesse Burke was oblivious to the cold that was typical in northern Nevada in January. The icy waves of grief consuming him were far greater than the lowering temperature from the approaching storm. He stared at the matching caskets that would soon be lowered into the ground and covered with dirt, never to be seen again.

Jesse dropped his chin to his chest and sighed as he shoved his hands into the pockets of his black trousers.

An achy sensation seized his throat and his eyes burned with unshed tears.

Dear God, he thought, his beloved parents were dead. Dead. He knew it was true and yet…how could this have happened? How could this be real? They'd waved goodbye to him as they drove away from the ranch. They'd been heading into town for the weekly shopping that was part of their normal routine. But they never came home. Because they were dead.

A raging storm had seemed to come out of nowhere, turning the dirt road into a slippery path of mud. The truck coming toward his parents' vehicle had skidded in the sludge and hit them head-on. And in that fateful second caused by nature's fickle touch, Joe and Phyllis Burke were no more.

"God," Jesse said, then shifted his gaze heavenward, struggling to retain control of his emotions as he drew a shuddering breath.

"Jesse."

He turned his head to see a small woman in her seventies standing a few feet away, shivering in her lightweight black coat. She hunched her bony shoulders against the cold.

"Maddie," he said. "This has got to be hell for you. My folks were your best friends for many years."

Maddie Clemens nodded and dashed an errant tear from her wrinkled cheek.

"At least they went together, Jesse," she said, her voice quivering. "They would have been lost without each other."

"Somehow," Jesse said, with a snort of disgust, "that doesn't make me feel any better. They were good, decent people, the best. They worked so damn hard for so long on that patch of land, scraping out a living, and for what? To die on a muddy road in the rain? Is that it, Maddie? Dad has a heart attack three years ago, I come back home, give up my dreams to work with him on that damnable ranch because I owe them that, could never really repay them for being such loving parents. Then in a blink it's all gone, it's over. They're dead."

"Jesse, honey, we need to go back to the house," Maddie said. "The neighbors are gathering there, bringing food. They'll want to see you, offer their sympathies, share a meal with you."

"I'm not in the mood for a party, Maddie."

"It's custom, Jesse, what your mother and father would expect you to do."

"I don't have a mother and father," Jesse said, nearly yelling as he spun around to face her. "I'm thirty-two years old and I have nothing. My parents are gone, my career is a forgotten dream, I can't stomach the thought of staying on that ranch and having a heart attack in a few years like my dad did. He loved the land. I hate it. I hate it, Maddie. God, I feel so empty. Alone. I have nothing left."

Fresh tears spilled onto Maddie's cheeks and she pressed trembling fingertips to her chapped lips for a moment.

"I can't bear to see you like this," she said. "I love you so much, Jesse, like a son I never had. I watched you grow up to be such a fine man, loving your folks just as they did you. They were so proud when you became the assistant district attorney over there in Culver.

"When you gave that up to come home to help your father after the heart attack, they were torn, wanted to tell you not to come, not to walk away from what you'd worked so hard for, yet thanking the good Lord every day that you'd made it possible for them to stay on the ranch. The land was part of their souls, Jesse, and you made them happy, right up until…until they weren't with us anymore."

Tears streamed down Maddie's face and along her neck. "Hang on to that, Jesse. Know in your heart what a fine, fine thing you did for Phyllis and Joe. Cherish it. You were a loving son to loving parents. That's a rare and beautiful thing."

"Yeah, right," he said, a rough edge to his voice. "And what do I have to show for it? Nothing. Hell, Maddie, I know I'm standing here feeling so damn sorry for myself, but I can't explain how alone I feel, how empty and useless and… Ah, hell, forget it. I'm whining like a kid. I'm alone and I'd better start accepting that fact." He looked at the caskets again. "Somehow."

"No, no, no," she said, shaking her head as a sob caught in her throat. "This is wrong. Phyllis and Joe wouldn't want you to be suffering like this, feeling as you are. No. It's time you knew the truth. It's time. Phyllis and Joe would want me to ease your pain, I know they would. You're not alone, Jesse. You're not."

"What are you talking about, Maddie?" Jesse took a step toward her. "It's time I knew the truth about...about what?"

"Jesse, honey, listen to me," Maddie said, wrapping her hands around her elbows as she seemed to consider her words. "You're not alone because...Jesse, Phyllis and Joe weren't your birth parents. No. I brought you to them when you were no more than a day old. They loved you like their own, cried tears of joy when I placed you in Phyllis's arms, but..."

Her voice grew stronger and she squared her shoulders as she relived the past. "They were in their forties then, you know that. Had tried for years to have a baby, and there you were. So perfect, so beautiful. It was meant to be, don't you see?"

"Are you saying I was adopted?" Jesse said incredulously. "That's crazy. Why would they keep something like that a secret from me? Why would they allow me to believe that all these years they were my natural parents?"

"It had to be that way."

"Why, Maddie?"

"Because you might have wondered about your birth parents later on. Gone looking for the adoption papers and discovered there weren't any. You would have had questions that your folks and I agreed should never be answered. But now? They'd want you to know you're not alone."

"You're not making any sense," Jesse said, frowning. "You're speaking in riddles, Maddie. Come on.

Talk to me. I want to hear whatever this hidden truth is."

Maddie lifted her chin. "Not now. You should be at the house where you belong, greeting those who care about you, who loved your folks and want to express from their hearts how much they'll be missed. You do what's right, and when the neighbors all leave later, I'll sit down with you and tell you what it's time you know."

"Now look—"

"That's my final word." She turned and started away, stumbling slightly on the uneven ground.

"Hell," Jesse said.

He looked at the caskets one last time, then nodded at the two men in the distance who were waiting to complete the work that would make two fresh graves in the shabby cemetery.

Jesse walked slowly toward the rusty pickup truck he'd driven from the house. He'd insisted that his parents take his sturdy SUV into town that fateful day, but even the bigger, heavier vehicle hadn't been able to save their lives. Nothing had.

His parents, he thought, as he watched Maddie chug away in her pickup, which was in worse condition than the one he was using. His *adoptive* parents? Was Maddie getting senile, losing touch with reality? Her story was crazy—that he'd been adopted, but there weren't any legal papers to prove it, or some such nonsense. In that moment when he'd been whining like a child about being left all alone, had she mentally scrambled for something to make him feel better?

But then again…

He could remember asking his folks why he didn't look a bit like them, why he was six feet tall when his dad was no more than five-eight and his mother four inches shorter than that. Why he had dark brown hair when his mother was blond and his father had gone through his school years with nicknames like Carrot Top and Fire Head because of his flaming red hair.

They'd shrugged off his questions with the explanation that he took after other Burkes who were no longer living. His wide shoulders and muscular build compared to their slight frames were a throwback to other generations.

Why did the family photo albums begin with pictures of him as a newborn baby, with no snapshots of his mother pregnant with the coming child? They hadn't owned a camera before he was born, he'd been told. They'd taken precious coins from the sugar jug on the kitchen counter to buy a camera when he arrived so they could have a record of him growing up.

Their answers had seemed logical, Jesse thought, as he slid behind the wheel of the truck. He'd asked his questions once and had been satisfied with what he'd heard. That had been that.

But now Maddie was saying he was adopted? Jesse's mind raced. *She'd* brought him to Phyllis and Joe when he was one day old? Ah, damn, that could have been possible because Maddie had been a midwife in those days, delivered babies all over the county.

Jesse smacked the steering wheel with the palm of

one hand, then turned the key in the ignition. The engine started on the third try and he drove away in the rattling truck, allowing himself one last look at the cemetery in the rearview mirror.

Ten minutes later he slowed as he approached the small wood-frame home where he'd grown up. Cars lined the driveway and the edge of the dirt road in front of the house.

People he'd known all his life were waiting for him, he thought, and he no doubt would have found a modicum of comfort in their embraces and from the kind words they'd speak. But not now. Not after what Maddie had said. And he wasn't going to learn this elusive truth from her until the last of the neighbors had gone.

"Everybody go home," Jesse said aloud, although there was no one near enough to hear him. He shook his head.

Nice, Burke, really classy, he admonished himself. These were good, down-to-earth people who had loved and respected his folks and treated him like one of their own family his entire life. He owed these neighbors sincere gratitude for being here, owed it to his parents to behave in the proper manner.

His parents? he thought, as he parked on the side of the road. His adoptive parents? If that was really true, how many people waiting for him inside the house knew that? Wouldn't someone, at some point over the years, have slipped up, said something to him that might make him realize that the Burkes' newborn son had been brought to them by Maddie the midwife?

How could a whole community of people keep a secret like that?

Ah, damn, so many questions. So many. And he intended to get the answer to every single one of them.

Jesse slammed the door to the truck and strode toward the house.

The following hours were a blur. He was, Jesse realized, performing as expected. People smiled at him, hugged him, said things that he couldn't remember seconds after the words were spoken. He offered tissues to weeping women and shook the work-roughened hands of countless men. A plate of food materialized in front of him when he'd been told to sit in his father's favorite threadbare chair. He consumed the offering, having no idea what he was eating.

He continually checked to be certain that Maddie was still there, made sure she didn't leave before keeping her promise to finish her bizarre tale when the company finally made their way home.

The threatening storm arrived at last and rain beat against the house, rattling the windows and hammering on the patched roof. People began to peer out to check the condition of the dirt road, wondering aloud if it might be best to leave while the routes were passable.

Yes, Jesse mentally yelled. Go. Thanks for everything, but for God's sake go.

And at long last, they went.

Women covered the food and placed it in the refrigerator, telling Jesse not to worry about returning dishes, that they'd be checking on him in the days ahead and each would reclaim what was hers. The men offered to help him on the ranch in any spare time they could find.

More hugs. More handshakes. More expressions of gratitude for their kindness, for coming to say good-bye to Phyllis and Joe Burke. His parents.

Then silence as Jesse closed the door behind the last of the neighbors and turned to find Maddie standing in the middle of the small living room. The rain had slackened to a slow, steady drizzle, and the house was gloomy and dark with the approaching evening.

Jesse snapped on a lamp, casting a circle of light that left Maddie in the shadows. He took off his suit coat and tossed it onto the faded sofa, then added his tie.

"Sit down, Maddie," he said roughly. "I've kept my part of the bargain and now it's your turn. I want the truth. All of it."

His breath caught as the old woman moved into the circle of light. She seemed to have aged even more since they'd spoken at the cemetery. Her wrinkled skin was pale, and dark smudges stood out in stark relief beneath her tired eyes. She sank onto an easy chair and clutched her hands in her lap. Jesse sat down on the sofa, leaning forward to rest his elbows on his knees, and lacing his fingers together as he stared at her.

"You're exhausted," he said. "I should do the right thing and tell you to go home and get some rest. That we'll discuss all this tomorrow. But I can't do that, Maddie."

"I know, Jesse," she said, weariness evident in her voice. "I believe with all my heart that Phyllis and Joe would want me to tell you the truth, because they couldn't bear to know how alone you feel now that they're gone."

Jesse nodded.

"The Phyllis and Joe Burke that you knew," Maddie said, "were happy, fulfilled people because they had you as a son. But before you came into their world Phyllis was a sad and brokenhearted woman because she couldn't have children. Oh, how she yearned for a baby, cried in my arms so many times because she didn't have a child. Joe was sorrowful, too, but he had a little easier time of it because he worked so hard on this land, was able to blank his mind for hours at a stretch.

"They tried to adopt, but none of the pregnant girls who saw their application chose them because they had so little to offer in the way of opportunities for a baby. Once Phyllis and Joe were in their early forties they knew there was no more hope of being picked. My heart just ached for them."

Maddie stopped speaking and stared into space as she mentally relived old memories.

"Go on," Jesse said finally.

"There was a storm, much like the one today, which came in fast and made the roads impossible to drive on," Maddie continued. "A young couple got stuck in the mud and saw the lights of my house in the distance. They walked through the rain to get to my door.

"The woman was pregnant, eight months along, and the hard trek had brought on her labor. They were cold and wet and scared to death because their baby was coming too early. How relieved they were when I told them I was a midwife. I could tell from their clothes, the quality of their wedding rings, just the way they talked and carried themselves that they were wealthy, not like folks in these parts. They spoke of a two-year-old son back home, staying with his grandparents.

"These people, I thought, have everything. Money, social status…and they were about to have their second child, while my poor Phyllis was living hand-to-mouth, with no baby to hold in her arms. Life seemed so unfair when I dwelled on it all.

"Anyway, the woman had a long labor. The man was frantic, wanted her taken to the hospital, but there was no way to get an ambulance to my place on those roads. She finally gave birth to a tiny but healthy baby girl she said they were naming Sarah. I gave the woman a whiff of ether so she could sleep, get the rest she needed, because she was exhausted. The man sat in my rocker by the fire in the living room, holding his new daughter.

"But then while the woman slept, she gave birth to another baby they didn't even know was there. A boy. You. I didn't think it through, Jesse, I just acted from my heart…for Phyllis, for Joe. I wrapped you in a blanket and set you on my own bed in the other room. You were small but so fine, so beautiful, and slept like an angel. I didn't tell those people about you."

Jesse felt the color drain from his face. "You…you

stole their son? They didn't know they were expecting twins so you just kept one and… My God, Maddie, how could you do such a despicable thing?"

"If you could have seen the look on your mother's face when I placed that baby in her arms you'd know the answer to that," Maddie said, her voice rising. "I've never seen such pure joy, such happiness, as I did when I brought you to your parents."

"They weren't my parents," Jesse yelled, lunging to his feet.

"They were, Jesse. From the moment they saw you, held you, you were their son. Oh, how they loved you. You know that. You grew up in this house with that love. You know what you meant to them."

"And what about the woman who gave birth to me?" Jesse splayed one hand on his chest. "Did you give one thought to her, to her husband? Think about how they would feel if they knew what you had done?"

"The ambulance finally got through to my house," Maddie said, "and off they went to the hospital, so happy with their new daughter. They had everything, don't you see? Everything. It wasn't fair, Jessie, that your folks had nothing. Not fair. I had a chance to fix that and…and I did."

"My God," Jesse repeated, dragging one hand through his hair. "I don't believe this. And my folks knew you had stolen, kidnapped me, and they went along with it? They didn't think about that couple, ei-ther?"

"They loved you, Jesse," Maddie said quietly.

"They didn't have the right to love me," he yelled. "I wasn't theirs to have." He began to pace around the small room, breathing heavily as he replayed in his mind what he had just learned. "And the neighbors? All those people who were here today? Didn't anyone question how the Burkes suddenly had a newborn baby?"

"Your parents and I worked out our story and I went to the neighbors, one by one. I said a young, unwed mother had come to me to give birth, and wanted to place her baby up for adoption. I said she panicked for some reason and left my house before I could get the proper papers signed. I swore everyone to secrecy because I knew the authorities would come for you if they knew there weren't any legal documents and… You were never told the truth…by anyone…until now. Oh, Jesse, you know what happy parents you had and—"

"Don't call them my parents," he said, slicing one hand through the air. "Phyllis and Joe Burke were not my parents. They were party to a terrible crime that you committed, Maddie. I loved them and you unconditionally all of my life and now I realize I really didn't know you people, what horrendous things you were capable of doing.

"And God help me, I don't even know who *I* am." Jesse stopped his pacing and came close to where Maddie sat, towering above her. "No wonder I didn't look anything like my…like them. No wonder I was never really content working this land. I was forced into a mold where I didn't fit, didn't belong. I gave up my ca-

reer for my…for Joe, to help him after his heart attack
because I felt I owed them that for loving me as they
did. *But they loved a child they had no right to have,
no right to call their son.*"

"You had a good life here, Jesse."

"It wasn't my life to live," he said, throwing out his
hands. "I belonged with that couple, my real parents,
with my twin sister and that other child they had. They
were my family, Maddie. They held the key to my
identity, to who I am. How could you and my…Phyl-
lis and Joe live with yourselves, knowing what you'd
done to those people, to me? How did all of you sleep
at night with that on your conscience?"

"We loved you. That's all that mattered."

"It was all a lie," Jesse said, his voice flat and weary.
"My entire life has been a lie. I'm not Jesse Joseph
Burke, son of Phyllis and Joe. I wasn't raised by decent, honest people who… You, them, you're evil. You
ripped a child away from where he belonged. Who
were they, Maddie? Who are my real parents?"

"MacAllister," she said, her eyes filling with tears.
"I can't remember the man's name. The woman was
Debra or Deedee, I don't know for sure anymore, and
the baby girl was Sarah. They were from California.
Rich people from California. The kind of people who
get everything they want just by wishing for it.

"They didn't suffer from what I did because they
never knew you existed. I didn't cause them any grief,
but the happiness you brought to Joe and Phyllis can't

even be described in words, it was so beautiful. You were *their* son, Jesse. It was meant to be."

Jesse stared up at the ceiling for a moment to gain control of his emotions, then looked at Maddie again.

"No. I was not their son. You listen to me, Maddie. Hear me speaking to you very clearly. I don't want to hear the names Phyllis and Joe Burke again, and I don't want to see you. I'm selling this ranch and leaving this lie behind me.

"I'm going to find my real family. I probably won't even approach them, speak to them, because they don't deserve to suffer the pain now of what you did so many years ago. I just want to see them, learn what they look like, how they live, with the hope that when I do I'll have a sense of who I am. Now? I'm an empty shell without an identity. I'm no one."

Chapter 2

Two Months Later

Jesse sat in the rather nondescript dark rented car and stared at the large, ranch-style house a short distance down the street. Darkness had fallen and the warm glow of muted, welcoming light was visible at the windows, where the drapes had been drawn.

This was the third day in a row he'd done this, he mused, and so far he hadn't seemed to attract any worried attention from people in the neighborhood. For the third day and into the night he'd attempted to come to grips with the realization that the woman he saw coming and going from the well-kept home was his sister, Sarah.

His sister. His twin sister. They had been born on the same stormy night in Maddie Clemens's house and should have been raised together by the parents he now knew were Ryan and Deedee MacAllister.

He and Sarah should have shared birthday parties marking their matching day of celebration, and been together for Christmas and Thanksgiving holidays, plus the day-to-day living with the special bond that twins had. Oh, yeah, that's how it should have been. They had an older brother, too, named Teddy.

Jesse shook his head and forced himself to unclench his jaw and dispel the anger that consumed him each time he dwelled on what Maddie had done and what Phyllis and Joe Burke had been a party to. God, thirty-two years of lies and deception by people he'd loved unconditionally, trusted, respected. People who were not who they'd presented themselves to be. What they had done was unforgivable.

Jesse sighed, then drew a steadying breath.

He'd put the ranch in Nevada up for sale, including all the shabby furniture in the house, and had set out on his quest. It had taken him weeks to find the right MacAllister family in California. *His* family.

He'd driven by Ryan and Deedee's attractive home, his parents' home, but hadn't garnered the courage to wait and watch for a glimpse of what they looked like. He wasn't ready for that yet, so had concentrated on his twin sister, Sarah.

They certainly didn't look a bit alike, but that wasn't unusual for fraternal twins, he supposed. Sarah was about five foot six, slender, and had short, curly black hair. From what he could discern across the distance when she emerged from the house, she was very beautiful. Very, *very* beautiful.

She had a great rapport with the three children she drove away with each morning. He could see them all smiling, and knew they often laughed. Sarah was obviously a terrific mother. But where was the father of those kids? Sarah's husband? There had been no sign of a man coming or going during the hours Jesse had sat there drinking in the sight of his sister.

The facts were pointing to Sarah being a single mother. Divorced? Widowed? She was devoted to her family and had apparently taken a job that would allow her to be with the kids before and after school. An attractive woman who appeared to be in her early sixties arrived at the house each day in the late afternoon, and Sarah left, returning close to midnight. Then the older woman drove away.

Jesse had considered following Sarah yesterday, but canceled the thought in the next instant, deciding to stay put and be assured she arrived back home safely. He didn't want to get too close to his sister, run the risk of his willpower going south, to the point where he found himself speaking to her.

No. He'd made up his mind that it would be a cruel and selfish act to confront the MacAllisters with the truth of his existence, tell them the horrendous story of what had happened that long-ago, rainy night, rip them up emotionally the way he was. No, he wasn't going to do that. They didn't know he existed and there was nothing to be served by revealing his identity now. They would suffer the kind of pain he was experiencing, and he had no intention of doing that to them.

So he lurked in the shadows and stared at his sister, nephews and niece. When he felt mentally stronger he would repeat this routine in front of Ryan and Deedee MacAllister's house, soak up the sight of the parents he'd never known.

The purpose in all of this, Jesse thought, was to attempt to achieve a sense of who he was, an identity to replace the one torn brutally away by the words Maddie had spoken on the day of his…of Phyllis and Joe's funeral.

He was Sarah's twin brother. Teddy's younger sibling, although he'd been unable to uncover any clue as to where his brother lived. Jesse was Ryan and Deedee MacAllister's son. *Their* son. Not Phyllis and Joe Burke's child. He was a MacAllister. But the MacAllisters would never know that.

The MacAllisters, Jesse thought. The results of his research, once he had found the right ones, had been a real eye-opener. The Ventura MacAllisters were a huge bunch of people, an extremely large family.

They were movers and shakers, too, involved in a multitude of charities and a variety of occupations. They obviously possessed a great deal of money and power, and were held in high regard by the citizens of Ventura. Jesse could be proud to be a MacAllister even though he would never take his place among them.

Well, *Jesse Burke*, he thought, how many days and nights are you going to do this stare-at-Sarah routine?

How many hours would he spend dwelling on what should have been? He knew who he was now, who he could and should have been, and once he'd etched the images of his real parents indelibly in his mind he would leave Ventura and start over somewhere else. Alone.

Alone, Jesse mentally repeated. The enormous Mac-Allister clan was not his to have, to be a part of. It would be too cruel to disrupt and devastate so many lives the way his had been. This would be his last night of spying on Sarah MacAllister Barstow, married or apparently no longer married to a man named Barry. Jesse would soak up the sight of his…his mother and father tomorrow, and that would be it. He'd leave this town and never come back again. He'd leave as he'd come—alone.

Jesse shifted in the seat, his muscles cramped and achy from the endless hours he'd spent sitting in the car. In the next instant he tensed in shocked surprise as the driver's door was flung open and a large hand clamped onto his upper arm.

"Okay, buddy," a man said, "the game is over. Get out of the vehicle slow and easy."

"Who—"

"Do it," the man said, increasing the pressure on Jesse's arm to the point of pain. "Now."

A flash of fury rose within Jesse and his first instinct was to strike out with his free hand. In the next instant he registered the fact that there was another man standing behind the first one, reducing the odds of his being able to escape from being robbed or having his car stolen, or whatever these two wanted from him.

Granted, the interior light of the vehicle made it possible for him to see that both guys appeared to be in their early sixties. But the strength in the hand gripping his arm said this one at least was in excellent physical condition. Better to go along with their demands for now and watch for a chance to make his move.

Jesse got out of the car and yanked his arm free. The man slammed the car door.

"Assume the position," he said.

"What?" Jesse exclaimed.

"Put your hands on the trunk and spread your legs," the man ordered.

"The hell I will." Jesse felt a muscle ticking in his jaw. "Who are you guys and what do you want?"

"We're retired cops," the man said, "which gives you a choice. Deal with us or we call for a squad car and you can explain everything to the boys in blue downtown."

"Explain what?" Jesse said. "I haven't broken any laws. You're harassing a private citizen, buddy."

"Right," the man said. "A private citizen who has been sitting in this vehicle for the past three days and nights, watching the house where my daughter and grandchildren live. You're either waiting for a chance to rob the place or you're a pervert after my grandkids.

Or maybe a stalker with a thing for Krista Kelly. Start talking, hotshot."

His daughter? Jesse did a double take. His grandchildren? Dear God, this man was Ryan MacAllister. This man was…was his father!

"Well?" Ryan MacAllister said.

"I've got nothing to say," Jesse stated, "because I've done nothing wrong."

"Let's go into the house, Ryan," the other man said. "We can call for the uniforms when we get inside."

"Now wait just a damn minute," Jesse said. "There's no law against a man sitting in his vehicle." He couldn't go into that house, Sarah's home. No. It was difficult enough to realize that he was inches away from his real father without… "I'll leave and I won't come back. Okay? Satisfied?"

"Not even close," Ryan said. "We're all going inside the house. We can do it the easy way or the hard way, it's up to you. Don't get cocky because Ted and I are eligible for senior discounts, sleazeball. You've got some stuff but there isn't enough of you to take on the two of us."

Jesse's gaze flickered quickly between the two men, seeing the width of their shoulders, the size of their hands, the flat bellies and broad chests beneath the polo shirts they wore. Those were definitely well defined muscles on those arms and… Hell.

"Okay, okay," Jesse said. "But let's just talk out here. There's no need to go inside."

"Let's hear what he has to say, Ryan," Ted said.

"Oh, I'm all ears," Ryan said, crossing his arms over his chest. "Let's start with your name."

"Burke. Jesse Burke."

"Well, Jesse Burke," Ryan said, "why are you so interested in my daughter's home?"

"I'm not," Jesse said quickly. "What I mean is, I wasn't concentrating on one house. I don't know your daughter, or your grandchildren or whoever Krista Kelly is. See that sticker on the windshield of my car? It's a rental. I'm considering moving here…with my wife and kids, and wanted to get a feel for the neighborhood, decide if it's a decent place to bring my family."

The two men exchanged looks, then Ted smiled and shook his head. "That is so bogus," he said.

No joke, Jesse thought, but it was the best he'd been able to come up with that fast.

"In the house, Mr. Burke," Ted said. "But first you're going to spread 'em like a good little boy because we're asking you so politely to do that."

Jesse sighed, then turned and planted his hands flat on the trunk of the car. Ted patted him down with what was obviously expertise, then Ryan gripped his upper arm again and the trio started across the street.

"Get your hand off of me," Jesse said, a rough edge to his voice.

"Ah, you blew it," Ryan said. "You didn't ask politely the way we did. Too bad."

Oh, Lord, Jesse thought, sweat beading his brow. He was about to enter his sister's home. And that was his *father's* strong hand cutting off the circulation in his arm. *His father.* He couldn't handle this. It was just too much to deal with all at once. At least Sarah wasn't home yet from wherever she went every night.

What in the hell was he going to do? They hadn't bought his ridiculous story about why he'd been parked on the street for three days. Maybe the best thing was to just let himself be hauled off to jail for loitering or whatever, get away from these people—his family— before he blurted out the truth and destroyed their lives. Okay. Yeah. That was good. That was his plan.

As the three men went up the walk leading to the house, the front door opened and a woman appeared.

"We got your guy, Deedee," Ryan said. "Says his name is Jesse Burke."

Your guy, Deedee? Jesse's heart hammered. *He was her son.*

Moments later Jesse was propelled into a large, nicely furnished living room and planted firmly in an easy chair. He drew a deep, steadying breath, then raised his head slowly to look at Deedee MacAllister. *His mother.*

Oh, man, she was so pretty, he thought. Her hair was a soft gray and she had big brown eyes. Her features were delicate and a few freckles dusted her nose.

He'd seen her come here each evening but hadn't paid much attention to her appearance other than to conclude that she was attractive. But now he knew he was staring at the woman who had been in Maddie's house that stormy night so long ago. The woman who had had her baby boy stolen from her, a son she never knew she had.

"You made a mistake, young man," Deedee said. "You chose the wrong house, the wrong people. I was a police officer's wife for many, many years and there was no way you were going to go unnoticed by me. I suggest you cooperate with my husband and Ted and tell them—us—what your intentions were."

"He did." Ted chuckled. "He was deciding if this was a safe neighborhood to move his family to."

"Oh, dear," Deedee said. "That's very far-fetched. Couldn't you do better than that, Mr. Burke?"

"I have nothing more to say," Jesse replied. "Call your cop friends and have them take me downtown. I'll deal with them, not you."

"A chip on your shoulder is not going to help the present situation," Deedee said. "We don't want to cause you problems with the police if it isn't necessary, but you must admit that your behavior the past few days has been rather questionable."

Jesse shrugged.

Deedee tilted her head to one side and narrowed her eyes. "You know," she said, "you look familiar to me, somehow. I can't quite put my finger on what it is but I feel as though I've seen you before."

"No," Jesse said quietly. "Believe me, you haven't ever seen me before right now." He paused. "Look, I understand that my actions appear suspect, but I assure you that I had no intention of harming anyone in your family, Mrs. MacAllister."

"Oh?" Ryan said. "What about Krista Kelly?"

"I've already told you that I don't know anyone named Krista Kelly," Jesse said.

"You've been watching her come and go with the kids and what have you for the past three days," Ted said.

Jesse frowned. "That was this Krista Kelly person? I thought it was Sarah— What I mean is…ah, hell."

"That's it," Ryan said. "I'm calling for a squad car. This scum is after Sarah, Deedee, for heaven only knows what reason. Thank goodness Sarah and Barry have been away for a few days."

"Wait a minute," Deedee said. "This doesn't make sense. How can he be after our daughter when he didn't even know what she looks like? He thought Krista was Sarah." She shifted her gaze to Jesse. "Mr. Burke, this is confusing and frightening. I want the truth right now."

No, you don't, Jesse thought. The truth would shatter their world as they knew it, and he wasn't going to do that to them. That wouldn't begin to make up for what Maddie and his…what she, Phyllis and Joe had done. But it was all he had to give them, these people, his real family.

"I…I've just always been fascinated by the MacAllisters," Jesse said. "There have been so many articles in the newspapers and magazines about all of you over the years. I was passing through Ventura and thought I'd see what larger-than-life people looked like going about their daily lives. It was a stupid thing to do and I'm sorry I caused you any upset."

"Oh." Deedee looked at her husband. "Ryan? That sounds reasonable, don't you think?"

"Honey," Ryan said, "you thought it sounded reasonable when Teddy was late for our family curfew when he was sixteen and he said he had had four flat tires at once. He went on and on about how it had taken a long time to change all of those tires, which was pretty amazing, I said, since there was only one spare in the trunk of the car.

"No, Deedee, this story of Mr. Burke's is as lame as the first one he told. Ted, let's call the station and have them run this joker through the computer. You keep an eye on him while I use the phone in the kitchen."

"Yep," Ted said.

Deedee sighed and settled onto the sofa, her gaze riveted on Jesse as Ryan strode from the room.

"I still think you look familiar, Mr. Burke. Mr. Jesse Burke. How ironic that your name is Jesse. Our daughter, Sarah, insisted on naming her and Barry's third child, their second son, Jesse. It wasn't even a name on the list of possibilities she and Barry had made. She just suddenly decided moments after she gave birth to that baby and saw him for the first time that his name would be Jesse. Jesse Robert Barstow."

Jesse's heart beat so wildly he could hear the raging tempo echoing in his ears.

Twins, he thought numbly. He and Sarah were twins, connected in that mysterious way twins were, operating on the same wavelength. Sarah had named her son Jesse for him. *Him.*

God, what an incredible thing, what a beautiful gift that was, and he would never be able to hug her, hold her, thank her. Never be able to pull that little Jesse onto his lap and say "Hey, I'm your uncle Jesse and you were named after me."

Here he sat in a house—no, a home—with his real parents, with his nephews and niece sleeping right down the hall, and he felt so chillingly alone. So alone. He had to get out of here. He couldn't take much more of this.

A telephone rang in the distance and Jesse jerked as the sudden noise pulled him from his tormented thoughts.

"Here we go," Ted said. "They're calling back already with the info we need on this guy. Now maybe we'll get some pieces to this puzzle."

A few moments later Ryan came back into the room with a frown on his face.

"Nothing," he said. "Okay, hotshot, let's see some identification. For all we know you made up the name Jesse Burke. We'll start over from the top."

Jesse shifted in the chair, retrieved his wallet from his back pocket and handed it over. Ryan flipped it open, checked the license and the name on the two credit cards inside. He shoved the wallet back at Jesse, who slipped it into his pocket.

"So much for that," Ryan said. "Well, you're from Nevada. Your address is a rural route box number. Meaning what?"

"I live…lived on a small ranch that is now for sale,"

he admitted, his voice flat and low. "I have no intention of ever going back there. I also have a law degree, if you want to check that out. I was an assistant district attorney in Culver, Nevada, for a year, but returned to the ranch because my…because I was needed there."

"An assistant district attorney?" Ted said. "In other words, you were putting away the bad guys."

"Trying to, yeah," Jesse said, nodding. "I wanted to do my part to make sure that lowlifes were kept off the streets."

"How strange," Deedee said. "You not only have the same name as Sarah and Barry's son, but your mind is on the same track as Ryan's…and Ted's, too. Put that together with this continuing feeling I have that you look familiar and it's enough to give me goose bumps."

"Don't romanticize this, Deedee," Ryan said. "This guy was staking out the house for three days. Let's go back to Krista, Burke."

"I told you," Jesse said. "I don't know a Krista Kelly. I thought the woman I was seeing with the kids, then leaving in the afternoon and coming home late, was Sarah MacAllister Barstow. The articles I read about the MacAllisters sometimes had pictures, but other than a clear photo of Robert MacAllister, the eldest member of the family, the group photographs weren't all that clear. Plus I was across the street and…I just thought I was looking at my—I mean, looking at Sarah."

"You said 'my,'" Ryan growled, taking a step closer to Jesse. "My what? The object of your perverted sexual fantasies? What did you picture yourself doing to my daughter?"

"Nothing," Jesse yelled, lunging to his feet. "Don't you dare insinuate that I would ever harm Sarah, or... That's sick."

"Down," Ted said, moving behind Jesse and yanking him back onto the chair. "Don't try anything like that again or you're toast."

"Ted," Deedee said, "you sound like a bad movie. Besides that, the saying 'you're toast' went out-of-date ages ago." She sighed. "This is getting ridiculous. We can't keep Jesse in that chair all night. It's time to make a decision."

"Oh, now you're calling him Jesse like you're old pals?" Ryan said.

"Don't get grumpy, Ryan," she said. "We have a grandson named Jesse. The name comes easily to me, is comfortable to say. Besides, I think Mr. Burke looks like someone who would be named Jesse. Of course, I've thought from the beginning of this fiasco that he looks like someone I *know*.

"I'm just having a difficult time believing he meant any of us harm. I can't explain why I feel so positive about that but... Okay, ignore me. I'm blathering. But let's get this finished one way or another."

"You're right, honey," Ryan said. "Ted? What do you think?"

"That we should wait until Krista gets here," Ted said. "I want to know if she's seen this guy hanging around the studio. This whole bit about being interested in the MacAllister clan could be a smokescreen for a typical celebrity stalker who is actually after Krista."

"I told you over and over," Jesse said, throwing out his hands, "I don't know anyone named Krista."

"In case you haven't noticed, Burke," Ted said, "we aren't believing a whole helluva lot of what you have to say."

Ted shook his head. "What bothers me, Ryan, is that if we have the uniforms come pick him up, he'll post bail for a charge of loitering or some low ticket thing and be back on the street in hours without us knowing why he was hanging around in the first place. That doesn't work for me. We need answers *now*."

"I just heard a car pull in," Deedee said, glancing at her watch. "I didn't realize it was so late, but just because so much time has passed certainly doesn't mean we've been having a barrel of fun. That must be Krista outside, though."

"Good," Ryan said.

A few moments later the front door opened and everyone turned in that direction. Jesse started to rise, but halted when he felt Ryan's hand land firmly on his shoulder.

"Hello, everyone," the woman who entered the house said cheerfully.

"Hello, Krista," Deedee said, managing to produce a small smile.

Jesse's heart thudded in his chest as he stared at Krista Kelly.

Watching her from a distance, he'd come to the conclusion that she was a beautiful woman. Very beautiful. But now? Standing only a few feet from him, she took his breath away. Blue. Her eyes were blue and, man, they were the most gorgeous blue eyes he'd ever seen, especially accentuated by her dark hair and fair skin.

She was wearing a mint-green suit with a silky white blouse, and there would never be doubt in anyone's mind that she had a lovely, womanly figure. And those lips. Oh, talk about made for kissing. She was really something, this Krista Kelly.

"My goodness," Krista said smiling, "it's a tad late for a party, but the gang's all here." She walked closer and smiled at Jesse. "This family never ends, does it? Hi, I'm Krista Kelly, and my ever brilliant journalistic eye tells me that you are yet another MacAllister. You look enough like Ryan to be his son. So, MacAllister-I-haven't-met-yet, which one are you?"

Chapter 3

Krista turned to look at Deedee when the woman gasped and stared at the man sitting in the chair.

She snapped her head back around to see that Ryan and Ted had shifted their positions so they, too, could focus on the stranger. His shoulders slumped, then he shook his head and sighed.

He was an extremely handsome man, Krista thought, but then all the MacAllisters were attractive people. Even though he was sitting down she could tell he was tall. He had wide shoulders, thick brown hair, the MacAllister dark brown eyes and rugged masculine features. Oh, yes, very handsome, indeed. And he certainly did resemble Ryan.

But for reasons that were totally confusing her, the

fact that she had stated the obvious had caused an instantaneous tension to crackle through the air. No one was speaking. They were just staring at the man, and the color had drained from Ryan's face.

"What's going on here?" Krista said. "I feel as though I came in in the middle of a movie and I don't have a clue as to what the plot is."

"We—we don't know what it is, either," Deedee said, her voice trembling slightly. "I knew Jesse looked familiar but…" She drew a steadying breath.

"Jesse?" Krista said. "Sarah and Barry named their Jesse after him?" She looked at the man. "You?"

"No, they didn't," he said. "I'm Jesse Burke and I've never met Sarah and Barry. Before tonight I hadn't met anyone in this room. I'd appreciate it, Ms. Kelly, if you'd tell them that you've never seen me hanging around whatever studio you work in. They need to be assured that I'm not stalking you like a celebrity groupie or whatever."

"Stalking me?" Krista said, her eyes widening. "Why would a member of the MacAllister clan be stalking me? And for the record, I'm not really a celebrity. Well, sort of, I suppose, because people do recognize me when I go out in public. But that's due to the fact that I'm the anchorwoman on the local television station and I'm in their living rooms every day, delivering the news at 6:00 and 10:00 p.m."

Krista waved one hand in the air. "That's not important. I'm very confused as to why all of you appeared so shocked when I said this man…oh. It's nice to meet you, Jesse Burke. As I said, I'm Krista Kelly. Now, where was I? Confused, that's where I was. I said Mr. Burke is obviously a MacAllister, looks enough like Ryan to be his son, and everyone went into supershock, or some such thing. Would someone care to enlighten me?"

"Ryan," Deedee said, attempting to stand, then realizing her legs wouldn't support her. "Jesse *does* look like you did when you were younger. Not a mirror image, but enough that I was certain I'd seen him before. I felt a connection to him, too, knew he didn't mean any of us harm. I just knew. Ryan?"

"What are you thinking, Deedee?" her husband asked, dragging a restless hand through his hair. "That I had an affair years ago and this guy is the result of it? I've never cheated on you, honey. If he looks like me, or any of the other MacAllisters, it's a fluke, a strange coincidence."

"Right," Jesse said quickly. "That's absolutely right. I'm Jesse *Burke,* remember? From Nevada."

"And your parents?" Deedee said. "Who are your parents?"

You and Ryan. Jesse's mind roared the words. I'm your son, Deedee.

"Phyllis and Joe Burke," he said, shifting his gaze to the floor. "They were killed in an automobile accident over two months ago. If you check that out through your police sources you'll find that it's true, and that their obituary listed Jesse Burke as their surviving son. They owned a small ranch outside a dinky town named Eden and—"

No, he thought frantically in the next instant. He shouldn't have divulged the name of the town where—

"Sarah was born in a rural area near Eden," Deedee said, finally managing to get to her feet. "She came early and was delivered by a midwife named Maddie Clemens. We were so lucky, blessed, really—to find her living in a little house we saw in the middle of nowhere during a raging storm. Do you know Maddie Clemens?"

"I've…I've heard the name," Jesse said, keeping his eyes averted from Deedee's.

"There was no hospital in Eden," Deedee continued. "When the roads were passable Sarah and I were taken by ambulance to the next bigger city, which was Prosperity, Nevada."

Jesse shrugged.

"Deedee, hold it," Ted said. "Your imagination is starting to put together something eligible for the *Twilight Zone*. A MacAllister baby was born in that area…and what? The next kid born nearby looks a little bit like a MacAllister because the genes are so powerful they winged through the air? Give me a break. Burke living near where Sarah was born is just one of those weird things that emphasizes how small the world is, or something."

"When is your birthday?" Deedee said to Jesse.

"Deedee, stop it," Ryan said.

"No, I won't stop," she said. "Something very strange is going on here, Ryan, and I want to know what it is. You looked at Jesse's driver's license. When is his birthday?"

"I didn't notice," Ryan said.

"Then look again," Deedee said.

Jesse got to his feet. "I've had enough of this. Either call the cops and have me hauled downtown or forget it. If you're not going to have me arrested for loitering, then I'm leaving. Right now."

"No, you mustn't go until we make some sense of this," Deedee said. "Why do you look like a MacAllister? Why did I feel such a connection to you? Why did Sarah name her son Jesse? Why did you suddenly appear in our lives, coming from the same place where Sarah was born thirty-two years ago? How old are you, Jesse?"

"Thirty…two, but a whole helluva lot of people on this earth are thirty-two."

"And what month and day were you born?" Deedee asked.

"A multitude of babies are born on the same day in this country," Jesse said. "You're making such a big deal out of—"

"What day?" Deedee yelled.

"July first," Jesse admitted, looking up at the ceiling for a moment.

"Dear God," she murmured, sinking back onto the sofa. "That is Sarah's birthday."

"Which means nothing," Ryan said. "Ted's right, sweetheart. You're letting your imagination run away with you. Hey, yeah, all of this is a bit weird, but weird happens, you know?"

"Excuse me," Krista said, "but as a journalist, I have

to admit that after hearing all of this I'd definitely be digging deeper for facts before I turned my back on this story. There are just too many coincidences. Now before you decide to hate me forever, Ryan, I am *not* suggesting that you had an affair ages ago and Jesse Burke, here, is the result of it. But I have to say *this*. There are a lot of MacAllisters in your family and you all have enough of a resemblance that a person could pick you out of a crowd."

"You're insinuating that one of my brothers or—"

"I'm not saying that, exactly," Krista interrupted. "This could all be just…weird, to overuse the word that's being applied here. But don't you want to know so you can put this to rest?"

"Yes," Deedee insisted.

"No," Ryan said at the same moment.

"Wait a minute," Jesse said. "You're all discussing this over and around me as though I'm not here. You have no right to dig into my past, into my…my parents' lives."

"Don't you want to know the truth?" Krista asked.

Jesse looked directly into her eyes. "I know the truth," he said quietly.

She took Jesse's hands in both of hers and continued to meet his troubled gaze. "Don't you think," she said gently, "that Deedee and Ryan have the right to know what that truth is, Jesse?"

No, he thought. Yes. God, he couldn't think straight. Krista's eyes, those incredible blue eyes, were pinning him in place, making it difficult to breathe, to even string two rational thoughts together. He was sinking into that sea of blue, a place of peace away from the turmoil and stress in this room, the demands these people were making on him.

And now…yes, now there was desire beginning to churn within him, with coils of heat low in his body. He wanted to wrap his arms around Krista and nestle her to him, kiss those lips that beckoned so enticingly, savor the taste and aroma and feminine softness of her.

He had never in his life experienced anything like this. What was this woman doing to him? What magical spell was she weaving around him? She was dangerous, this Krista Kelly, but he didn't care. He wanted her.

"Jesse?" Krista said, her voice trembling.

And Jesse knew that she was as shaken as he was by the mysterious connection that was happening between them. That knowledge gave him strength, made him feel as though he wasn't so alone. At least for this instant in time, he wasn't alone.

Jesse shifted his gaze to his and Krista's entwined hands, then slowly, very slowly pulled his free, squared his shoulders and looked at Deedee and Ryan, who were now standing close together.

"I believed with my whole heart," he said, then cleared his throat as he heard the emotion ringing in his voice, "that the kindest thing I could do for you would be to keep the truth buried. I saw no purpose in you being devastated by it as I had been, still am.

"I just wanted to see you from a distance, with the

hope that I would gain a sense of identity again, of who I am and… But I messed that up so badly by staying too long and appearing to be a threat to Sarah, or your grandchildren, or Krista. I never intended for you to know I'd been in Ventura. No, it's more than that. I never intended for you to even know that I existed."

"Who…who are you, Jesse?" Deedee asked, clutching Ryan's hand.

"Look," Jesse said wearily, "it's after one in the morning. This isn't the time to get into all of this, not when we're all exhausted and emotions are on the edge of control. We need to get some sleep."

"That's a good point," Krista said.

"That's a lousy point," Ted countered. "We agree to get some rest, then meet back here later and Burke doesn't show. He figures with our police resources we'll blow holes in whatever scam he's trying to pull and he cuts and runs."

"I'm not attempting to put a scam into motion here," Jesse said. "I didn't intend to even speak to any of you."

"So you say," Ted said, crossing his arms over his chest. "But you hung around long enough to get our attention, didn't you? I think you're as phony as a three-dollar bill, Burke. You saw photographs of the MacAllisters in the newspaper, realized you resembled them for some quirky reason, and decided to cash in on that. Well, nice try but no cigar."

"Fine," Jesse said, raising both hands as he glowered at Ted. "We'll go with that, say you're right. I'll walk out the door and that will be the last you'll see of me. I have no problem with that because I wasn't going to make my existence known to these people in the first place. I really don't give a damn what you think of me, Ted."

"Then hit the road," he said, "and consider yourself lucky that we didn't have you hauled downtown as a possible stalker. It was not a pleasure meeting you. Goodbye, Burke."

Jesse spun around with the intention of leaving the house, hesitated for a second to look at Krista, shook his head, then started toward the front door.

"No, no, please, don't go," Deedee said. "Jesse? Wait."

He stopped and looked back at her over one shoulder.

"Ted," she said, "you had no right to do that. Yes, you're considered a member of the MacAllister family, have been for so many years I think we've all forgotten that you really aren't a blood relative. Would you think for a minute, Ted? What if Jesse had such a strong resemblance to you that it was obvious that he was related to you in some way? Wouldn't you want to know the truth? Know why he looked enough like you to be your son?"

"That would be way out in left field, Deedee," Ted said, "and you know it. The case of mumps I had when I was a teenager rendered me incapable of fathering a child. This imaginary scenario you're cooking up would be impossible, and explained away as a crazy fluke of nature, which is exactly what you should be doing about him looking like a MacAllister."

"Oh, there is just no talking to you, Ted," Deedee said, with a frustrated shake of her head. "I want, I intend to hear what Jesse has to say."

"Take it easy, honey," her husband said.

"Don't patronize me, Ryan," she said, none too quietly. "I'm not going to be treated like an hysterical female whose emotions are out of control. I want answers. I want to hear the truth from Jesse."

"And how do you know he'll be telling the truth?" Ryan said, matching her volume. "Con men who are any good at their chosen profession spend a lot of time doing their homework. Did you notice how he slipped in that he is from Eden? That, oh, yeah, he's heard of Maddie Clemens? And what a slick move it was how he handled the bit about his birthday? Oh, so reluctant to tell you the date, then giving in and, son of a gun, if he wasn't born on the same day as Sarah. He's smooth, I'll give him that but…ah, hell, this is ridiculous. Deedee, we're not getting suckered in here. No."

"Amen to that," Ted said.

"I feel a connection to Jesse, Ryan," Deedee said, her eyes filling with tears. "I do. I can't explain it, but it's there. Don't let him leave until we hear what he has to say." A sob caught in her throat. "Please, Ryan."

Look what he'd done to Deedee, to his…God, to his mother, Jesse thought. He was tearing her apart emotionally and causing discordance within this family by just being there, existing. What if they knew the truth? Knew what horrible injustice had been done to them so many years ago? He couldn't do this to them. He just couldn't.

"I'm leaving," he said, a rough edge to his voice. "I wasn't planning on having to put up with so much weeping and wailing, with people going nuts. It was supposed to be easy to work my way into the position where I wanted to be, but it isn't worth this kind of hassle. You win some, you lose some. Quit blubbering, lady, I'm outta here."

"Big-time scam," Ted said, nodding. "Bingo. I was right. Hit the road, Burke, before I decide to take you apart."

"Right, old man, like you could really do that," Jesse said. "You people are a waste of my time."

He strode to the door, gripped the knob, then stopped, unable to move as the soft sound of his name being spoken reached him.

"Jesse," Krista said.

His hold on the doorknob tightened.

"What you're attempting to do right now," she said, "is so kind, so giving, but it's not working because it's not true. You're not a con man who has run out of patience with the emotional reactions you're creating. You're a MacAllister. How that came to be is something only you know at this point. You can play the role of the bad guy from here to Sunday, but I'm hearing the pain in your voice, can see it on your face, in your eyes. You're willing to leave to protect these people, and that is so admirable, but it's too late for that, don't you see?

"I agree with you, though, that everyone is exhausted and emotions are raw. We all should get some sleep, then meet here in a few hours—say, at nine o'clock, after I deliver the children to school. And then, Jesse Burke, you must divulge the truth. You know that."

Jesse's shoulders slumped and a wave of bone-deep fatigue consumed him, causing him to take a shuddering breath. With his back still to the room, he nodded, then turned the knob and left the house, closing the door behind him with a quiet click.

"No way," Ted said, starting forward. "I'm camping on that phoney joker's doorstep and making damn sure he shows at nine. You're making a big mistake, Krista. He's a con artist and I want to hear him admit it again before we send him packing. If I don't stick close to him he's going to get the hell out of Dodge right now."

Krista lifted her chin. "Jesse will be here at nine o'clock, Ted. Guaranteed. When he comes, he's going to explain how he is connected to the MacAllister family, how he became one and why he hasn't come forward before now. And every word that Jesse says, Ted, will be the truth."

"Yes," Deedee said softly. "You're absolutely right, Krista. Ryan, I'd like to go home now and get some sleep, so I'll be better prepared to hear what Jesse has to say, to hear the truth that he'll speak."

"Ah, Deedee," Ryan said, shaking his head. "Your womanly instincts are off target this time, honey. And you, Krista? I saw the long looks you and Burke were engaging in, could practically feel the romantic tension building, crackling between the two of you. Honey, you got the hots for the wrong guy this trip."

"Amen, amen," Ted said. "I'm going home to bed. It was an interesting evening but it's over. I won't get to hear Burke admit again that he's a scam man because he's headed for the highway while we're standing here."

"I'll see you at nine, Krista," Deedee said. "Whether Ryan and Ted choose to be here is up to them."

"Nine o'clock, Deedee," Krista said decisively.

"Women, women, women," Ryan said, rolling his eyes heavenward. "You're off the hook, Ted, but I'll have to be here to protect my checkbook when the scum hits Deedee up for money."

"Oh, I'll be back at nine," Ted said smugly, "so I can say I-told-you-so when Burke doesn't show." He paused. "Well, it's been an interesting evening, I'll say that much for it. Wait until I tell Hannah what went down here. Unreal. Sarah's going to be ticked that she missed this performance. Oh, don't forget to e-mail Teddy in Italy and fill him in. He'll get a kick out of this one. Good night, all."

Forty-five minutes later Krista pulled the blankets over herself in the bed in the guest room and snapped off the light on the nightstand. She sighed wearily, then stared up at a ceiling she couldn't see in the darkness.

What an unbelievable night this has been, she thought. *The entire scenario was like something cre-*

ated by an author's imagination, in a book. But this was real, was actually happening.

Who in heaven's name was Jesse Burke?

Well, she thought dryly, she did know a few facts about the mysterious Mr. Burke, facts that were rather unsettling, to say the least.

He had evoked a sensual reaction within her like nothing she had felt before. When he'd looked at her, directly at her, with those fathomless dark brown eyes of his, she'd felt as though she was being transported to another place where only the two of them existed.

She had been acutely aware of her desire for Jesse, too, the heat that had thrummed within her, consumed her, made her breasts feel achy and in need of a soothing touch. Jesse's touch.

Her response to him had not been just physical, it had been emotional, as well. She knew, somehow just knew, that he was not a despicable con artist as Ted had stated. No, not Jesse. Every heartfelt word he had spoken had been true, except, of course, when he was attempting to project himself as the evil person Ted was accusing him of being.

Jesse would arrive back at the house at nine o'clock as promised. There was no doubt whatsoever in her mind. Why did she know that? When it came to men, she wasn't a very trusting woman, that was for sure. She did, in fact, have carefully constructed walls built around her heart and mind in regard to the opposite sex, due to the pain and disappointment she'd suffered in the past.

But with Jesse it was different. So many things were different—new, exciting and terrifying in the same breathless moment.

"Oh, Jesse Burke," Krista whispered, "what are you doing to me? And who are you, Jesse? How did you become a MacAllister? Which member of that large family helped create you over thirty-two years ago?"

Jesse had been determined to protect the MacAllisters from the devastation the truth would cause, but that was no longer possible. Lives were going to be irrevocably changed by what Jesse had to say. In just a few hours the truth would be known.

How strange, Krista thought. *She* wasn't a MacAllister. She'd started out as a friend of Sarah's and had been welcomed by the other MacAllisters as time passed, making her feel like a part of their warm and loving family. Jesse's words would have no direct impact on *her* life, because like Ted and his family, she was an adopted member of the large clan.

But even so, the arrival of Jesse Burke had already thrown her off-kilter, shaken her deeply.

Because he was there, she knew she would never be quite the same again.

Chapter 4

The next morning Krista delivered the three chattering Barstow children to school and returned to the house, arriving just after eight-thirty.

Her breath caught as she turned off the car's ignition and glanced toward the porch, where Jesse Burke was standing with one shoulder propped against the front door.

She'd known Jesse would keep his word, she realized as she got out of the car. And he had.

Now if she could follow the firm directive she'd given herself at some point in the night, and quit over-reacting to the masculine magnetism of this man, she'd be all set. She gotten enough sleep to feel once again in control of herself, and there would be no more adolescent behavior on her part in regard to Mr. Burke. Fine.

"Good morning, Jesse," she sang out, as she approached the house. "You're early for the time we all agreed on. Would you like a cup of coffee?"

"Yes," he said, nodding. "Sounds good, but I'm here before the others arrive because I wanted to have a chance to talk to you privately."

"Oh?" Krista unlocked the door and entered the house, knowing Jesse was right behind her.

On top of everything else, she thought, why did he have to have such a deep, rumbly voice, so male it caused shivers to course down her spine? The man just didn't play fair.

"Kitchen," she said, then inwardly groaned when she heard the squeaky noise that used to be her voice.

In the large, sunny kitchen she waved one hand in the direction of the table, then poured two mugs of coffee, placing one in front of Jesse, then sitting down opposite him with her own.

"Sugar and creamer are on that lazy Susan thing," she said, not looking directly at him. "There are some spoons there, too, and napkins. Oh. Would you like some cookies? Toast? I'm no great shakes as a cook but I managed not to poison the kids in the week I've been here so—"

"Krista," Jesse said.

"What?" She nearly shouted the word as she finally looked at him. "You did that on purpose, didn't you? Made your voice another octave lower when you said my name, made it so damnably…male that my bones are dissolving and…oh, good Lord." She plunked one elbow on the table and dropped her forehead to her palm. "I've never been so mortified in my entire life."

Jesse chuckled, and Krista raised her head to glare at him.

"Sorry," he said quickly. "If it makes you feel any better, you've thrown me for a loop, too, Krista Kelly. I don't know how you do it, but you push buttons in me that I didn't even know I had."

"Really?" She smiled, then in the next instant frowned again. "This is ridiculous. Erase everything that happened since we came in the house, and back up to your wanting to talk to me."

"Don't you think we should discuss this strange effect we have on each other?"

"I certainly do not," she said, with a little sniff. "There are far more important matters taking place. Pandora's box was opened last night and it can't be closed again."

"Yeah, I know," he said with a sigh. "I messed everything up so badly it's a sin. I never intended…well, I've said that bit enough to sound like a broken record." He paused. "Look, I arrived early because I wanted to have a chance to thank you for trusting me, believing in me, refusing to think I'm some kind of despicable con man. It meant a lot to me, Krista, that you stood by me last night, and I wanted to tell you that."

"Don't give me too much credit for that, Jesse, because I don't have a clue as to why I did it. I just somehow knew that—oh, I don't know. I don't trust men in general, not easily, but...never mind."

"Why don't you trust men in general?"

"It's not important," Krista said. "What *is* important is what will take place here a very short time from now. The truth you're going to tell will result in lives being turned upside down, maybe even shattered. Am I right?"

Jesse nodded.

"Oh, dear," Krista said.

"I could still leave, be out of here before the others arrive," he said. "They'd never hear what I am being forced to say."

"It's too late for that, Jesse. You can't turn back the clock and pretend you never came here."

"And met you."

"Don't go there," Krista said, shaking her head. She got to her feet. "I'd better make a fresh pot of coffee so there will be enough for everyone. And I have to make a pot of tea. Deedee likes tea. Sarah must have a teapot someplace so I can—"

Jesse left his chair to stand in front of Krista, gripping her shoulders as he looked directly into her eyes.

"Calm down," he said. "You're falling apart by inches. I realize I've created a terrible situation for the MacAllisters by being here, but to have whatever this strange attraction is between us cause you to be so upset is more than I can handle. I'd like to know what this is, Krista, but not at the cost of your peace of mind."

"No, I'm the one who's sorry," she said, meeting his gaze. "I'm a wreck worrying about what you're going to tell the family, and I have nowhere to put how you make me feel when you…oh, mercy. Tell me to shut up, Jesse."

"There's a better way than telling you," he said. Then he lowered his head and kissed her.

Well, it's about time, Krista thought, then blanked her mind and returned Jesse's kiss with total abandon.

Her arms floated upward to encircle his neck as he wrapped his arms around her to nestle her close to his body.

Burke, he yelled silently, what in the hell are you doing? He didn't go around hauling a woman he hardly knew into his arms and kissing the living daylights out of her. But this wasn't just any woman, this was Krista and she was…she was…

All rational thought fled as he drank in the taste, the feel, the aroma of Krista Kelly. Heat rocketed through his body, coiling to the point of pain as the kiss went on and on. He raised his head a fraction of an inch to draw a ragged breath, then claimed Krista's lips once more.

Control, he thought hazily. He was slipping to the edge of his control. He wanted her, wanted to make slow, sweet love to her for hours, see her blue eyes turn smoky with desire, hear her whisper his name as they became one and… He had to stop. Now.

He broke the kiss and eased Krista back from his aroused body, the inches now separating them feeling like torturous miles.

Krista lifted her lashes, which had fluttered closed so she could better savor the wondrous sensations sweeping throughout her. She smiled softly, feeling as though she were encased in a sensuous mist that allowed room only for her and Jesse Burke.

In the next instant she blinked and landed back in the kitchen with a thud as reality swished the heavenly mist into oblivion. She took a step backward and wrapped her hands around her elbows.

"That…that should not have happened," she said, hearing the thread of breathlessness in her voice. "I don't do things like this."

"I don't, either," Jesse said, his own voice gritty. "I'm sorry. No, cancel that. I'm not one bit sorry. Those kisses were sensational and you shared in them equally, Krista."

"I know," she said miserably.

Jesse laughed. "You don't have to sound like it's the end of the world, for Pete's sake. We didn't break any law that Ryan and Ted can get us arrested for. We're normal, healthy human beings who—"

"Could we quit discussing this to death?" Krista said.

"Oh, okay. I'll just think about it, then. I'll relive how you tasted. Remember your aroma, which is like a flower garden, and how you fit against me so perfectly it's as though you were custom-made just for me. Then I'll—"

"Stop it," Krista cried, with a burst of laughter. "You don't play by any sort of rules."

"I'm not playing games," he said, serious again. "That statement you can take all the way to the bank."

Before Krista could reply, the doorbell rang and her eyes widened. "They're here."

"I wish *I* wasn't," Jesse said, with a sigh. "The Mac-Allisters are obviously fine, decent people. They don't deserve to have their lives as they know them to be ripped to shreds. God, I hate this. It was so selfish of me to indulge in my need to see them, just get a glimpse of…" He paused and produced a meager smile. "Maybe they'll decide to kill the messenger and take care of this burden of guilt I'm lugging around."

The bell chimed again.

"Zero hour," Krista said, then turned and hurried out of the kitchen.

Jesse followed her slowly, forcing himself to put one foot in front of the other. As Deedee and Ryan came into the house, Jesse stared at them, once again struck by the incredible fact that these two people were his parents, the couple who should have left Maddie Clemens's house with newborn twins so many years ago. But instead, their son had been stolen from them by those who'd put their own selfish needs before what should have taken place.

Ted entered the room, accompanied by an attractive woman in her early sixties with salt-and-pepper hair and a slender figure. This was Hannah, Jesse assumed, Ted's wife, whom he'd referred to last night.

"Good morning, Jesse," Deedee said, with a small smile. "I'd like you to meet Hannah Sharpe, Ted's wife."

"Hello," he said.

"Hello, Jesse," Hannah replied. "Please know that I'm not here out of simple curiosity, but to give support to Deedee and Ryan, who are like family to me. I must say that you definitely do look like a MacAllister."

"May I offer you coffee or tea?" Krista said. "I can prepare both if you like."

The four shook their heads in the negative. The MacAllisters and Sharpes settled onto the sofa, while Krista sat down in an easy chair.

Jesse hesitated, glanced at the door with the thought that he could still bolt, and knowing in the next instant that is was far too late for that. He sat in an easy chair opposite Krista.

A heavy silence fell over the room.

"Okay, Burke," Ted said finally. "Tell your story. No, wait—I have a question. Why are you driving a rental car? Would a check of the license number on your own vehicle reveal that your name isn't really Jesse Burke?"

Jesse sighed. "No. I'm Jesse Burke. Phyllis and Joe Burke were driving my SUV when they were killed in the accident, and my vehicle was totaled. I received a check from the insurance company to replace it, but have been using the money to locate the MacAllister family. Any funds I had when I returned to the farm, ranch, whatever you want to call it, are long gone because it was needed to help keep a roof over our heads."

"I'll accept that answer for now," Ted said.

"Oh, hey, don't strain yourself," Jesse said, glaring at him.

"Please, let's not start with tempers flaring," Deedee said. "Talk to us, Jesse, and we'll listen."

"Whether or not we'll believe you remains to be seen," Ted said.

"Hush, Ted," Hannah said. "That's enough. Go ahead, Jesse."

Go ahead, Jesse, his mind echoed. Slice and dice these people. Destroy their peaceful existence, their happiness, their life as they know it and worked hard to have. Oh, sure, go right ahead, Jesse.

"Jesse," Krista said softly. "It's time."

He nodded and drew a steadying breath before beginning to speak.

"On the day of the funeral for Phyllis and Joe Burke," he said, looking at a spot just above the heads of Deedee and Ryan, "I was feeling very sorry for myself. I'd lost my...my parents, had given up a career I had intended to dedicate myself to so I could return home to help them out, even though I hated working the land. I stood at their grave site filled with immature self-pity and a chilling sense of being totally alone, having nothing, no one.

"I told Maddie Clemens how I felt, and she became very upset by what I said. She had been friends with Phyllis and Joe for many, many years and believed they would be brokenhearted if they knew how desolate I was.

"She was convinced that Joe and Phyllis would want

me to know the truth, want me to know that I *wasn't* alone, not really. And so she told me what had taken place on the night I was born. On the night that Sarah and I were born at her house."

"What?" Deedee whispered, reaching for Ryan's hand.

In a voice ringing with painful emotion, Jesse revealed the truth, told everyone in that room what Maddie had done and what Phyllis and Joe Burke had been a party to. The color drained from Deedee's face, while Ryan's became ruddy with fury. Hannah gasped. Ted shook his head in disbelief and mumbled an expletive.

"The neighbors were told," Jesse said, "that a teenage girl had come to Maddie to have her baby delivered and put up for adoption, but that she'd left before she signed the legal papers. Everyone was sworn to secrecy because if the lack of documents became public knowledge I would be taken away by the authorities.

"I grew up surrounded by lies," Jesse said angrily. "When I found that out, I lashed out at Maddie, told her I never wanted to see her again, never wanted to hear the names Phyllis and Joe Burke again. I despise them all for what they'd done, to you, to me. I stood there stripped of my identity, the very essence of who I was. Alone? God, I had never been so alone.

"I had to see you and Sarah—my twin sister, Sarah— from a distance, to hopefully get a sense of who I was. I didn't intend for you to know what had been done to you, because it would serve no purpose to cause you such pain. I was wrong to come here, was thinking only of myself, what I needed, believing you'd never know I existed. But it didn't go that way, because I stayed too long."

"Oh, my God," Deedee said, tears streaming down her face. "I was carrying twins? I didn't know. I just didn't know. Maddie Clemens stole my baby? My son?" She looked at Ryan. "Our son, Ryan. She never told us that he—"

"Hold it," Ted said. "Why didn't Ryan hear you crying when you were born? So, okay, Deedee was put to sleep with some ether, but Ryan was wide-awake. Newborn babies cry, Burke. Did you forget that little detail?"

"It was raining very hard," Ryan said, his voice strained. "Beating down on the roof of that little house, rattling the windows. Plus I was sitting in a rocking chair, holding Sarah in front of a noisy, roaring fire in the hearth.

"When Maddie came into the room, I didn't hear her until she was right next to me. I wouldn't have heard the cry of a newborn in the bedroom where Deedee was sleeping from where I was sitting."

"All these years," Deedee said, a sob catching in her throat, "we had a son we knew nothing about? Sarah had a twin, Teddy had a younger brother, and we didn't know? How could people do something so cruel, so heartless? My God, I can't believe this."

"No joke," Ted said. "Deedee, don't buy into this crap. This is the most far-fetched tale of lies I've had to stomach in a long time. You heard Burke say he's stone broke, doesn't have two nickels to rub together. He's here to get some MacAllister money, can't you see that? By a quirk of nature he happens to look like a MacAllister, and he's attempting to cash in, literally, on that.

"Tell her, Ryan. Come on, man, she's falling apart for no reason. This jerk isn't your son. He's a con artist who has done his homework very, very well and performed the I-didn't-intend-for-you-to-know-I-existed bit like the pro he is. He's outta here. I'll make certain of that. Take Deedee home and forget this junk ever took place, because it's a crock."

Ryan held up one trembling hand to silence Ted as he stared at Jesse.

"Deedee's doctor didn't have the equipment to do an ultrasound," Ryan said, "and we saw no reason to go somewhere else to have one. The doctor heard only one heartbeat, but Deedee was appalled at how big she was compared to when she carried Teddy.

"We...we joked about wouldn't we be surprised new parents if she had twins. That they might have been in a position that only one heart was heard each time the doctor listened. We laughed about us both being up in the night, each tending to a baby because we'd gotten two instead of one. Been...blessed with two. Blessed."

Ryan swallowed heavily.

"And we were," he added gruffly. "Blessed with two. With twins. A daughter. A son. It makes sense. Deedee's size, the labor starting early, which is common with twins. The tiny size of Sarah despite how big Deedee had gotten."

"And she stole our baby, Ryan," his wife said, anguish nearly strangling her. "She took him and gave him to people who knew they had no right to have him. Evil, horrible people who…" She covered her face with her hands and wept.

Ryan wrapped his arms around her and pulled her close, burying his face in her hair.

"I'm sorry," Jesse said. "I'm just so damn sorry. Look what I've done to you. I'll never forgive Maddie, Phyllis and Joe for what they did, and I'll never forgive myself for what I just did to you. *I'm sorry.*"

"Hell," Ted said. "Hannah, talk to Deedee. Say consoling stuff to get her to listen to you, to realize that none of this is true."

"No," Hannah said slowly, her gaze riveted on Jesse. "It's true. Everything that Jesse said is the truth. I know it here." She splayed one hand on her heart. "Jesse is Deedee and Ryan's son, Sarah's twin brother."

"Yes," Krista said, hardly able to speak. "He is. It's hard to fathom how people could do what was done but…it's true. Jesse is a MacAllister."

Jesse lunged to his feet. "It doesn't matter now. It's too late, thirty-two years too late. I'm a stranger to all of you and that isn't going to change, not really. Revealing the truth to you has caused you nothing but pain, just as I knew it would. I've got to leave Ventura and never come back, or you'll relive this nightmare every time you look at me."

"No," Deedee said, freeing herself from Ryan's embrace. She got to her feet and went to Jesse, gripping his upper arms. "No, you can't go. I won't lose you again, Jesse. You're my son, my baby boy."

"No, I'm a grown man you don't even know," he said. "You can't expect me to just slip into place in the MacAllister family as though I've been here all of my life. I'd make everyone uncomfortable, edgy. You'd look at Sarah, remembering her first steps, when she cut her first tooth, said her first words. Then you'd ache with the knowledge that other people witnessed those events when I did them. You'd be continually reminded of the horrendous thing that was done to you and it would rip you up. I can't stay here and allow that to happen."

Deedee spun around. "Ryan, don't let him go. Please, Ryan, he's our son. Make him understand that he belongs here with us. We'll spend hours and hours together, getting to know each other, listening to Jesse talk about what kind of a little boy he was. We'll get back as much as we can of what we missed out on. The family will accept him as a MacAllister, make him feel loved and welcomed, you know that. Ryan?"

Her husband got to his feet. "Deedee is right, Jesse. If you leave now you'll cause us even more pain than you feel your staying will create. You belong here with us."

"You're playing right into his hands, Ryan," Ted said. "Let's talk about a DNA test, shall we? How do you feel about that, Burke? You've won this round because you've snowed Deedee and Ryan to the point they're begging you to stay. But while you're laughing up your sleeve, a nifty little DNA number will be under way. Having second thoughts? Think maybe you should hit the road?"

"I have no problem with a DNA test, Ted," Jesse said angrily. "None at all, because every word I've spoken here today is the truth. But I still feel that my presence is a source of pain to these people. *That's* why I should go, not because I'm afraid of a DNA test."

"Yeah, right," Ted said, with a snort of disgust.

"Ted, stop," Hannah ordered. "You're overstepping. This is Deedee and Ryan's decision, not yours."

"They're not thinking clearly, Hannah," he argued. "Somebody has to protect them from this con artist, and I'm the only one in this room who isn't being suckered in by this guy."

"I'll take your damn test," Jesse said. "No man worth his salt is going to be called a liar, a con artist, without fighting back. You want proof, Ted? Then fine, let's do it. It won't change my mind that the best thing for everyone concerned is for me to leave. But, by God, I'll go with the pleasure of having seen you eat crow."

"Then you'll stay, Jesse?" Deedee said, fresh tears filling her eyes.

"Only long enough to prove that I'm an honest man," Jesse said.

"Okay, okay," Ryan said, raising both hands. "We'll

settle for that for now. I don't believe that DNA test is necessary, but if it means we'll have your word you won't leave during the weeks it will take to get the results, it will serve a purpose."

"Oh, I'll stay. You have my word on that," Jesse said. "I'll also expect an apology from Ted when the test results are in. Then I'll go."

"Fat chance of that test proving you're a MacAllister, Deedee and Ryan's son," Ted said, shaking his head. "It's not going to happen."

"Ted," Hannah said wearily, "shut up."

"Now, listen to me, all of you," Ryan said. "Krista, this is especially important where you're concerned, because of you working for the television station. No one is to know what's taking place here. We MacAllisters are too well known in this town. If this leaks out it will be sensationalized, a hot topic, a big deal story. We'll all be hounded by reporters."

Krista nodded. "You're right. The MacAllisters are household names in Ventura. The arrival of Jesse on the scene would be headline news and exploited to the hilt. The public would be clamoring for every detail that could be unearthed. Don't worry about me, Ryan. I won't let anything slip at the station. But you must be very careful, give thought to who you can trust to take blood samples and get the DNA tests run."

"Kara still works a few hours a week at the hospital, even though she's retired from practicing medicine," Deedee said. "She'll take care of that part for us."

Krista nodded. "Perfect."

"Jesse?" Deedee said. "Will you stay at our house with us?"

"That's it," Ted said, rising. "I can't take any more of this. The free handouts are starting and I'm outta here. Come on, Hannah, we're going home."

"Fine," she said. "Then I can give you a hefty piece of my mind in private, Ted Sharpe."

Hannah hugged Deedee and Ryan, smiled at Jesse and Krista, glared at Ted, then left the house with her husband.

"Jesse?" Deedee said. "Will you? Collect your things from wherever you're staying and settle in at our home? *Your* home."

"No, I don't think so," he answered, running one hand over the back of his neck. "That would just add fuel to Ted's fire. I'm already causing discord within your family, and because there are so many of you it could end up being a split camp, one side pitted against the other in their beliefs. I don't want to be responsible for that."

"Then you should stay with me," Krista said.

What? she thought in the next instant. Had that really come out of her mouth? Had she lost her mind? But then again, it made sense because…

"I'm not a MacAllister," she explained. "I've been welcomed into the fold as though I was, but technically I'm not. If you stay with me, Jesse, it gets you out of a motel room, which I imagine is nothing to shout about, since you explained your financial situation.

"Plus, it will give Deedee and Ryan time to approach the members of the family and explain what has taken place, allow them all to digest things, get used to the idea, without cluttering their minds with the fact that you're bunking in at Deedee and Ryan's."

"But I want him to—" Deedee began.

"No, honey," Ryan interrupted, "what Krista is saying makes sense. Some of the clan might see things as we do, but others might jump to the conclusions Ted has. If that contingent hears that Jesse is getting room and board from us, more fires will be fueled. Krista, is the painting of your apartment on schedule?"

"Yes. They finished yesterday and Sarah and Barry get back from their trip tomorrow morning."

"Dear heaven," Deedee whispered. "Sarah. This news is going to be terribly upsetting to her. She should have grown up with a twin brother and...oh, dear."

"Which is all the more reason for Jesse to stay with Krista," Ryan said. "Sarah needs time to let all of this sink in before she meets him. She should be allowed to determine when she's ready for that introduction. If Jesse is at our house we'd be—no offense meant, Jesse—we'd be shoving him down her throat before she might be prepared to handle it."

Deedee sighed. "Yes, all right."

"Jesse, if you'll give me the number of your motel, I'll phone you with the time and place to have your blood drawn, after I've talked to Kara." Ryan paused. "Well, I don't know about you, Deedee, but I'm exhausted. Let's head on home, shall we?"

"But when will we see Jesse again?" Deedee said.

"There's so much I want to ask him, to discover. I want to sit and gaze at my son, Ryan."

"I have tomorrow night off from the station," Krista said. "Why don't you come for dinner at my apartment—which hopefully won't smell too much like paint. Six o'clock? Would that help, Deedee?"

"Yes, yes, it would. Thank you, sweetheart." She looked at Jesse again. "May I hug you goodbye?"

"Well, uh, sure, I guess," he said with a slight shrug.

"No, I'm sorry," Deedee said. "That wasn't fair of me. I'm a woman you don't know, even though I am your mother. I didn't mean to make you uncomfortable. The hugs will come later. Oh, Jesse, I can never forgive what was done, but at least you're here now. Welcome home."

"Until tomorrow night then," Ryan said, taking her hand. He got the telephone number of Jesse's motel, then tugged on the hand of a reluctant-to-leave Deedee, drawing her toward the front door. Krista followed and shut the door with a quiet click behind them. She turned and leaned her back against the panel as she drew a long breath.

"I feel as though I've run in a marathon," she said. "You must be wrung out completely, Jesse."

He leaned back on the sofa and stared at the ceiling.

"Yeah, I am." He lifted his head and looked at Krista when she sat down beside him. "I have a knot in my stomach the size of a bowling ball, because it would be understandable if the majority of the MacAllisters feel as Ted does. I don't blame him at all for being as suspicious of my motives as he is. I wouldn't believe me, either, because my story sounds like something out of a bad movie."

"Your story is true," Krista said firmly.

"But shouldn't have been told." Jesse dragged both hands down his face, then shook his head. "Why, why, why was I so selfish? So determined to see what my real family looked like? I'm going to tear the MacAllisters apart, Krista, and I'm already on guilt overload for what Maddie, Phyllis and Joe did."

"The MacAllisters are strong, resilient people," she said. "You come from sturdy stock, Jesse. Yes, there might very well be upset and arguments, but it will all smooth out. The DNA test will prove without a doubt that you're Deedee and Ryan's son."

"Deedee. Ryan. My mother and father. I can't bring myself to refer to Phyllis and Joe as my parents anymore because I'm so appalled at what they were a party to. They're Phyllis and Joe Burke, who weren't even close to being who I thought they were. I've stripped them of the title of Mother and Father in my mind, but I'm having a difficult time passing that baton to Deedee and Ryan. I'm sure not prepared to call them Mom and Dad."

"It's too soon for that," Krista agreed, placing one hand on his shoulder. "They wouldn't expect that of you at this point, Jesse. Look how understanding Deedee was about your not being ready to hug her. They'll be patient, you'll see."

"What if I can never bond with them, trust and believe in them like a son should? Hey, we're your parents and we love you and we're terrific people and…hell, I bought into that all my life with Phyllis and Joe Burke, and it turned out there was a dark side to them that I can't forgive them for. I feel as if a part of me has just shut down, as far as trust goes."

"Give it time," Krista said.

"Yeah, well…okay, new topic. Don't you think you were a bit hasty in saying I should stay at your place? You're a celebrity in this town. There must be a gossip column in the Ventura newspaper. What if they get wind that a man is living with TV anchorwoman Krista Kelly? That might cause you grief with your bosses, your public, the whole nine yards."

"Let me worry about that," she said. "It's more important that *your* story, your being a MacAllister who was kidnapped at birth and on and on, doesn't get leaked to the media somehow. I'm not such a big deal that reporters keep an eye on me and my comings and goings. It's the best solution, Jesse. It gets you out of the motel, but gives the family some breathing room to come to grips with the fact that you exist." Krista paused and frowned. "Unless, of course, you'd rather not stay at my apartment. What do *you* want to do?"

Jesse got to his feet and began to wander restlessly around the living room.

What did he want to do? he thought. He wanted to take Krista into his arms and kiss her again, be transported to that place where nothing and no one existed but the two of them. He wanted to make love with her for hours, then hold her close as they slept. He wanted to shut out the world and the turmoil and the pain and just be…with Krista.

Jesse stopped his restless wandering and turned to look at her. "I'd much rather stay at your apartment than in that gloomy room at the motel," he said. "I'm grateful for your generous offer. But I feel I should re-assure you that there won't be a repeat performance of what happened in the kitchen earlier.

"I'm not sorry that happened, that we shared those kisses, but I won't touch you again, make you edgy in your own home, make you worry about whether I'm going to…" He paused, smiled suddenly and raised one hand. "I swear I'll behave as a proper gentleman should."

How very noble, Krista thought dryly. But how could she be certain that she would behave as a proper lady should?

Chapter 5

Just before five o'clock the next evening, Deedee entered the living room to find Ryan sitting on the sofa reading the newspaper. She stopped and gazed at him, savoring the fact that after all the years they had been together the mere sight of him could still cause her heart to flutter.

Oh, how she loved Ryan MacAllister, she thought. He was a devoted husband who continually made her feel special and wanted, feminine and even still beautiful. He was also a wonderful father, had been an equal partner with her in the care of Teddy and Sarah.

Sudden and unexpected tears filled Deedee's eyes.

Ryan should have also had the years of joy that raising their second son, Sarah's twin brother, would have brought into their lives. And she, too, should have had the role of mother to three miracles, not just two.

Jesse.

Thirty-two years of their son's life had been taken from them, Deedee realized, dashing an errant tear from her cheek. Dear heaven, it was so difficult to fathom that something so horrific could have happened to them, been carried out by Maddie Clemens and sanctioned by Phyllis and Joe Burke. How had they lived with the knowledge of what they had done? It was so evil, cruel, it was almost impossible to comprehend. Yet it was true. They had stolen her and Ryan's newborn baby.

Ryan glanced up and saw the stricken expression on Deedee's face.

"Hey." He tossed the newspaper aside, hurried to her and wrapped his arms around her.

"I'm sorry," she said, nestling her head on his chest. "My tears are so close to the surface right now that it doesn't take much to cause them to spill over. A part of me is so grateful that Jesse wanted a glimpse of us, was caught in the act, so to speak. But when I think of how much we missed, how much *he* missed… So many years, Ryan. I get so angry, so…" She sniffled.

"I know, sweetheart," he said, tightening his hold on her. "But we can't turn back the clock, change what happened. All we can do is live in the present and hope that the future finds Jesse willing to stay in Ventura as part of the family. This is extremely difficult for him, too. If he chooses to leave we can't stop him."

Deedee tilted her head back to look up at her husband.

"I can't bear the thought of losing him again," she said, fresh tears filling her eyes. "We have to make him realize how much we love him, that all the MacAllisters will welcome him into the family, that he isn't alone."

"Whoa, honey," Ryan said. "Let's be realistic here. We can say we love Jesse based on the fact that he's our son, that that love is automatically in place. But we have to face the fact that we may not like him. He's a grown man with opinions, values, outlooks that might be so removed from what we believe in that we can't connect, can't bond."

"Ryan," Deedee said, stepping backward and out of his embrace, "how can you say such a thing? Jesse is our son, just as Teddy is our son and Sarah our daughter. We don't agree with everything they say and do, but that doesn't diminish the love we have for them."

"True," he said, nodding. "But we raised them from the minute they were born. We know who they are inside, the essence of them. Honey, please, you've got to accept that Jesse Burke is a stranger to us. He is, Deedee."

"No. He's our son, Ryan. He deserves our unconditional love just as much as Teddy and Sarah. A mother knows her son."

"Okay." Ryan crossed his arms over his chest. "What's his favorite color? Does he hate broccoli with a passion the way Sarah does? If Jesse found a wad of money on the floor in a bank would he turn it over to a teller, or put it in his pocket, finders-keepers? Does he want to have a wife and children in his life, or does he prefer an existence with no responsibilities of that nature? Pick one question, Deedee, and tell me the answer."

"I…I don't know the answer to any of those questions."

"Of course you don't," Ryan said gently, "because Jesse is a stranger. By the same token, he doesn't have a clue as to who we are, either, except for things he read in old newspapers and magazine articles about the ever-growing MacAllister family.

"This whole process of getting to know each other is going to take time and patience, and at any given moment Jesse could decide that the world we have to offer him is not what he wants…and he will leave. Titles of son, mother, father just don't carry their usual weight in a situation like this one. The key word here is *strangers,* because that's what we are to each other. You've got to face that, Deedee."

"Oh, darn it, Ryan, you're right, and I wish so much that you weren't. I'm his mother and I love him, but that might not be enough to keep him with us."

Ryan laughed, closed the short distance between them and dropped a quick kiss on her lips. "Don't ya just hate it when the old man is right?"

"At the moment I do," she said, producing a small smile.

"One day at a time, my love," he murmured. "That's

the only way to do this." He paused. "We'd better get going or we'll be late for dinner at Krista's."

"Do you think Sarah will come to Krista's? She was so upset when we told her about Jesse, about what those despicable people did. She was devastated."

Ryan sighed. "I know. I couldn't begin to guess as to whether she's ready to meet Jesse now. You heard her say that she wanted to stay with the children after being away, and if she felt she was prepared to see Jesse she'd come to Krista's later in the evening, after the kiddos were in bed. We'll just have to wait and see what she does."

"Yes, all right," Deedee said. "I wish we'd been able to reach Teddy in Italy when we phoned him. He's been very difficult to connect with lately."

"Yep," Ryan said, wiggling his eyebrows. "Do remember that he said the woman heading up the computer department in the company there is extremely intelligent and very attractive. That's interesting data."

"Oh, my," Deedee said, smiling. "What a marvelous thought. All Teddy did here in Ventura was work, work, work at the computer company. He needs a wife, children, a home."

"Which you tell him on a regular basis," Ryan said, chuckling. "I don't have a clue as to why he's hard to reach by phone these days, but it did occur to me that he'd made reference to that woman more than once."

"Rosalie," Deedee said. "Her name is Rosalie." Her eyes widened. "Oh, mercy, what if he married her and decided to live in Italy? That would be terrible."

"I should never have opened that can of worms," Ryan said. "Now you'll stew about it. We're out the door, Deedee, and off to Krista's. Concentrate on the situation we're facing right here."

"Jesse," Deedee whispered. "Our son."

Krista frowned as she peered in the oven, then shut the door and shrugged. "The chicken is getting brown and crispy," she said, turning to look at Jesse. "This is my one and only complete meal I know how to prepare. Baked chicken, potatoes, gravy and a veggie. Whoopee. Very basic. Very boring. Julia Child I am not."

"It sure does smell good," Jesse said, pushing himself away from the counter he was leaning against. "I finished setting the table. That's about the extent of *my* kitchen abilities."

Krista laughed. "We'd better not get married or we'd either starve to death or eat microwave food in boxes for eternity, the way I do now."

"Why *aren't* you married, Krista? You're a beautiful, intelligent woman. Are all the eligible men in Ventura complete idiots?"

"Yep. You got it in one," she said breezily. "Okay, everything is under control for now. Let's relax in the living room before the others arrive."

Jesse followed Krista from the good-size kitchen.

She sure had skittered around the subject of marriage, he mused. There was no way that a woman like Krista wasn't sought after. Cancel her quick agreement that Ventura men were dopes.

There was something about the subject of marriage that Krista didn't intend to divulge, a secret something. Oh, sure, she'd joked about how they shouldn't be married because neither one of them could cook, but when he'd gotten serious on the issue she had verbally run like hell in the opposite direction. Why?

"Did you get settled into your room all right?" she asked, sitting down on one end of the sofa.

"Yep," Jesse said, choosing the opposite end. "I really appreciate your letting me stay here. Your apartment is big, bright and sunny, and welcoming. Everything that motel room wasn't."

"Well, my guest room is actually my office, with a bed stuck in the corner. I wouldn't call it plush accommodations."

"Looks great to me." Jesse paused. "You know, Krista, I'm going to feel like I'm under a microscope with all the MacAllisters peering at me and passing judgment. It's not a very comfortable image in my mind's eye."

"Just be yourself."

"That was why I was determined to locate the Mac-Allister family in the first place—to discover who I am, have an identity again. It's very unsettling to find out after thirty-two years that you're not who you were told you were.

"But now that I'm here I realize it's not going to be that easy to feel like a MacAllister, either. I look at Deedee and Ryan and all I see are strangers, people I don't know anything about except what I've read in newspapers and magazines. There was no instant connection like there was, well, like there was with you."

"You're comparing apples and oranges, Jesse. You and I felt an attraction, a man and woman thing, which we are not going to discuss further. As for Deedee and Ryan, I don't think it's realistic that you'd feel a link to them at this point. It's going to take time."

"So you think that Deedee's emotions regarding me are based on the simple fact of me being her son rather than a true intuitive connection?"

"Oh, now you're stepping into a mysterious arena," Krista said. "The love of a mother for her child is not easily explained because it's so intense. I can't help you there because I'm not a mommy."

"Do you want to be? A mother?" he said.

Krista shrugged. "Someday, I suppose. I'm thoroughly enjoying my career right now, concentrating on that. I'm only thirty-one. There's plenty of time for marriage and babies if I choose to go that route. I'm not positive I will, though."

"Why not?"

She frowned. "Why do you keep circling around to the subject of my marital status?"

"Because you get fidgety whenever I mention it," Jesse said, "and I can't help but wonder what it is about the subject that makes you edgy."

"And I can't help but wonder why you think it's any of your business," she said, lifting her chin.

"Whew," Jesse said, smiling. "I will consider myself just having been popped in the chops for being too pushy about a taboo topic."

Krista laughed and got to her feet. "Well, good. Score one point for me. I'd better go check on my dinner. I have this irrational idea that the chicken will fly away if I don't make certain it's still in the oven. That shows you how much confidence I have in myself as a chef. Zip. Nada. None."

A short time later Deedee and Ryan arrived, and a wave of sadness swept through Krista as she watched the interaction between them and Jesse as they all sat in the living room.

They were trying so hard to relax and be comfortable with each other, she thought, but there was a tension between them, a hesitation before they spoke, as though they were carefully picking their words so as not to offend or push too hard.

Ryan was holding Deedee's hand, giving her support in a difficult situation. Krista wanted to do that for Jesse, let him know she was there for him, was willing to help him in any way she could. Oh, gracious, her emotions were running amok regarding Jesse Burke, totally out of control.

Get a grip, Krista, she ordered herself, *and go put dinner on the table.* About the only useful thing she could do right now was fill empty stomachs. Big deal.

Krista left the living room with no one noticing her exit, and a short time later announced in a cheerful voice that dinner was served. Everyone settled on chairs around an oak dining set in the alcove beyond the kitchen.

"Oh, this looks marvelous, Krista," Deedee said. "Thank you so much for going to all this work."

"I hope it tastes as good as it looks," she said, laughing. She picked up a bowl and handed it to Jesse. "Since Sarah isn't joining us for dinner I felt safe in serving broccoli. I know better than to have those green things on the menu when Sarah is at the table."

Jesse accepted the bowl, hesitated, then passed it on to Deedee without putting any of the vegetable on his plate.

"Uh-oh," Krista said, smiling. "I blew it."

"You don't like broccoli, Jesse?" Deedee said, leaning slightly toward him.

"No, I don't," he said. "No offense, Krista, but I can't even take a bite of broccoli to be polite. I'm really sorry."

"Did you hear that, Ryan?" Deedee said. "Jesse hates broccoli just as Sarah does. Isn't that marvelous? Even though they're fraternal twins they still have a bond, a link. It's going to be wonderful to discover what else they share as far as opinions and attitudes and—"

"Deedee," Ryan said, gently, "let's not go ballistic over broccoli. Okay?"

"But—"

"Jesse," Ryan continued, "when we phoned and told Krista to let you know that Sarah might need some time to come to terms with the fact that you exist before she met you, did you understand that? We don't want you to be hurt by it."

"Sarah has every right to protect her emotions," Jesse said, "who she is, her life as she's always known it. If she never wanted to meet me it wouldn't seem unreasonable. There might be a lot of MacAllisters who feel that way."

"Oh, no, no, that won't happen," Deedee said. "Sarah, and perhaps some of the others, just might need a little time to take it in, that's all. Eventually they'll be thrilled that you're finally here, where you belong."

"As thrilled as Ted?" Jesse asked, frowning.

"I'm sorry about Ted's attitude." Deedee sighed. "But once the DNA tests are back, Ted will realize how wrong he was about you. We spoke to Kara and she's thinking about the best way to have those tests done to assure total secrecy, so there's no chance that the media gets wind of this."

"Ted wants proof of my identity," Jesse said, "and I don't blame him. Others in your family will probably feel the same way."

"They're your family, too," Deedee said, "and you must take comfort in knowing that Ryan and I believe you are our son. Krista has no doubt that you're telling the truth, either. Ryan and I love you, Jesse."

"That's not possible," he said, his voice rising slightly. "I'm a complete stranger to you."

"No you're not," Deedee said. "Well, yes, you are in a way but—"

"Let's slow down here and enjoy this delicious meal," Ryan said. "Pass the chicken on over here, Krista. It's calling my name. By the way, that was a nice job of reporting you did on the news about the police going to schools to teach the kids about stranger danger."

"Thank you," Krista said. Bless you, Ryan, she thought. Some light chitchat was really called for here. There was a frantic edge building in Deedee's voice, and Jesse was getting more tense by the minute. "I think the public could see from the film clips we showed that the little ones were listening, giving those officers their full attention."

"Absolutely," Ryan said. "Mmm. This dinner is hitting the spot."

"Yes, it's great," Jesse said.

"As long as no one plunks any broccoli on your plate," Krista said, laughing.

"True," he said, smiling at her. "I'll make up for it by having an extra serving of potatoes and gravy. It's been a couple of months since I've had a home-cooked meal and I'm enjoying every bite."

"Jesse, may I ask you what your favorite color is?" Deedee said.

Oh, dear, Krista thought, so much for casual chitchat. Deedee was so eager to get to know her son, try to fill in the gaps, make up for all the years he hadn't been with her, that she was running the risk of pushing Jesse too hard, possibly making him feel as if he were being grilled under a bare lightbulb.

"Blue, I guess," Jesse said, directing his attention to his plate. "I've never thought about it that much."

"Blue?" Deedee said. "That's Sarah's favorite color. When she married Barry the bridesmaids wore blue and Sarah's bouquet was blue and white flowers. We must remember to tell her that your favorite color is blue just as hers is. She'll like that, I know she will."

"Deedee, stop it," Ryan said firmly. "Sarah will not give a rip right now about matching favorite colors. She is trying to come to grips with the fact that she has a twin brother."

"But…" Deedee sighed and nodded. "I'm sorry. I really do apologize, because there's no excuse for my behavior. I think some irrational part of my mind believes that if I talk loud enough and fast enough, and ask a zillion questions, it will help erase all the years that Jesse… Well, just tell me to put a cork in it when I get off on one of my tangents."

She glanced around. "Krista, they did a lovely job painting your apartment. Everything looks so fresh and clean, and you must be pleased. Oh, and I've been meaning to ask you how your parents are doing in Florida. Weren't they planning to go on a cruise?"

What class, Jesse thought. Deedee MacAllister, his…his mother, was one very classy lady. She was pulling herself together under extremely difficult circumstances.

"They're on the cruise as we speak," Krista said. "It's the dream vacation they've fantasied about for years, and I'm thrilled for them. They'll be stopping at various islands to sightsee and shop, then on they go. They'll be gone an entire month."

"Good for them," Ryan said. "Deedee and I went on a cruise years ago and it was...um..."

Deedee laughed. "You were bored out of your mind, Ryan MacAllister. The ship went so slow, and the activities available were not to your liking. The only time you perked up and showed some enthusiam was for another one of those fabulous meals they served."

"Well, it isn't natural to hold someone captive on a ship that just creeps through the water," Ryan said. "I mean, for Pete's sake, how many games of shuffleboard can a man play? How many hours can he sit in a deck chair and say things like 'this is the life'? Nope, cruises are not my cup of tea."

"I had a fabulous time," Deedee said, smiling at her husband.

Ryan leaned over and gave her a peck on the forehead. "Then my suffering was worth it, my love," he said.

"Oh, that is so sweet," Krista said, smiling. "Ain't love grand, as the saying goes."

"It is, indeed," Deedee said, "and I'm sure your mother reminds you of that fact on a regular basis. Mothers have an extra gene that makes them want to see all their children happily married and producing bouncing baby grandchildren for us to spoil. We can't help ourselves when we nag about the subject."

"Is that a fact?" Jesse chuckled. "That reminds me of a case I prosecuted once where the public defender was scrambling so badly to attempt to get his guilty-as-sin client off that the defense was that the owner of the liquor store that was robbed created an attractive nuisance by having a huge sale and was obviously bringing in beaucoup money on the night in question. Hey, it wasn't the guy's fault that he did it."

Everyone at the table laughed in delight at Jesse's story.

"I assume you won that case," Ryan said finally.

"Yes, I did." Jesse smiled. "The biggest concern was whether the judge was going to hyperventilate and pass out from lack of oxygen because he was laughing so hard. I took a lot of razzing back in the office about being the next F. Lee Bailey."

"Somehow I don't think I would have been given copy in my hot little hand to report that trial on the news," Krista said.

"You enjoy being a prosecuting attorney?" Ryan asked.

"I do," Jesse said, nodding. "Very much. I plan to return to that career as soon as I can."

"We have attorneys in the MacAllister family," Deedee said pleasantly.

"There are so many MacAllisters," Jesse said, "it's probably difficult to name a career arena where you don't have at least one."

She laughed. "That's probably true. We even have royalty among us due to several marriages that took place."

"I came across those stories while doing my research on all of you," Jesse said. "It was the stuff of which fairy tales are made."

"And I got to report it on the 6:00 and 10:00 p.m. newscasts," Krista said. "I could practically hear the wistful sighs coming from the female populace of Ventura while I was still talking to the little red light on the camera."

"Your fans would sigh again if your engagement to your own prince charming became news, Krista," Deedee said. "People adore love stories and happy endings. I'm just tossing that in because your mother isn't here to do it."

"Which prompts me to ask if everyone is ready for dessert." Krista got to her feet.

"Well, I tried," Deedee said. "Do remember that I can't be held responsible."

"Because of the extra gene you have," Ryan said.

"And the fact that unmarried adult children are an attractive nuisance that can't be ignored," Jesse said.

"Exactly," Deedee said, beaming.

Laughter filled the air again and Krista felt a rush of deep respect for Deedee.

Oh, yes, Krista thought, as she carried plates back into the kitchen, the MacAllisters had dignity, class and grace. And Jesse was a MacAllister.

The conversation remained light and breezy as everyone enjoyed a dessert of cherry cheesecake and coffee. Krista laughed and admitted that she'd made the coffee from scratch but her favorite bakery a few blocks away had produced the cheesecake. Deedee had just offered to help tidy the kitchen when a knock sounded at the apartment door.

They all stiffened and heads snapped around in the direction of the sudden noise.

"It's Sarah," Deedee whispered, reaching for Ryan's hand. "Sarah has come to see Jesse. She's ready to meet her twin brother."

Chapter 6

Krista's heart began to race as she got to her feet to answer the knock at the door.

"Krista," Deedee said, "would you mind if Ryan and I greeted Sarah?"

"No. No, of course not." She sat back down. "Go right ahead."

Deedee and Ryan hurried from the room and Krista looked at Jesse, seeing the tight set to his jaw and the stiffening of his shoulders.

"Oh, Jesse," she said, "this isn't fair. No one asked *you* if you were ready to meet your sister. Your feelings and emotions should be taken into account, too."

"No, I lost the right to that consideration when I got caught in front of Sarah's house, stayed there too long.

Ah, Krista, I'm upsetting so many people, turning their lives upside down." Jesse shook his head. "I should never have come to Ventura. It was so selfish of me and—"

"Hello, Jesse," a soft, feminine voice said. "I'm Sarah. Your twin sister."

Jesse planted his hands flat on the table and pushed himself to his feet, his gaze riveted on the woman standing in the doorway.

Sarah, he thought. There she was. She looked so much like Deedee—slender, with big brown eyes, delicate features, even the same dusting of freckles on her nose. Her hair was a tumble of strawberry-blond curls to her shoulders. Sarah. His sister.

They had been born that same night thirty-two years ago at Maddie's, only to be ripped apart, not knowing the other existed. He had been robbed of the chance to grow up with this sister, have the special bond between twins, share loving parents and the big brother who they probably would have trailed after like little pests.

"Hello, Sarah," Jesse said, his voice strained with building emotions. "I...I'm very sorry that I've caused you such upset by suddenly appearing in your life." His gaze flickered to Deedee and Ryan. "In all of your lives."

"You mustn't feel that way," Sarah said, walking forward. "You belong here with us. You're a Mac-Allister, Jesse. You have every right to take your place within this family."

He shook his head.

"Let's all sit down, shall we?" Sarah said.

When everyone was settled at the table, Sarah looked directly into Jesse's eyes.

"MacAllister eyes," she said. "You have them. Big and brown." She paused. "I want to share a couple things with you, Jesse. When Barry's and my third child was born they placed him in my arms in the delivery room and I said that his name was Jesse. Barry was confused because we had narrowed down our choices to a couple of names and Jesse wasn't on the list.

"I don't know. I looked at that baby and said he must be named Jesse. Now I realize that I was somehow picking up signals, mental waves, whatever label you want to put on it, from you. We're twins—fraternal twins, yes, but there is still a special link between fraternal twins, just as there is between identical ones."

"I don't know much about that type of thing," Jesse said, "other than what I read in an article in a magazine about the special bond twins have. I didn't pay much attention to the information because I wasn't aware that I had a twin sister."

Sarah nodded. "There's something else I need to tell you that no one knows because I've never shared it with anyone. For as many years as I can remember I've had a dream at night every few weeks. The very same dream. I'm in a towering field of corn that stretches in all directions as far as I can see. I'm searching for something, pushing aside the stalks, frantically trying to find what I'm seeking, but I never do, nor am I sure what it is I'm looking for. I've had that dream over and over and over."

"Corn?" Jesse said, feeling the color drain from his face. "We grew corn on the farm, the ranch. Several acres every year with tall stalks. You saw the cornfield in your dreams?"

"Yes, and now I know I was searching for you," Sarah said. "And here you are at long last." Tears filled her eyes. "Welcome home, Jesse. We're all so glad you found us. I can't forgive the people who took you from us, but at least you're home now. I want you to meet my husband, the children, especially your namesake, Jesse. He's five years old and I can't wait to see him sitting on your lap and—"

"No," Jesse said, getting to his feet again. "Sarah, stop and think a minute, please. I'm a stranger, don't you see? Would you allow a stranger into your home, trust him to interact with your children, welcome him as a member of your family after having nothing more than a brief conversation with him? No, you wouldn't."

"You're my brother," Sarah said, her voice rising. "My twin brother."

Jesse sliced one hand through the air. "Titles mean nothing under these circumstances. Mother. Father. Son. Brother. Sister. They're words, just words. For God's sake, we didn't even know each other a few days ago. Don't just automatically trust me, believe in me, label me a MacAllister and expect me to become one with no difficulty. *I don't know who you people are.*"

"Do you trust us?" Deedee said softly. "Believe our feelings for you, that our desire to welcome you into our hearts, our family, our homes, is genuine? Do you trust us, Jesse?"

He drew a shuddering breath. "I don't know. I trusted and believed in Phyllis and Joe Burke my entire life and now I know that it was all lies. They weren't who they presented themselves to be. What am I supposed to do? Say 'Well, those Burke parents were duds, so I'll just take on Deedee and Ryan MacAllister as my next set and see how they turn out'? It's not that easy. It's not."

"But—" Deedee said, extending one hand toward him.

"Of course it's not that easy," Krista interrupted. "This is all going to take time and patience on everyone's part. This is an extremely emotional situation and it can't be rushed. People can't be pushed and pressured. Sarah, you came here tonight because you were ready to meet your brother. Did anyone ask if Jesse was ready to meet you? I think it's forgotten at times that he has a great deal to handle here, too. Jesse has suffered a devastating blow by discovering that he was deceived by the most important people in his life, the ones who raised him from infancy. Have any of you given thought to the pain he's suffering because he…he…"

Her voice trailed off as she suddenly became aware that everyone was staring at her with stunned expressions on their faces.

"I'm sorry," she said, sighing. "I'm overstepping and…oh, dear."

She looked tentatively at Jesse, and her heart skittered as she saw a smile begin to form on his lips and a warmth glow in the depth of his dark eyes. He mouthed the words *thank you* and she nodded slightly.

"You're right, Krista," Ryan said, breaking the silence that had fallen over the group. "You are absolutely right. We're all centered on ourselves, what we want, what we're feeling, and losing track of the fact that Jesse is as overwhelmed by all of this as we are."

Ryan shifted his gaze to his son. "I apologize, Jesse, on behalf of all of us. From now on you'll have an equal voice in what takes place. If you're not up to meeting more MacAllisters at a given moment, then that will be respected."

"Thank you, sir," Jesse said.

"Sir," Ryan said, frowning. "I can't find a place to put that title. Look, why don't we agree that you'll call me Ryan and your mother—I mean, Deedee—is Deedee. Are you comfortable with that?"

"Yes. Fine." Jesse nodded. "Ryan."

Sarah opened her purse and removed a small leather folder. "This is a photograph of Barry and me with the kids," she said. "Would you like to have it? That smallest boy is Jesse."

"Thank you," Jesse said, accepting it and flipping it open. "You're a beautiful family. Jesse looks a great deal like I did around that age, according to the pictures I've seen."

"Where are those photos of you growing up?" Deedee asked eagerly.

"They're in albums in a box I stored in a friend's garage in Nevada, along with my extra clothes, books, personal things. I'm selling the ranch as is, leaving the furniture in the house. I didn't take much when I left."

"I would dearly love to gaze at each photograph in those albums," Deedee said, a wistful tone to her voice. "I could see you as an infant, then a toddler, then on to a busy little boy and—"

"And it could be very painful to do that, Deedee," Ryan said. "Let's not think about those pictures at this point. I'd say we all have enough on our emotional plate as it is right now."

She sighed and nodded.

"Enough for one night," her husband continued. "We're out of here. Sarah, go home to Barry. He must be concerned about how you're holding up over here. Thank you for dinner, Krista, and for everything else you're doing."

"Sarah," Deedee said. "Jesse hates broccoli."

Sarah laughed. "Of course he does. We agreed on that while we were still in your tummy, Mom."

With that lighthearted statement the trio left, smiling, Krista waving a farewell from the doorway. She closed the door, locked it for the night, then turned and saw Jesse standing in the middle of the room looking at her.

"That wasn't so bad, was it?" she said.

He chuckled. "No, not after you went on a rip and reminded them that I had feelings, too. That I wasn't just a windup toy or something. You're a scary lady when you put your mind to it."

"You'd better believe it," she said, laughing. "What I made clear needed to be said, but I'll admit I got a tad carried away with my rather loud sermonette."

"I appreciate what you did," he said, serious again, "and I want to repeat my sincere words of gratitude for allowing me to stay here rather than in that bleak motel. You're a very thoughtful and caring woman, Krista. Add beautiful and classy to that description, too."

"Classy," Krista said thoughtfully. "That was how I was painting Deedee in my mind tonight."

"So was I, as a matter of fact, but you should include yourself in the painting."

"Thank you, Jesse." Krista paused. "Would you like a snack?"

"No, I'm still full from that delicious dinner. I'm also drained, really exhausted. I think I'll call it a day and attempt to get a solid night's sleep. The tricky part will be turning off my mind, not dwelling on the people I've met, what they said, how they look."

"Your family," she said softly.

"There's another one of those titles that is just a word at the moment," he said, frowning. "Maybe that's all any of them will ever be—just words. I don't know." He opened the leather folder he was still holding, stared at the picture of Sarah, Barry and the three children, then closed it again. "I just don't know."

Krista crossed the room to stand in front of him. "Give it time," she murmured. "Don't let anyone rush you. Take all the time you need."

"That's excellent advice and I'll keep telling myself

to remember it but…" Jesse placed a hand on her cheek "…when it comes to you, Krista, I don't want any more of that famous time to pass before I kiss you again, hold you." He stroked her soft skin with his thumb. "I'm sorry. I shouldn't have gone there. I'll say good-night now."

"But I…" Krista began, then stopped speaking. *I want you to kiss me, hold me and, heaven help me, make love with me, Jesse.* Oh, mercy, what was happening to her? "Yes, good night."

Jesse looked directly into her eyes for another long, heart-stopping moment, then dropped his hand from her face and walked out of the room, disappearing down the hallway.

Krista drew a shuddering breath, then placed trembling fingertips on her cheek, savoring the warmth still there from Jesse's tender touch.

In the middle of the next morning Kara telephoned to say that if it was convenient, she would come to Krista's herself and take a blood sample from Jesse for the DNA testing, which she would have done at a private laboratory.

After Kara had slipped the vial of blood in a small box and put it in her purse, she smiled at Jesse. He was sitting on the sofa, with Krista at the opposite end. Kara sat down in an easy chair across from them.

"Having this test done is nonsense," she said, "because all a person has to do is look at you to know that you're a MacAllister."

"Try telling Ted that," Krista said. "I imagine there will be other doubters in the family, too."

"Maybe." Kara nodded. "Word about you is spreading through the clan like wildfire, Jesse. Personally? I'm just sick at heart when I think about what took place when you were born, but I'm finding some comfort in the fact that you're at least here at long last."

"It's not that simple," he said. "I'm a stranger, remember?"

"That's right, buster," Kara said, laughing. "For all we know you're an ax murderer, by golly."

"Well, I could be," Jesse said, matching her smile.

"Oh, honey," Kara said, "I'm sixty-eight years old and I've been a doctor for more years than I can count. I've learned to size up people very quickly in my profession. You're a fine man with MacAllister genes. You're Deedee and Ryan's son, and that's good enough for me.

"I was adopted into this family when I was a teenager—a kid with a chip on my shoulder a mile wide, Jesse. I hate to even imagine what would have become of me if the MacAllisters hadn't made me one of their own.

"All I'm saying is, give them a chance. I realize they're strangers to you, too, but you can trust and believe in them. I didn't buy into that way back when, but time took care of my doubts and fears."

"Ah, that word again," Jesse said, frowning. "Time. The great solution to all dilemmas."

"Maybe not all," Kara said, getting to her feet, "but

a whole big bunch. Well, I'm off. Nice to see you again, Krista. And Jesse? That chip on my shoulder that I spoke of? It got very heavy to tote around. Think about it."

Krista saw Kara to the door, then returned to sit on the sofa.

"That's what I call a straight-shooting lady," Jesse said.

"With some more of that MacAllister class," Krista said.

Jesse nodded. "That, too." He planted his hands on his knees and pushed himself to his feet. "I think I'll go for a walk and get out of your way. You're not accustomed to having someone underfoot and I don't want to be a nuisance, keep you from your normal routine."

"All I planned to do was a load of wash," Krista said. "Besides, I enjoy your company." She paused. "I hope you won't feel deserted this evening while I'm at the station. My being there from about four to close to midnight sort of turns my workday upside down from the norm."

"I'm used to being alone," he said, starting to wander around the living room.

"Do you prefer that, Jesse? Being alone?"

"Do you?" he said, stopping his trek to look at Krista.

She laughed. "You must be an excellent attorney. You have that answer-a-question-with-a-question bit down pat."

"Actually, at the risk of sounding full of myself, I *am* a good attorney. I'm eager to get back to that career." He nodded. "I really am. My life was on hold when I returned to the ranch to help out. Now? It's on hold again because I've created this complicated situation with the MacAllisters.

"But, oh, man, I just had to know who I was, have an identity of some kind again after I discovered I really wasn't Phyllis and Joe Burke's son. What a joke. Who am I? A complete stranger to a whole bunch of people who will probably come to wish that I'd never surfaced and messed up their well-ordered lives. Ah, hell, what a crummy situation I've stirred up."

"That's not true," Krista said, getting to her feet. "You have a family, Jesse. You're a MacAllister who has returned to take your rightful place among them. Yes, it's startling, upsetting, hard to comprehend what happened all those years ago, but you're here now, where you belong."

"I'm not sure about that," he said. "Hey, enough of this. Let's go out to lunch with the agreement that we're two people enjoying a meal together, and not mention this, quote, crummy situation even once. Deal?"

Krista smiled. "Deal."

At six that evening, Jesse knew he was smiling as he watched Krista reporting the news on television.

Sensational, he thought. Not only was Krista Kelly beautiful, she was an excellent anchorwoman. She knew exactly what tone and expression to use for each story she related to the public. The lady had class.

And those incredible blue eyes of hers. Every person glued to their set must feel as though she was looking directly at them, caring and sharing.

Her dark curls shone in the lights from the cameras, and she was wearing the prettiest shade of rose-colored lipstick, which brought memories of the kisses he'd shared with her front row center in his mind.

Jesse shifted in the chair he was sitting on.

Correct that, he thought dryly. The memories of those kisses, her aroma, the feel of her body pressed to his were now causing heat to coil low in his body, tight and aching. Oh, how he wanted her. He wanted to make love to Krista for hours, through an entire night, where no one would exist but the two of them.

He frowned.

How many other yahoos had the same kind of thoughts as they watched the news delivered by Krista? How many sleazeballs fantasized about her, about making her theirs? No wonder Ted and Ryan had accused him of being a possible stalker of celebrity Ms. Kelly. It was a reasonable fear, by damn.

Maybe he should go down to the station and escort her safely to her car. Or even better, while he was staying here at her place he could take her to work and pick her up again. He could make certain that no one hassled his Krista, or put her in harm's way. Yeah, he could...

His Krista?

"Whoa," he said aloud, stiffening in the chair.

Where had *that* come from? he wondered. *His* Krista? She wasn't his. Granted, he felt closer to her than he did to any of the MacAllisters who were actually his family, but his attraction to Krista was an understandable man and woman thing. He just wasn't connecting with the MacAllisters in an I'm-a-member-of-the-family way. And maybe he never would.

So, sure, he and Krista felt that sexual pull toward each other. Why not? They were healthy adults with natural urges and desires. Where this *his* Krista stuff was coming from he had no idea. It was just that the idea of a city full of faceless men watching her on TV every night and wanting her the same way he did made him mad as hell.

"Oh, Burke, you're losing it, buddy," he said, shaking his head.

Besides, he mused, mentally rambling on, suppose, just suppose that he fell in love with Krista—though it wasn't going to happen. That would get him nothing but a busted heart, guaranteed, because for reasons she obviously wasn't going to reveal, the lady had a negative mind-set about marriage.

Why? Why did she feel so strongly about that? What had happened to her in the past? Who had hurt her so much that she had slammed the door shut and locked it tight on the subject of commitment and forever? Would she ever trust him enough to tell him?

Trust. Now there was a peachy word. Trust that your loving parents, the ever-famous Phyllis and Joe Burke, are everything they appear to be as you're growing up. Yeah, right.

And trust that Deedee and Ryan MacAllister are just thrilled out of their socks that their long lost son has returned to the fold, wrecking the lives they'd worked hard to create. Yeah, right again. For appearances sake they had to go through the motions of welcoming him, acting as though he was a gift from the heavens or some such thing. The classy MacAllisters would do nothing less than the expected.

But what were they really thinking and saying behind closed doors, in the privacy of their own home?

Trust? Oh, yeah, right.

The only person he really and truly trusted in the entire city of Ventura, California, was Krista Kelly. Beautiful, beautiful Krista.

Chapter 7

During the next three days, which included the weekend, there was no contact from any members of the MacAllister family. Jesse felt himself beginning to unwind and relax for the first time since the day of Phyllis and Joe Burke's funeral.

He was, he knew, playing ostrich, but indulged himself and focused on Krista and the pure joy of being with her, seeing her smile, hearing her laughter, watching her blue eyes sparkle. His desire for her was growing steadily, but he evoked every bit of willpower he possessed and kept his word that he would "behave as a proper gentlemen should."

On Sunday afternoon Krista and Jesse sat on a blanket in a lovely park. They had packed a picnic lunch and eaten every bit of the delicacies they'd purchased at a nearby deli. They had also bought a kite to fly in the picture-perfect weather, which included a kite-flying breeze.

"Our pretty kite is probably bobbing along over San Francisco by now," Krista said, laughing. "I can't believe the string broke. I mean, come on, that was official kite string, for Pete's sake. You don't suppose it had anything to do with the dolts who were yanking on it, do you?"

"Us?" Jesse said, matching her smile. "Don't be absurd. There was definitely a flaw in the string. They just don't make kite string like they used to." He flopped back onto the blanket. "Ah, man, what a great day. Look at those clouds."

Krista hesitated a moment, then settled next to him, looking up at the sky.

"Did you find pictures in the clouds when you were a little boy?" she said.

"Sure. I always saw dragons and great sailing ships. Guy stuff."

"I found princesses in beautiful dresses. And teddy bears. There was always a teddy bear."

They lay in silence for several minutes, each searching for pictures in the fluffy white clouds.

"Jesse?" Krista finally said.

"Hmm?" He turned his head to look at her.

Krista met his gaze, her heart quickening as she realized how close he was.

"The last few days have been so nice," she said.

"I've enjoyed being with you more than I can say. It's as though we closed a door on the world beyond, ignoring for a while wherever we were, whatever we were doing."

"I know."

"The MacAllisters should be commended for giving you some space, not pressuring you to meet more of them," she continued. "But I imagine these past few days have been especially difficult for Deedee. As your mother she must be aching to see you again, talk to you, hope you'll come to believe in her and Ryan, and want to take your rightful place within the family."

"Your point?" Jesse said, frowning.

"It appears that the MacAllisters are waiting for you to take the next step to connect with them. At the risk of your becoming angry at me, I'm asking if you plan to do that soon?"

Jesse rolled onto his side and propped his head on his forearm.

"I can't imagine ever becoming angry with you, Krista," he said. "I know I can't go on just pretending the MacAllisters and the whole mess I created isn't out there waiting for me, but I've been savoring every minute we've shared, just the two of us."

"But?"

"But you're right. It's time for this ostrich to pull his head out of the sand." Jesse paused. "You know, this may sound weird, but the person who keeps flitting into my mind is that little guy Jesse, Sarah's son. I think…yeah, I think I'd like to meet him. The way she came to name him after me is special, you know? A bit strange how it happened, but special."

"Then that's where you should start," Krista said. "With Jesse. He is so cute, and talk about a bundle of energy. He is one hundred percent boy. Sarah says she cringes on wash day when she has to empty Jesse's pockets before putting his jeans in the machine."

Jesse chuckled, and a shiver slithered down Krista's back at the deep, rumbly, oh-so-male sound.

"Well, I can't expect Sarah to allow me to take Jesse for an outing," he said. "She'd be crazy to do that. I'm a stranger."

"Sarah obviously doesn't feel that way."

"She's riding on emotions, not good sense," he said. "I'll have to gear up to see Sarah again, meet her husband, the other two kids, in order to have a chance to interact with Jesse." He paused. "Okay. I'll do it. I'll call Sarah and ask her if I can come over there after school tomorrow when the kids get home."

"I'd be glad to go with you for support, but I have to work tomorrow afternoon," Krista said.

"I've already taken advantage of you, Krista," Jesse said quietly. "I'm staying in your home, infringing on all your free time, using being with you to give me a chance to gain at least a modicum of inner peace. I'm long overdue to stand on my own two feet and square off against this situation."

"You haven't used me, Jesse. Don't say such a thing. If I hadn't wanted to spend this many hours with you

I would have spoken up. I've enjoyed this time we've had very, very much."

"Thank you for saying that," he said, then laughed. "How many points do I get for being the proper gentlemen I promised I would be?"

"Do you want me to answer that as a proper lady should, or tell you the truth?" Krista said, no hint of a smile on her face.

"Truth is good," he said, looking at her intently. "Yes, truth is a very good thing."

"I…I wanted you to kiss me again, Jesse. Hold me in your arms as you did before, and make me feel so alive and feminine and beautiful. I even fantasized about what it would be like to make love with you. I have not had 'proper lady' thoughts regarding you, Jesse Burke. I'm not prepared to make any promises, commitments, nothing even close to that arena. All I know is that I've wanted you, and I guess that's borderline tacky…or something. Good heavens, I can't believe I just said all that."

"I…" Jesse started, then cleared his throat. "I don't think there is one tacky thing about what you just told me. It was honest and, believe me, I put a lot of emphasis on truth, honesty, these days."

He looked up at the sky for a long moment, then met her gaze again.

"Krista, it's taken every bit of willpower I possess to keep from taking you into my arms and kissing you, holding you close. I've tossed and turned at night, aching for you, wanting to make love with you. I can't think about the future until I figure out how to solve the enormous problems I've caused the MacAllisters. All I know is that I enjoy being with you, memorize every minute we spend together, and I want you more than I can even put into words. That isn't tacky. That's me being just as honest with you as you have been with me." He smiled. "Hey, how can a guy resist a woman who sees teddy bears in the clouds?"

Krista matched his smile. "Well, then kiss me, Jesse Burke."

And he did.

Under the brilliant blue sky that held clouds forming pictures of sailing ships and teddy bears, Jesse lowered his head and claimed Krista's lips in a searing kiss. He shifted to pull her close as they lay on the blanket, then delved his tongue into the sweet darkness of her mouth.

Heat rocketed through their bodies in an exquisite pain of desire and anticipation of what was yet to come, what they would share. Passions soared to meet the clouds that seemed to encase them in a private, misty place.

"Hey, get a room," a strange voice yelled in the distance.

They jerked apart, then Krista buried her face in Jesse's shirt and laughed. "Oh, how embarrassing," she said, her voice muffled. "We're acting like teenagers on a hormone rush."

Jesse chuckled. "We're adults on a hormone rush, or whatever. But you're right, we did get a bit carried away, considering where we are."

"Which means," Krista said, wriggling out of his embrace, "that we should go home to continue this...discussion."

"Are you sure about this, Krista?" he asked. "I couldn't handle it if you had regrets, were sorry later that we—"

"Shh," she said, tapping his lips with one fingertip. "I'm sure. Very sure. I won't be sorry, Jesse. I promise you that."

Jesse nodded. "Then let's go home."

The gathering of the picnic things and the drive to Krista's was a bit of a blur. Anticipation of what was to come seemed to actually crackle through the air, heightening their desire and causing their hearts to race.

At last in Krista's apartment, they dumped the blanket and picnic basket on the living room floor and stepped eagerly into each other's arms. They shared a kiss that caused a whimper to escape from Krista's throat and a groan to rumble in Jesse's chest.

Krista broke the kiss, drew a trembling breath, then took Jesse's hand and led him down the hallway to her bedroom. He absently registered the fact that he hadn't seen this room before, and that it was pretty, very feminine just as Krista was.

She'd decorated it in mint green and pale yellow, soft, soothing colors that no doubt helped Krista relax and sleep when she returned so late from the television station. Now the afternoon sun cast a golden glow over the room.

"Oh, dandy," she said, with a wobbly little laugh. "I'm suddenly very nervous, Mr. Burke. There's that honesty again, right out on the table."

"And it means so much to me," he said, framing her face in his hands. "I'm a tad nervous myself, Ms. Kelly."

"I like to think it's because I care for you, like and respect you. I'm not *in* love with you, but my feelings are such that I'd like to think we're going to make love."

"Ditto," he said, then lowered his head to claim her mouth.

The nervousness fled along with all rational thoughts. They parted only long enough to shed clothes that had too many buttons and zippers for fumbling fingers, then stood in naked splendor, each drinking in the sight of the other.

"You are so beautiful," Jesse said, his voice raspy. "You're exquisite, Krista."

"So are you."

He swept back the spread and blanket to reveal mint-green sheets. They tumbled onto the bed, reaching for one another, holding fast, kissing until their breathing was labored as their hands explored—her body soft and womanly, his rugged and male.

Jesse splayed one hand on Krista's flat stomach, then laved the nipple of one of her breasts with his tongue. Krista sank her fingers into his thick hair and urged his mouth more firmly onto her breast, closing her eyes to savor the sensuous sensations coursing throughout her. He moved to the other breast, and a sigh of pure feminine pleasure whispered from her lips.

"Oh, Jesse," she said, "I feel so… I want you. Now. Please."

"Yes."

He moved over her and into her, slowly, carefully, watching her face for any sign of discomfort, but seeing only her blue eyes, smoky with desire for him. *Him.* He filled her with all that he was, and she welcomed him into the moist, feminine haven of her body.

Their gazes met for a long, special moment, then he began to move within her, increasing the tempo more and more until it became a thundering rhythm that she matched beat for beat.

It was ecstasy. It was wild and earthy. It was holding nothing back. Giving. Receiving. Rejoicing in the wonder of it. Tension coiled low in their bodies as they climbed higher, reaching for the summit, closer now…closer and closer and then…

"Jesse!"

"Oh, Krista."

Only seconds apart, they burst upon the place they had been seeking, in an explosion of sensations and bright, dancing colors. They clung tightly to each other as wave after wave of wondrous release swept through them.

Then, the vibrant colors replaced by fluffy clouds like those they'd seen in the sky at the park, they drifted down, down to the bed again, the room, the golden sunlight encasing them.

Jesse used his last ounce of energy to move off of Krista, then tucked her close to his side. He rested his lips on her dewy forehead as she splayed one hand on the moist hair on his chest.

"Oh my," she whispered.

"Unbelievable," Jesse said, awe ringing in his voice. "Just unbelievable."

"Yes."

Krista shivered and he drew the blankets up over them. And then they slept, heads resting on the same pillow, dreaming of sailing ships and teddy bears and each other.

In the middle of the next morning, Jesse paced around Krista's living room with her portable telephone pressed to his ear. It rang on the other end once, twice.

"Hello?"

"Sarah?"

"Yes."

"This…this is Jesse Burke."

"Oh, hello. I was just thinking about you, Jesse."

"I was wondering if I might come by your place this afternoon. I'd like to meet your son Jesse. Well, I mean, I'd like to meet all your kids but—"

"But Jesse holds special significance for you because of his name and the way it came to be."

"Yes."

"That would be fine, wonderful," Sarah said. "The two older kids have soccer practice today. Jesse will be here without his brother and sister about three o'clock. Does that work for you?"

"That would be perfect. Thank you, Sarah."

"No, I thank you, Jesse. See you then. 'Bye."

"'Bye." Jesse pushed the off button on the phone. "Whew. That was a lot tougher than I thought it would be."

"That's understandable," Krista said, from where she sat on the sofa.

"Sarah said that the older kids will be at soccer practice. I suppose she's calling Deedee now," he said, placing the phone on the coffee table and sinking onto the sofa next to Krista. "Word will spread like wildfire that the mysterious Jesse Burke has taken a step toward the family. That's not a family, it's an army. Why does there have to be so many of them?"

Krista laughed. "Well, some of the clan are honorary members, like I am, but I agree that the number is rather daunting. Don't think about that part. You've met Sarah. Barry is at work. Rick and Emma will be off kicking a ball around, so the only new face will be little Jesse."

"Oh, man," he said, sitting bolt upward. "This is such a stupid thing to have done. I have never in my life carried on a conversation with a five-year-old. What do I say to him? Hi, kid, what's your opinion on the state of the economy?"

Krista laughed. "You have nothing to worry about. Ask him about his collection of those tiny cars, whatever they're called, and he'll take it from there. You'll be given a full description of each and every one until your eyes cross. Jesse is very proud of those cars."

"Oh." He sank back. "That doesn't sound so hard. Cars are good—guy stuff, you know? I can relate to cars."

"One hundred and seventy-two of them?"

"You're kidding. I'll be brain dead."

"Been there, done that," Krista said, smiling. "I've had the full tour of Jesse Barstow's car collection. Oh, I'm so sorry I have to go to work and won't be there to hear it all again."

Jesse laughed and lifted Krista onto his lap. "Oh, you are so good for me, Ms. Kelly. Whenever I start to stress out, you work your magic and make me laugh, sort of diffuse the bomb, as it were. That's a rare and special gift you have, and I thank you."

Krista laced her hands behind Jesse's neck and smiled at him warmly. "You have rare and special gifts that you give me, too, Jesse. You make me feel so feminine and lovely, and you have a way of listening to me when I speak that makes me feel as though what I am saying is the most important thing you've ever heard. There are more things on the list, but I don't want you to get a big head, you know."

"Heaven forbid."

"Do you think heaven would forbid…" Krista lowered her head toward Jesse's "…this?"

Her mouth melted over his and he drank of the sweet taste of her, inhaled her aroma as it surrounded him, was acutely aware of the instantaneous flash of heated desire that coiled within him.

Krista raised her head slowly, reluctantly, then drew a shuddering breath. "Goodness."

"Oh, yes, ma'am," he said, his voice gritty. "You are one very potent lady, ma'am."

"You're not too shabby yourself, sir," she said, scooting off his lap and getting to her feet. She turned to look at him. "I do like you, Jesse Burke. I like you very, very much. No, it's more than that. I care for and about you. Oh, that doesn't seem like an important enough word, either. I hope you can understand what I'm saying, even though I'm fumbling around here."

Jesse rose. "I do understand, because I feel the same way about you, and I'm not certain I could find the proper word to describe it myself."

"At least we're on the same wavelength on the subject."

Jesse smiled. "On a lot of subjects."

"Mmm," Krista said, wiggling her eyebrows. "Now, if you will excuse me, sir, I will tend to the exciting task of shifting my clothes from the washing machine to the dryer. Ta-ta."

"Farewell," Jesse said, bowing dramatically.

He watched as Krista left the room, then chuckled as she added an exaggerated sway to her hips just before she disappeared from view. He sank back onto the sofa, rested his head on the top and made no attempt to hide his smile as he stared up at the ceiling.

These stolen days and nights with Krista—for lack of a better way to describe them—were like nothing he'd experienced before. It was sort of like playing house, acting out the roles of husband and wife. Earlier that morning Krista had dusted and he'd vacuumed the floor. He'd done a load of his wash, now she was doing hers.

They laughed their way through their attempts to make appetizing meals together, declaring themselves total duds in the arena of culinary arts.

And the lovemaking they shared? Incredible. That caring they had just spoken of added something wondrous to their joining. They'd reached for each other upon wakening, so eager to journey to the special place again, forget that the world around them existed. There was just the two of them in the entire universe.

It was all so perfect.

Jesse frowned, sat up and rested his elbows on his knees. He made a steeple of his fingers and tapped his lips.

Perfect, he thought. Every aspect of what he had with Krista qualified for that description. Did that mean he loved her? Was in love with her? Was this what love did? Gave you that feeling of rightness, of perfection, of knowing you wanted to be with that other person so much you nearly ached with the intensity of it? That's how he felt, all right.

Did that mean he was in love with Krista Kelly?

Wouldn't a thirty-two-year-old man know if he had fallen in love with a woman? Maybe not. He wasn't exactly an experienced pro at this stuff. He'd engaged in little more than casual dating during college, then had been almost too busy to date at all when he'd been working in the district attorney's office. Once he'd gone back to the ranch there had been no eligible women in the area to even take out for a cup of coffee.

What if he *was* in love with Krista?

Jesse sighed.

It really wouldn't matter, he thought. She had made it crystal clear that she was not interested in any type of serious relationship. Why? She still didn't care to divulge that information.

Not only that, he didn't have one thing to offer her. He was nearly broke, was unemployed and didn't have a clue as to where he might work or live once this fiasco with the MacAllisters was settled.

No, there was no sense dwelling on what the depths of his feelings for Krista might be. No sense at all.

As far as the MacAllisters went? Oh, man, he didn't have the mental energy to concentrate on that right now. He'd just focus on meeting little Jesse and his one hundred seventy-two tiny cars.

At exactly three o'clock that afternoon, Jesse pulled into Sarah's driveway and turned off the ignition to the rental car. He crossed his arms on top of the steering wheel and stared at the house.

He didn't want to go in there, he decided. What if he said or did something to upset the kid? Sarah was all enthused over the concept of her long-lost twin brother suddenly turning up, but now she was going to see him interacting with one of her precious children.

If little Jesse didn't like him one iota it would no doubt diminish big Jesse in the eyes of his sister.

Why did that thought disturb him so much? He'd already established in his mind the fact that titles like "sister" were just words attached to strangers. So what difference would it make if Sarah thought he was a dud? None. Except...

"Okay, okay," Jesse said aloud, getting out of the car. "So I don't want to fall short in Sarah's eyes. Why? I don't have a clue."

As he reached out to press the doorbell, the door swung open to reveal a smiling Sarah.

"Guilty," she said. "I've been watching for you to arrive. Come in, Jesse."

"Thanks," he said, managing to produce a small smile as he entered the large home.

"Let's go into the kitchen," she suggested. "Jesse is out there and I thought we could all have a snack."

"Does he have his tiny cars with him?"

Sarah laughed. "Krista warned you about those cars, didn't she? Yes, I'm afraid you're in for a complete description of the car collection."

"Sarah, wait a minute," Jesse said, stopping.

"Yes?" She turned to look at him questioningly.

"What did you tell Jesse about me? I mean, who am I supposed to be?"

"Barry and I told all the children that you are a relative we didn't know about and that we're thrilled that you found us. We also said that we think it's very special that you and Jesse have the same name. He informed Rick and Emma that you were going to be *his* new friend because you were both named Jesse. Okay?"

"Whatever works."

In the bright, sunny kitchen Jesse halted in his tracks and stared at the little boy lying on his stomach on a braided rug, surrounded by a multitude of miniature cars. He scrambled to his feet when he became aware that his mother and the man named Jesse had entered the room.

Whoa, Jesse thought, his heart thundering. Little Jesse was a carbon copy of himself at that age. It was as if one of the photographs in those albums he had in storage had come alive and jumped off the page right in front of him. This was so strange. It was also rather…special.

"Hi," little Jesse said. "Are you Jesse?"

"Yep. Are you?"

"Yep."

"Cool." Jesse extended his hand. "It's nice to meet you, Jesse."

The child shook it willingly.

"I have freshly baked chocolate chip cookies," Sarah said. "Jesse, would you like soda, milk, iced tea?"

"Soda," little Jesse said.

"Iced tea, please," big Jesse said, at exactly the same time.

Sarah laughed. "This is going to get confusing. My dear son, you are having milk." She paused. "To keep things straight, I think we'll call big Jesse…Uncle Jesse."

"'Kay," little Jesse said, shrugging.

"Sure, why not?" Jesse said. "Uncle Jesse it is."

"After we have our snack, Uncle Jesse," the boy said, "would you like to see my cars? I have the bestis collection of cars in the whole wide world."

"No kidding?" Uncle Jesse said. "Wow. That's really something. I sure would like to see the bestis car collection in the whole wide world." He smiled. "You know, I'm really looking forward to it. Let's dig into these cookies so we can get to those cars."

"Yeah," Jesse said. "Can I sit by you at the table in the very next chair 'cause we're both named Jesse and you're my new friend? Can I sit right next to you, Uncle Jesse? Please?"

A strange, foreign warmth tiptoed around Jesse's heart as he looked at the little boy, who was meeting his gaze with wide eyes and an expression of hope and anticipation.

How was it possible, he thought, that such a young, innocent child could make a grown man feel ten feet tall? Man, this was something. The little munchkin had staked a claim on Uncle Jesse's heart in record time. Amazing. And again, very, very special.

"I'd be honored to sit by you, Jesse," Uncle Jesse said, his smile genuine, "and I'm also very glad that you're my new friend."

Chapter 8

Italy

Teddy MacAllister dragged a restless hand through his thick brown hair, frowning as he listened to his mother on the heavy, old-fashioned black telephone.

"That's quite a story, Mom," he said, when she paused to take a needed breath. "I've seen a movie or two with this plot and the long-lost relative always turned out to be a fake, someone after the family money."

"That isn't true in this case, Teddy," Deedee said. "Jesse is Sarah's twin, he truly is, and he's your younger brother."

"Because he looks like a MacAllister? I imagine a

lot of people do if we would take the time to glance around. Our features aren't *that* unique. I'll believe it only if the DNA test proves this Jesse's identity. How long before the results are back?"

"I don't know. Kara asked them to rush it, but it's a complicated procedure. Oh, Teddy, you're being as cynical as your uncle Ted, who you were named after. I'm telling you that Jesse is my son. A mother knows these things.

"Sarah believes in Jesse. He's been over there several times this week, and little Jesse adores him. Uncle Jesse, to avoid confusion, has met Barry and the other kids, too, and they all like him very much."

"Yeah, well, Sarah is a sucker for a sad story," Teddy said, "and Barry is so crazy about her he'd go along with anything she wants. I'm with Uncle Ted on this one. This Burke guy is phony."

"No, Teddy, you're wrong," Deedee said. "If you were here, could meet and speak with Jesse, you wouldn't feel that way."

"Uncle Ted did the meet and speak bit. Did he change his mind?"

"Well, no, but—"

"Mom, you're setting yourself up to be very badly hurt by that jerk. Is Dad there?" Teddy asked, an edge to his voice. "May I talk to him?"

Deedee sighed. "Yes, all right, I'll put him on. By the way, we've had a difficult time reaching you over the past days. That's why we haven't told you about Jesse until now. Is everything all right?"

Before Teddy could answer, the door to the apartment opened and a beautiful woman entered, smiling at him. She was slender, about five feet four inches tall, with a tumble of wavy black hair that reached just below her shoulders, tawny skin and dark eyes. She wore a flowered skirt with a peasant blouse and carried a cloth bag, where a long loaf of bread could be seen along with fruit and vegetables.

"Everything is just fine here," Teddy said, smiling at the woman. "I moved to a quaint, charming village ten miles out of the city to get away from the hustle and bustle. The apartment is on the second floor and there's a balcony overlooking the town square. It's like something you'd see on a postcard. I should have e-mailed you from work to let you know what was going on, but it's been hectic there."

"I see," Deedee said. "And Rosalie? How's Rosalie, Teddy?"

The lady in question blew Teddy a kiss, then went into the small kitchen to unpack the purchases in the cloth bag.

"She's a brilliant computer whiz," Teddy said, "as I've mentioned before. A very nice, very lovely woman who is a joy to…work with."

"And have dinner with?" his mother said. "Go dancing? Strolling in your quaint little village? Don't try to fool your mother, Teddy. I hear a special sound in your voice whenever you speak of Rosalie. Why don't you take a picture of her with that fancy camera you have that lets you send photos on the computer, so we can see your Rosalie?"

Teddy rolled his eyes heavenward. "Mom, you were going to put Dad on the phone, remember?"

"Will you send a picture of her?"

"First chance I get," he said.

"Fine." Deedee paused. "Oh, Teddy, you've been in Italy for over six months and we miss you terribly. I know you said you didn't know how long you'd be gone, but is the end in sight now?"

"Not really," he said. "The exchange of technical information is going extremely well and we're expanding what we plan to share."

"Oh, dear," Deedee said. "I wish I could at least circle a date on the calendar indicating when you'll be home."

"I'll let you know when I know," Teddy said. "May I speak to Dad now?"

Deedee sighed. "Yes, yes, naggy son. Say hello to Rosalie for us."

"Oh, okay." Teddy chuckled. "You always have the last word on a subject, Mom."

"Of course, dear. It's in my job description as a mother. Here's your father."

"Teddy?" Ryan said. "Have you had your fill of authentic spaghetti and are ready to head home?"

"No, not yet." He laughed, then was serious again in the next instant. "Dad, I don't get it. Why aren't you insisting that this Jesse Burke guy keep his distance from the family until the DNA test results are back?"

"Because I believe he's my son, that the information your mother related to you is true."

"Ah, man, you've got to be kidding. He's snowed you, too? His story is so off the wall it's a crime. Is Uncle Ted the only one in the family who can see this con for what it is?"

"It's not a con, Teddy." Ryan paused. "But your uncle Michael and uncle Forrest have been quite vocal about the fact that they are very skeptical. I'm not going to click off the entire MacAllister roster and tell you where each person stands because we'd run up the national debt on this phone call. Let's just say that some members of the family don't believe Jesse, some do and some are withholding judgment for now."

"Damn it," Teddy said. "That guy is dividing our family. There are going to be arguments about this, you know there are. This Jesse jerk could destroy the very foundation of our family unit."

"The foundation is stronger than that, Teddy."

"Is it? Under this kind of pressure? Try this on for size. Sarah obviously bought the story big time, has welcomed Burke into her home, lets him interact with the kids, the whole enchilada. Now suppose our cousins Jessica, Emily and Alice don't believe Burke for one second? That would definitely cause dissention between Sarah and the triplets. This is bad, very bad."

Rosalie came up behind Teddy and placed her hands on his shoulders. He reached up with his free hand to cover one of hers.

"Have a little faith in your family, son," Ryan said.

"Dad, why aren't you thinking like a cop, like Uncle Ted is, about Jesse Burke?"

"Because I'm Jesse Burke's father and I'm giving free rein to *those* emotions."

"Okay, I give up for now," Teddy said. "But keep me informed about this, will you? I want to be completely up to date on what is happening."

"Yes, of course we will."

"All right. 'Bye for now, Dad, and give Mom a hug for me."

"Sure thing. Goodbye, Teddy. We love and miss you very much."

Teddy replaced the receiver but left his hand on it, staring at it as he replayed in his mind the conversation that had just taken place.

"Teddy?" Rosalie said. "What's going on?"

He got to his feet and encircled her shoulders with one arm, pulling her close to his side.

"Let's go fix dinner together and while we're doing that, I'll tell you all about it. It's crazy. It really is nuts."

While Teddy and Rosalie prepared the meal of sautéed fresh vegetables, pasta and garlic bread, he related the story he had heard from his parents.

When they sat down to eat at the small, glass-topped table at the end of the kitchen, Teddy shook his head as he picked up his fork. "How's that for a plot that would be a box office flop? It's hard for me to believe that my father, who was a police officer for so many years, would fall for this garbage."

Rosalie took a bite of pasta before speaking. "Mmm," she said, "this is delicious. We're a good team in the kitchen, Teddy."

"We're a good team, period. You. Me. Together. I love you, Rosalie Louisa Cantelli."

"I love you, too." Rosalie paused. "But back to what you told me. The facts that your mother related provide a reasonable explanation as to how that midwife was able to steal your newborn brother without your parents even knowing he existed. It could have happened, Teddy."

"Jesse Burke invented a tale that would make it sound feasible, don't you see? Sharp con men make certain that they cross every *t* and dot every *i*."

"But your parents are convinced that Jesse is their son."

"Yes, and they're going to be devastated when they learn the truth," Teddy said. "I'm just worried about how much cash Burke will talk them out of before the DNA results come back.

"And another thing, Burke is bunked in at Krista Kelly's apartment. She's like one of the family, and I hate the idea that she's being used. She also makes good money at the television station. He's probably hitting her up for some of the green stuff, too."

"I don't know, Teddy," Rosalie said thoughtfully. "Mother love is a very strong and almost mysterious emotion. If Deedee says that Jesse Burke is her son, then…" She nodded.

"Oh man, you're falling for it, too," Teddy said, his voice rising.

"Why don't you just put it on the back burner until the DNA test results are in?" Rosalie said. "Stressing out about it isn't going to accomplish anything. The bottom line is that the test will determine the truth. Jesse Burke is either attempting to run a scam on your family, or he's actually your brother."

"But emotional damage is being done in the meantime," Teddy said. "I have concerns about how much money is being slipped to that jerk, too, but the important issue is what his lies will have done to my sister, her kids, our parents. And Krista and heaven only knows who else."

Rosalie leaned slightly forward. "You don't know for sure that Jesse Burke is telling lies."

"Ah, come on, Rosalie. A midwife stole him out from under my parents' noses when he was born? Stashed him in the closet or something while my mother was sleeping and my father was rocking Sarah in another room? That is so lame, so damn bogus. Things like that don't happen in real life. In dumb novels and grade D movies, maybe, but not in reality, for crying out loud. No way."

"We'll have to find some crows to make into a pie for you to eat if you're wrong," Rosalie said, smiling.

"I'm not wrong," he said, glaring at her.

"Okay, okay, the subject is closed for now." Rosalie paused. "Teddy, why haven't you told your parents about us? You made it sound like you moved into this place alone, when in actuality we are living together. We're in love with each other. I've certainly shared that information with *my* family. I want the world to know that I've fallen in love with a magnificent man who loves me in kind. But you're going out of your way to keep it a secret from all the MacAllisters. Why?"

"Because I don't feel like sharing you with them yet," he said. "I'd get the third degree. When are we getting married? And where? Can they expect me to arrive home with my bride, or do we plan to have the wedding in Ventura? Are we going to live in the house I own there, or have a new one built that we design together? On and on it would go, and I'm not ready to face all that."

"I see," Rosalie said, placing her fork on the side of the plate. "Yes, I can understand your reluctance to be put in a place where you'd have to answer those questions, especially since we haven't discussed them ourselves."

"Good point." He took another bite of pasta, chewed and swallowed, then sipped his wine. "All I care to dwell on at the moment is that I'm in love for the first time in my life. You, I love. I want to marry you, have lots of bambinos with you and live happily ever after. Now there's a plot that makes sense."

"Live happily ever after where?" Rosalie asked, making no attempt to finish her dinner.

"Ventura," he said. "That's where my career is, where I'm going up the corporate ladder at lightning speed, my sweet. Plus, my enormous family is there. They drive me nuts at times, but I love them all the same."

"I have a very large family here in Italy, Teddy," Rosalie said, "and I am also establishing a fine reputation in my chosen field in the corporation I work for. Why are you just taking for granted the fact that I'll leave my family, my career, and move to California?"

"Don't you want to have our babies, Rosalie? You can't be a mother and put in sixty-hour work weeks at your company the way you do now."

"Of course I want babies, Teddy, but having a family wouldn't mean I would have to give up my career completely. My company would allow me to work part-time. As the head of marketing and development, I worked together with Maria, my administrative assistant, to set up this information exchange program with your company, and it's proved to be very beneficial to both of our firms. Maria is engaged to be married, and I know she wants to have children. Everything is in place for us to share the operation of that department in the future. And what about my family? You just expect me to leave them without a backward glance?"

"No," he said, frowning. "I make very good money, Rosalie. We can fly back here as many times a year as you want to visit your people."

"Teddy, my boss has already offered you a position in the firm here. He's extremely impressed with you and wants you on his staff. You would make excellent money, as well, and we could fly to Ventura to visit your family several times a year.

"All that is true, yet you apparently aren't even considering it, haven't given one thought to the possibility that I want to stay in Italy, not live in America."

"But you'd be my wife and—"

"And what?" Rosalie said, pushing her plate to one side. "I'm supposed to bow three times, or perhaps salute, and do whatever I'm told because I have that title? I really resent your attitude."

Teddy leaned back in his chair and folded his arms over his chest. "What are you saying? That you won't live in Ventura as my wife?"

"I'm saying that equal consideration should be given to your living in Italy as my husband."

"That isn't how it's done," he said, nearly shouting.

"What century are you daydreaming in, Teddy Mac-Allister?" Rosalie said, matching his volume. "I'm just as important in this relationship as you are. My roots, my family, my career, the lifestyle I've known here all my life are not things I can easily walk away from, and it makes me angry that you're just assuming that is what I will do because you say so."

"Well, this is great," Teddy said, throwing up his hands. "I've met the woman of my dreams, the one I want to marry, have children with, live with until I die and she won't leave her mother."

"That's not fair," Rosalie said, getting to her feet. "You're twisting around what I said, and you know it, making me sound like a child clinging to my mother's skirts. You want to live close to your family in Ventura, go home to the life you've always known, but with a wife on your arm. Why am I wrong to want the same things here that you want for yourself there?"

"Wait a minute," Teddy said, raising one finger. "Before you go storming off in a rage, let's back up here a second. Remember that big family picnic we attended at your parents' house a couple of weeks ago?"

"Of course," Rosalie said, still standing next to the table.

"Then you must recall the sermon your mother gave while we were eating, about how homesick she was when she first moved here as a bride. But she got over it in time and this became her home, and a wife's place is by her husband's side no matter where he might choose to go. Everyone around that table, including you, Rosalie—oh, yes, including you—nodded in agreement with what your mother said."

"I know I did," she said, planting her hands on her hips. "That little speech was directed at me, and I didn't want to go another ten rounds with my mother on the subject and ruin the day. Believe me, she and I have discussed the issue in the past. Loudly."

"Oh," Teddy said, surprise evident on his face. "I thought—"

"I know what you thought," Rosalie interrupted, "and I don't blame you for that, because I did give the appearance that I was of the same mind as my mother and everyone else on the subject. But now we've discussed it and you're aware of how I really feel."

Teddy got to his feet and gripped Rosalie by the shoulders. "Sweetheart," he said, "we're in love with each other, want to spend the rest of our lives together. I won't lose you, what we have, over an issue, a bump in the road. We'll find an answer to this problem… somehow."

"Will we?" she said, unexpected and unwelcomed tears filling her eyes. "I want you to live here in Italy with me. You want me to live in America with you. We both feel very strongly about it. Where's the solution, Teddy? There's not even a compromise that can be utilized. It's all or nothing. We either make our home here or in California. It's a black-and-white situation with no gray area that we can explore."

"I need time to think this through," he said, pulling her close and wrapping his arms around her. "I didn't know we had a problem until tonight, because I just assumed that you would move to Ventura with me. So, okay, I was wrong. I'm sorry that I didn't discuss it with you before mentally deciding it was a done deal."

"I don't know what the answer is, Teddy," she said, then sniffled.

"Hey, don't cry. We'll figure this out, you'll see. When two people love each other the way we do, they can't be defeated if they stand together." Teddy eased back a bit and tilted Rosalie's chin up with the fingertips of one hand. "I love you, you love me. That's all we need to concentrate on right now."

"But…"

"And right now," he said, his voice dropping an octave, "because I love you, I want to make love with you. Right now. The problem can wait."

"What about dinner?" Rosalie said. "We hardly touched it."

"That's why microwave ovens were invented, and there's one in this charming apartment with a kitchen the size of a shoebox. We'll warm our meal and eat later. Much, much later."

Teddy lowered his head and claimed Rosalie's lips with his own. As always, she responded instantly, eagerly, neither of them seeming to be able to get enough of each other.

They made love in the creaky old bed in the one bedroom the apartment boasted. Made beautiful love. Exquisite love. They didn't think, they only felt, savored, memorized, declared their love in whispers, then shouted each other's name when they toppled over the edge of the place they were flung to seconds apart.

Afterward they didn't speak, just lay close, sated, as darkness fell and replaced the brilliant sunset that had streaked across the heavens.

Teddy dozed, but as Rosalie stay nestled next to the man who had stolen her heart for all time, a chill swept through her, a sense of foreboding that caused fresh tears to mist her eyes.

What were they going to do? she thought frantically. How were they going to solve this dark dilemma they were facing?

She loved Teddy so much, but she'd worked so hard to reach her goals. She'd sacrificed her social life, lost contact with lifelong friends because she no longer had time to nurture those relationships, missed countless family celebrations due to the long hours spent focused on the project she had been involved with at the time.

And now? Teddy wanted her to walk away from it

all and follow him to America, be satisfied with two or three visits a year to see her family, forget the success she was so proud of having achieved in her career.

She couldn't do it.

He was asking far, far too much of her in the name of love. But in all fairness, she was doing the same to him. If he loved her he would stay in Italy, take the position offered him at the firm where she worked, substitute her family for his own and make do with visits to see the many MacAllisters he loved so dearly.

Teddy was so certain there was a solution to this. An answer they just hadn't yet discovered. He was convinced they'd find a way to provide peace and contentment for both of them in the choices made about their future.

She hoped and prayed he was right. He had to be right. There was an answer for them waiting to be put into place. Oh, God, there had to be.

But as another chill swept through Rosalie, then settled like a cold fist gripping her heart, two tears of stark fear slid down her cheeks.

Chapter 9

Deedee peered in the oven, closed the door, then opened it again and took another look at the baking lasagna.

"It's doing fine," she said aloud, then wandered into the formal dining room and swept her gaze over the table. "And that looks fine. Everything is fine, except me."

"Because talking to yourself," Ryan said, coming up behind her, "is a sign of old age, and if you're getting there, then so am I and that will never do."

Deedee smiled as she turned to face her husband. "So, okay, I'm a nervous wreck about this dinner tonight," she said. "It has nothing to do with age, Mr. MacAllister."

"I should hope not, Mrs. MacAllister," he said, pulling her into his arms. "But you're nervous? Why on earth would you be nervous? Our son is coming for dinner. That is a very common occurrence across the country on any given evening."

"It sounds simple enough, doesn't it?" Deedee said, still smiling. "Except this son happens to be Jesse Burke, whom we haven't seen in nearly a month since we agreed to not push him to accept his place in the family.

"Others have popped in and out of Krista's to chat with him, or dropped by to see Sarah, Barry and the kids and found Jesse there. We, however, have sat on the sidelines and had no contact with him whatsoever."

"Well, that's changing as of this evening," Ryan said, linking his hands at the back of Deedee's waist. "We kept the promise we made to Jesse and it paid off. He called and said he'd like to see us, you extended an invitation for dinner and there you have it. There's nothing to be nervous about."

"Oh, and I suppose you're all calm, cool and collected?" Deedee said, raising one eyebrow.

"Sure. It's the bevy of butterflies in my stomach that need a tranquilizer or a stiff drink, not me."

"Got it." Deedee laughed, then frowned in the next instant. "Oh, Ryan, it's so sad and so incredibly wrong that I'm worried about what topics of conversation to bring up with our own son. I'd love to hear about his adventures as a little boy, but I don't know if that will upset him because it forces him to face what his parents—well, what the Burkes did all those years ago."

"Talk about the weather, my sweet," Ryan said. "That's always safe and should last at least thirty seconds. April in Ventura is lovely. The end." He paused.

"Seriously, I think we should allow Jesse to set the tone. It took several weeks for him to be ready to see us again, and I have a feeling the cousins of the butterflies in my stomach have taken up residency in his. I betcha a buck that he's as nervous about this night as we are."

He was nervous, Jesse thought, as he turned off the ignition to the car, then folded his arms on top of the steering wheel. Correct that. He was beyond nervous, was more like shaking in his shorts big time because he didn't have a clue as to what he was going to talk about with Deedee and Ryan MacAllister.

It had been Krista who had urged him to contact his *parents* and ask to see them again. She'd pointed out how many of the family he'd met and been accepted by, plus she'd emphasized the fact that Deedee and Ryan hadn't pressured him to spend time with them. So here he was, glued to the seat of the rental car because he was getting cold feet.

"Enough of this," he said, leaving the vehicle. "Get it together, Burke."

He started toward the front door of the large house with its circular drive.

Get it together, MacAllister, he thought. MacAllister. He was in actuality Jesse MacAllister, about to share a meal with his parents, Deedee and Ryan MacAllister.

Jesse slowed his step and shook his head.

That sounded as foreign and unbelievable as it

would if he was attempting to convince himself that he was a little green creature from Mars approaching the home of his little green mother and father from the red planet.

But, hell, what was he going to talk about with these people? He'd heard enough to know that Deedee would like details of his youth, what kind of kid he had been, but he didn't want to go there. No. To do so would be to relive the shock and devastation of what Phyllis and Joe Burke had done.

Jesse walked across the sweeping front porch and stood staring at the doorbell.

Maybe he'd flip a coin, he mused. Heads, he'd go through with this. Tails, he'd hightail it out of there. And he'd be willing to pay fifty bucks for a coin with tails on both sides.

"Shut up," he said, with a snort of self-disgust.

Jesse pushed the doorbell and heard the chimes echoing inside the house.

"Jesse is here," Deedee said, spinning around and out of Ryan's embrace. "Oh, dear heaven, Jesse is here."

"Calm down," her husband said. "Take a couple of deep breaths while I answer the door."

"Okay, I will." She followed him from the dining room. "I'm fine. There. Deep breath. I'm fine. No, I am not fine."

She stopped at the entrance to the living room and watched Ryan continue on, chuckling at her nonsense as he went. He opened the door and smiled at their guest.

"Hello, it's good to see you. Come on in, Jesse."

"Thank you," he said, stepping into the entryway.

Ryan closed the door and swept one arm in the direction of the living room.

"Deedee has prepared what I know will be a delicious dinner. We hope you're hungry. Would you like a drink?"

"No, I'm fine," Jesse said, glancing around the living room and seeing Deedee. "Hello."

"Hello, Jesse," she said, smiling as she walked forward. "Welcome to our home."

"It's a great house," he answered, nodding in approval. "It's large, yet still homey, comfortable."

"Well, it helps when you have architects in the family," Ryan said, "and a construction company. It gets the job done."

"Have a seat, Jesse," Deedee said, settling onto a smoky-blue chair. "Dinner won't be ready for another few minutes."

Jesse sat down on a dark blue sofa as Ryan sank onto what was obviously his favorite recliner, as evidenced by the fact it was the only piece of furniture showing signs of wear. A heavy silence fell over the room.

"So," Deedee said, a tad too loudly. "I understand you have your very own fan club in the form of Sarah's children, with little Jesse as president."

Jesse smiled. "They are super kids. I really enjoy being with them. I've never spent any time with children before and the working of their brains fascinates me. I like their honesty, too. They just hit you with whatever is on their mind, don't weigh and measure their words first, just wham, there it is, Uncle Jesse, deal with it. It's really refreshing."

"I suppose we were all like that as children," Ryan said, "then fell into the adult method of communicating without realizing it was happening. Now we have to work at being completely up front about what we say."

"Politically correct and all that rot," Deedee said, laughing.

"Exactly." Jesse nodded. "The other day little Jesse told me that he didn't think it was very nice of me to have waited this long to become his friend. See what I mean? That's how he feels, and he let me know."

"Whew," Ryan said.

"You've got that straight," Jesse said. "It was a simple, honest statement, so I responded in a simple, honest manner and told him I was sorry. He accepted that at face value and moved on to something else. That is one neat little kid."

"You obviously are going to be a marvelous father someday," Deedee said, "because you've discovered that you sincerely like children, enjoy and accept them just as they are."

"I haven't thought about…" Jesse began, then stopped speaking for a moment. "You know, you're right. I think I would be a halfway decent dad, for the reasons you just mentioned." He paused again. "Well, maybe not. There's a lot more to being a parent than just liking the way kids carry on a conversation."

"That's true," Ryan said, "but it's high on the long list of important things. I'm sure you've figured out by now from the size of the family that MacAllisters definitely like children. If that old saying about how it takes a village to raise a child is true, we're all set, because there are enough of us to create our own village."

"There you go," Jesse said, laughing and marveling at the fact that he was actually beginning to relax.

"I'll check on dinner," Deedee said, getting to her feet.

"Let me know if you need an extra set of hands to get it on the table," Ryan called after her as she left the room, then redirected his attention to Jesse. "Are you still driving that rental car?"

Jesse nodded.

"That's an expensive way to get around town," Ryan said. "I've got an old pickup truck that I haven't been able to bring myself to part with. Why don't you turn in that rental and use my clunker?"

"I appreciate the offer, Ryan," Jesse said, "but I don't think that would be a good idea. I know the Mac-Allisters who believe I'm a con man are waiting for me to make my move, see what I can get for myself before the DNA test results are back and prove that I'm lying about who I am. If they see me driving your vehicle they'll be convinced that I'm starting my crooked campaign."

Ryan frowned. "Don't worry about that."

"I have to," Jesse said, matching his frown, "because I'm the cause of the situation that is splitting the family into camps. I feel very badly about that, plus I'm carrying around a load of guilt because of the heartache you and Deedee must be going through because you've learned what happened the day Sarah and I were born. My presence just makes the two of you unhappy, because you continually have to face the reality that you missed watching one of your children grow up."

"Yes," Ryan said, nodding, "knowing what we were deprived of is difficult to deal with, but we're extremely grateful that you're here now. Please, Jesse, don't feel guilty because the family is momentarily unsettled. What happened all those years ago wasn't your fault, and you have every right to take your place among us as a MacAllister. The doubters will be satisfied that you're who you say you are once the DNA test results are in, and that will be that. Just be patient with those who are squinting their eyes at the situation."

"Have you told your other son about what is going on here?" Jesse said.

"Teddy? Yes, we finally tracked him down in Italy. He was in the middle of moving to a small town a few miles from the busy city where he's working."

"And?"

"Well, let's just say he's stuck on the same page as his uncle Ted."

"In other words," Jesse said, shaking his head, "he thinks I'm lying through my teeth. Because of me you're at odds with your firstborn son. How can I *not* feel guilty about that?"

Before Ryan could reply, Deedee reappeared.

"Gentlemen," she said, "dinner is served, and I hope you're hungry because I doubled the recipe of my ever-famous lasagna."

"Oh, lead me to it," Ryan said, getting to his feet. "Jesse, you're in for a real treat. Your mother makes lasagna from scratch that would put anything Teddy is having in Italy to shame."

Your mother, Jesse thought, as he followed Ryan across the room. That's who Phyllis Burke had claimed to be for thirty-two years—his mother. What a joke that was.

Deedee Hamilton had given birth to him. That was true. She was his biological mother. But what did that title mean when applied to her in regard to a man raised by someone else? Someone who had walked the floor with him when he was a baby, seen his first steps, heard his first words, taught him how to tie his shoes and ride a bike. Someone who'd read him stories at bedtime and assured him there were no monsters in the closet. Someone who had introduced him to strangers as her son.

Someone who had no right to have done any of those things, didn't deserve the title of mother because it hadn't been hers to possess.

No, Phyllis Burke hadn't been his mother, not really.

Deedee MacAllister was.

But she'd gained that title so late, too late. He didn't need a bandage on a scraped knee, help with his homework, comforting when he had a bad dream. A man his age stood on his own two feet. He needed nothing from Deedee. He had nothing to give to her.

They were grateful he was here among them at long last. Why? He didn't get it, he just didn't get it.

"Jesse?" Deedee said.

"What? Oh, I'm sorry. I was off somewhere."

"Have a seat," she said, smiling.

The food was delicious and Jesse complimented the cook several times. He got the feeling that Ryan was aware of him tensing up again, so deliberately kept the conversation light, talking about sports, the weather, the continuing growth of Ventura.

"How's Krista?" Deedee said, as they ate chocolate mousse for dessert. "We watch her at night on the news, of course, but we haven't seen her beyond that lately."

"She's fine," Jesse said. Beautiful. Sensational. Funny and fun and wonderful. She was like no woman he'd ever met before and she was stealing his heart one emotional inch at a time. "Just fine. Great. Really great and…" He cleared his throat. "She's fine."

"I see," Deedee murmured, looking at him intently. "Yes, I believe I do see."

"Pardon me?" Jesse said.

Ryan chuckled. "Now, Deedee, you asked the man a question and he answered it. Don't go off on one of your romantic matchmaking tangents, my sweet."

"I don't believe any matchmaking is needed," she said, with an indignant little sniff. "It would seem that Krista and Jesse have taken care of that type of thing quite nicely on their own."

"I didn't say that Krista and I…" Jesse paused, feeling a warmth creep up his neck.

"You didn't have to spell it out in so many words, dear. I just wish I could figure out so easily what is going on between Teddy and Rosalie," Deedee said. "Anyone care for more dessert? Jesse? Ryan?"

"I'm full to the brim," Ryan said.

"No, thank you," Jesse said. "Who's Rosalie?"

"She's Teddy's counterpart in the company in Italy where they are sharing computer data to run things more efficiently," Deedee said. "The exchange program is going so well that they're incorporating computers into more areas of the firm, which is extending Teddy's stay over there."

"What is driving your mother—Deedee—crazy," Ryan said, "is that she can't quite get a handle on the exact relationship between Teddy and Rosalie. He speaks of her often on the phone and in his e-mails, and we have a feeling the love bug may have taken a nibble there. But we aren't certain because Teddy isn't being forthcoming with details. Just hints, no real facts."

"Which isn't one bit fair," Deedee said, then paused. "Maybe I'll call Krista and ask if she's free to have lunch soon. We haven't had an outing in ages."

"Oh, man," Jesse said, laughing.

An Important Message from the Editors

Dear Reader,

Because you've chosen to read one of our fine romance novels, we'd like to say "thank you!" And, as a **special** way to thank you, we've selected <u>two more</u> of the books you love so well **plus** an exciting Mystery Gift to send you — absolutely <u>FREE</u>!

Please enjoy them with our compliments...

Pam Powers

Lift here

Peel off seal and place inside...

How to validate your Editor's
"Thank You"
FREE GIFT

1. Peel off gift seal from front cover. Place it in space provided at right. This automatically entitles you to receive 2 FREE BOOKS and a fabulous mystery gift.

2. Send back this card and you'll get 2 brand-new *Romance* novels. These books have a cover price of $5.99 or more each in the U.S. and $6.99 or more each in Canada, but they are yours to keep absolutely free.

3. There's no catch. You're under no obligation to buy anything. We charge nothing—ZERO—for your first shipment. And you don't have to make any minimum number of purchases— not even one!

4. The fact is, thousands of readers enjoy receiving their books by mail from The Reader Service. They enjoy the convenience of home delivery...they like getting the best new novels at discount prices BEFORE they're available in stores... and they love their Heart to Heart subscriber newsletter featuring author news, horoscopes, recipes, book reviews and much more!

5. We hope that after receiving your free books you'll want to remain a subscriber. But the choice is yours— to continue or cancel, any time at all! So why not take us up on our invitation, with no risk of any kind. You'll be glad you did!

GET A *Free* MYSTERY GIFT...

SURPRISE MYSTERY GIFT COULD BE YOURS ***FREE*** AS A SPECIAL "THANK YOU" FROM THE EDITORS

The Reader Service — Here's How It Works:

Accepting your 2 free books and gift places you under no obligation to buy anything. You may keep the books and gift and return the shipping statement marked "cancel." If you do not cancel, about a month later we'll send you 3 additional books and bill you just $4.74 each in the U.S., or $5.24 each in Canada, plus 25¢ shipping & handling per book and applicable taxes if any.* That's the complete price and — compared to cover prices starting from $5.99 each in the U.S. and $6.99 each in Canada — it's quite a bargain! You may cancel at any time, but if you choose to continue, every month we'll send you 3 more books, which you may either purchase at the discount price or return to us and cancel your subscription.

*Terms and prices subject to change without notice. Sales tax applicable in N.Y. Canadian residents will be charged applicable provincial taxes and GST.

If offer card is missing write to: The Reader Service, 3010 Walden Ave., P.O. Box 1867, Buffalo, NY 14240-1867

BUSINESS REPLY MAIL
FIRST-CLASS MAIL   PERMIT NO. 717-003   BUFFALO, NY

POSTAGE WILL BE PAID BY ADDRESSEE

THE READER SERVICE
3010 WALDEN AVE
PO BOX 1341
BUFFALO NY 14240-8571

NO POSTAGE
NECESSARY
IF MAILED
IN THE
UNITED STATES

"You'll get used to this type of thing in time, Jesse." Ryan smiled. "It goes along with being part of a large family, although I'm not certain this is one of the perks."

"Ryan MacAllister," Deedee said, "all I said was I'd like to have lunch soon with Krista. What's wrong with that?"

"Nothing," he replied, getting to his feet. "Some people might come to the conclusion that you're a meddling mother, Deedee, but I know better. You love all your baby chicks and need to be assured they're doing well. The bigger our family gets, the larger your heart becomes to make room for the additions. You're there for each and every one of them no matter what they need."

Ryan looked directly at Jesse. "You're never too old to cherish that kind of mothering love Deedee gives of so freely, son. Don't assume that because you came into our lives as an adult it diminishes how we, your parents, feel about you. I hope, in time, you'll realize that you can trust in our love, in us." Ryan paused. "Now then, let's pitch in and help clean the kitchen, shall we, Jesse?"

What had the man done? Jesse wondered, as he carried dishes from the table. Peered into his brain and seen what he'd been thinking? Then Ryan had proceeded to inform him that he was way off base and that he did, indeed, have much to gain by accepting these people as his parents.

Deedee had tapped into his mind, too, and clicked

right on to the fact that there was something going on between him and Krista. This was enough to give a guy the creeps. Or maybe not. Maybe this was what a real family was about. Maybe...hell, there was no maybe about how confusing this all was, that was for sure.

After the kitchen was sparkling clean the trio went back into the living room and watched a spring-training baseball game on television. There was no more heavy conversation, nothing beyond hoots and hollers directed at the players, and Jesse found himself once again relaxing and enjoying himself, enjoying being with Deedee and Ryan.

When it was time to leave, Deedee thanked him for coming, said they hoped to see him soon. She gave him a peck on the cheek, making no attempt to hug him or press him for a definite date when they would be together again.

Very classy people, Jesse thought, as he drove to Krista's. Nice people. People he could truly believe to be exactly as they presented themselves? The jury was still out on that one. He knew he was holding a part of himself back from them, being cautious, wary, but he couldn't help it. Yes, okay, they were his parents, but Phyllis and Joe had performed in that role for so many years and...

"Shut up, Burke," he said aloud. "Don't go over it again. Not again. Not tonight."

No, not tonight, he thought. He was going home to wait for his Krista to return from work. Going home? His Krista?

Yes, that's exactly how it was…now. This moment. The future? It was a blur, just a foggy, unclear entity. So he'd concentrate on the now and go home and wait for his Krista.

The moment Krista stepped into the apartment she was swept into Jesse's arms and kissed until she couldn't breathe, a kiss she returned with total abandonment.

"Welcome home," he said when he finally released her.

"And quite a welcome it was," she replied, smiling at him. "I'll change into something comfy, then I want to hear all about your evening at Deedee and Ryan's."

"We had great lasagna," Jesse called after her as she left the room. "End of story."

"You're not getting off that easily," she yelled back.

She returned in a few minutes wearing a full-length, coral-colored velour robe that zipped up the front and clung just enough to hint at her lush figure beneath.

"You expect me to carry on an intelligent conversation when you're wearing that robe?" Jesse said, from where he was sitting in a large easy chair. "You've got to be kidding."

"You've seen this creation before," Krista said, curling up in a corner of the sofa.

"I realize that," he said, chuckling, "and I know from experience that you have nothing on underneath it. I can't remember a thing that happened tonight beyond the lasagna I already told you about."

"Nice try, but forget it," Krista said, laughing. "Seriously, Jesse, how was the evening? I know you were nervous about going over there."

"It was all right. I tensed up a few times, but Deedee and Ryan kept things light for the most part. We watched a ball game after dinner."

Krista nodded.

"Ryan did make a point of telling me that even though I came into their lives so late it didn't diminish how they feel about me, and that I should trust in their love."

"And?"

"And I don't know," he said. "It all comes back to titles, Krista. They automatically love me because I have the title of being their son? Love is more complex than that. I believe they've convinced themselves they love me. But I really don't want to go through all of this again tonight."

"Jesse, if you don't start believing in them, in the other MacAllisters, too, you won't have a foundation to build on, a solid base to stand on as you take your place as a member of the family. Don't you see that?"

"You're getting ahead of where I am emotionally, Krista. I'm not that certain I can ever be a MacAllister."

"Oh, Jesse, don't make your family pay the price for what the Burkes did. You have so much love and caring to gain by joining the family that is rightly yours."

Jesse got to his feet and began to pace around the room. "Love and caring?" he said. "How will I know which MacAllisters really do love and care for me, and which are putting on a front to keep peace in the family?"

"Trust them."

"Yeah, right," he said, dragging a restless hand through his hair. He stopped and stared down at Krista. "I loved the Burkes so damn much. They treated me like I was the most important person on the planet, taught me to believe in myself, go after my dreams. I didn't like the lifestyle we had on that crummy little ranch, but when I realized that if I didn't go back and help out, give up my career, they wouldn't be able to keep the place going, I didn't hesitate. I went. I felt I owed them that for loving me the way they did, for making me feel secure, safe, all of my life."

Jesse stared up at the ceiling for a long moment, then shook his head and met Krista's gaze again. "I loved and trusted Phyllis and Joe Burke unconditionally, Krista, and despite the fact that they were doting parents, it turned out they didn't deserve my unconditional love and trust. Not by a long shot. They weren't even close to being who I thought they were. They took more from me than they gave, and that's very difficult to deal with."

"I know," Krista said softly.

"And now?" Jesse added. "You're saying to me that I should go down that road again. Trust and believe in Deedee and Ryan because they have the title of being my parents. Just lay my heart out there to be smashed to smithereens by them, or some other MacAllisters who may never come to accept me. It's just not that easy to step up and do. Can you understand that?"

Krista got to her feet and encircled his neck with her hands. "You trust me, don't you?"

"Yes. Yes, I do," he said, wrapping his arms around her waist. "I was wary at first, on guard or whatever, but yes, I trust you, Krista, and I care for you very, very much." He paused. "I wish you trusted me."

She frowned. "What do you mean?"

"Let's sit down."

Settled on the sofa, Jesse shifted so he could look directly at her.

"Krista," he said, taking both of her hands in his, "it's very obvious that you've built a wall around yourself, don't let yourself become too seriously involved with a man, have said you aren't interested in a heavy-duty commitment. Why? What happened to make you feel that way? Who hurt you and how? Why don't you trust me enough to share it with me?"

Krista pulled her hands free and wrapped them around her elbows. "I do trust you, Jesse, it's just that…it's so painful to talk about and…" She shook her head. "No, you're right. I trust you enough to give myself to you when we make love, yet I'm keeping a whole portion of myself from you. You can't pick and choose when it comes to trust. It's total and absolute or it's not really there."

He nodded.

"Jesse," she said, then drew a steadying breath, "what do you think about when you center in on the fact that I'm a minicelebrity in this town, that I'm rec-ognized when we go out, am a household word of sorts? Where does your mind go with that?"

"Directly to fear," he stated, with no hesitation.

"What?" Krista said, frowning. "Fear of what?"

"Fear for your safety. Hey, remember back to when Ryan and Ted thought I might be a stalker who was after you? I haven't forgotten that. There are some sickos out there, you know.

"I'd like to take you to work and pick you up every night so I'm certain you're all right, but I haven't told you that because you're so independent I figured you'd pitch a fit.

"Bottom line? I wish you weren't so well known, because it scares the hell out of me when I dwell on the issue of your safety. But I have to learn to handle it because you love what you do. Does that answer your question? And why are you staring at me like I just grew an extra nose?"

"That's it?" Krista said. "That's how you see your-self in regard to my career? As a man who is placed in a position of concern for my safety?"

Jesse lifted one shoulder in a shrug. "Yeah."

Krista framed his face in her hands, kissed him, then smiled at him with tears shimmering in her eyes.

"Oh, man," Jesse said, "you're doing a woman thing on me here that has me totally baffled, and I betcha a buck I'm going to end up in trouble because I don't un-derstand what's happening."

"No, you are not in trouble," Krista said, dropping

her hands from his face. "Far from it. You see, Jesse, I have trusted men in the past, have been in several relationships that I believed might lead to marriage, children, everything I dreamed of having. But I was wrong. Each time. I was very, very wrong."

"What happened?"

"Those men didn't love me, Jesse, they loved who I was—the celebrity, the person who could open doors for them, get them where they wanted to go. I was duped. So, yes, Jesse, you're right. I did build a wall around my heart and was determined never to trust again, never become involved. Then you came into my life. And, Jesse?" she said, sudden tears misting her eyes. "What if I hadn't let you into my life? Think of what we would have missed out on, the wonderful memories we're making, the joy we're experiencing by being together. I don't know where we're headed as far as the future goes, but this has been a precious gift to me. Thank you. Thank you so much."

"And I thank you for trusting me enough to finally share what you just did with me," he said, his voice raspy.

"Take it further, Jesse. Think about what you might gain if you trusted the MacAllisters."

"The MacAllisters aren't in this conversation, my sweet," Jesse said, reaching for the tab on the zipper to Krista's robe. "Something important just took place between us and it's ours, with no room for anyone else." He inched the zipper down slowly, enticingly, and Krista shivered.

"But they're your family and…oh!"

Krista gasped as he trailed a ribbon of kisses behind the lowering zipper.

"Yes?" he said.

"Oh, yes," she whispered.

Chapter 10

"I'm so glad that you could join me for lunch today, Krista," Deedee said. "Isn't this new tearoom delightful? My friends have been raving about it and I thought we should see it for ourselves. This onion soup is delicious, and just look at the variety of little sandwiches we have to choose from."

"It's a lovely place," Krista agreed, then laughed. "I doubt seriously if they'll get many male customers, though. The decor is definitely feminine and it would take several platters of those sandwiches to satisfy a man's appetite."

"Yes, I suppose you're right," Deedee said, beaming. "You've been sharing many meals with Jesse, haven't you? You know how much food a hungry man can consume at one sitting." She paused. "Ryan and I were so pleased that Jesse joined us for dinner the other night. It's only been a couple days now since we've seen him, but I'm already eager to be with him again. But I know, I know, I mustn't push him."

"You're wise to be patient, Deedee. Jesse is having a difficult time dealing with the duplicity of the Burkes, as well as really comprehending that he's a member of the MacAllister family. Being a MacAllister is like a shoe that doesn't fit him yet."

Deedee frowned. "The fact that there are members of our family who aren't accepting him on faith, are insisting on waiting for the DNA test results, isn't helping Jesse to feel welcomed, either."

"Oh, he has no problem with that," Krista said. "He admits his story sounds pretty far-fetched, even though it is the truth."

"Mmm." Deedee nodded. "You and Jesse obviously talk a great deal, share how you're feeling about things, communicate. That's extremely important in a relationship between a man and a woman."

"Oh, look," Krista said, taking a sandwich from the tray. "I am about to have my very first cucumber sandwich, just like on a movie set in England."

"Krista Kelly, you have no intention of telling me what is or is not going on between you and Jesse, do you?"

"No," she said, laughing. "Jesse warned me after he had dinner with you and Ryan that you are on a fact-finding mission regarding the subject of the two of us."

"You two don't play fair," Deedee said, then took

another sandwich. "I wonder what this is? Surely they wouldn't make a parsley sandwich. Well, only one way to find out." She took a bite. "It tastes fine, but I still don't have a clue as to what it is."

She paused. "Krista, surely you can understand that I'm simply a mother who wants her children to be happy. Jesse is my son. You're like another daughter to me. So? Don't you think I should be privy to at least a hint as to whether or not you and Jesse are—shall we say—attracted to each other?"

"Nope."

"Darn it," Deedee said. "I used to be so good at this. I can't wangle one bit of information from Teddy about Rosalie, either. I'm definitely losing my touch."

"Well, I will say this," Krista said quietly. "Jesse is the first man I've spent time with who doesn't have a secret agenda for wanting to be with me. My status as an anchorwoman, my connections in the industry and what have you, mean nothing to him. He simply likes me for being me, and that's very refreshing and special. It means a great deal to me.

"I didn't think I could trust another man, Deedee, because I've been badly hurt in the past by those who were using me, and I was too naive to realize it. But Jesse? I've come to trust him, believe in him. Enough said."

"Oh, my dear child, you've fallen in love with him," Deedee said gently.

"I didn't say that," Krista said sharply.

"You didn't have to. It's there in your voice, in your

eyes, in the expression on your face when you speak of him. Oh, sweetheart, now you look so stricken. What is so frightening about being in love with a wonderful man?"

"I'm not in love with Jesse Burke," Krista said, leaning forward slightly. "It would be a foolish thing to do, for heaven's sake, and I won't allow it to happen.

"Jesse is attempting to discover who he is, regain a sense of identity. He doesn't know if he'll ever feel like a real MacAllister, nor has he said one word about living in Ventura. No, I am not in love with your son, Deedee. I care for him, yes, a great deal, and I'd miss him if he left, but my heart wouldn't be broken, because it doesn't belong to him. And with that, Deedee, the subject is closed."

The older woman beamed. "Certainly, dear, whatever you say. Now then, shall we select something sinfully rich and fattening from that dessert cart that is coming this way?"

When Krista entered her apartment after the lunch date with Deedee, she was met by country-and-western music being played at a high volume, accompanied by the very off-key voice of Jesse singing along at the top of his lungs.

The cacophony was coming from the direction of the kitchen, and Krista went to the doorway without Jesse being aware that she had even arrived home, due to the noise.

Her eyes widened as she took in the scene before her.

Jesse had a dish towel tied around his waist and was vigorously stirring something in a bowl, resulting in what appeared to be flour floating up, then landing on the counter. There was an amazing number of dirty dishes in the sink.

Jesse continued to sing and stir, and a soft smile formed on Krista's lips as she watched him. A warmth consumed her and her heart began to beat so wildly she could hear the echo of the racing tempo in her ears.

In the next instant her smile disappeared and she took a step backward without realizing she had moved, answering the subconscious need to put distance between herself and Jesse.

Dear heaven, she thought frantically, Deedee was right. Oh, no, no, no, how had this happened? Krista had been so certain that she had her emotions under tight control and, oh God, this was terrible.

But there he was, Jesse Burke, singing like a drunken sailor and looking so endearing as he went about whatever disaster he was concentrating so intently on. There he was, the man who now held the power to smash her heart to smithereens.

There he was, Jesse, and she loved him with every breath in her body.

A wave of dizziness swept over Krista and she stretched out one hand toward the kitchen table. She moved forward cautiously and pulled a chair free, sinking onto it with a thud.

Jesse's head snapped around and another cloud of

white powder wafted up from the bowl. He reached over and snapped off the radio on the counter.

"You scared the hell out of me," he said, grinning at Krista. "I didn't hear you come in."

She managed to produce a small smile. "A football team could have stomped in here and you wouldn't have heard them."

"Yeah," he said, laughing, "but when I sing I put my heart and soul into it."

"What on earth are you doing over there?"

"Making biscuits," he said, nodding decisively. "I got hungry for homemade biscuits and remembered how my mother—how Phyllis used to let me stand on a chair and dump the stuff in a bowl, then stir until I made the right consistency of goo. The thing is I can't recall if I'm supposed to use baking powder or baking soda, so I added both to be safe."

"Oh, Jesse," Krista said, laughing and shaking her head.

Oh, Jesse, an inner voice shouted, *I love you. I love you so much. I didn't mean to fall in love with you, Jesse Burke, but I did, and I'm so frightened, and I don't know what to do, and for the rest of my life whenever I eat biscuits I'll think of you and...oh, damn it.*

"Hey," he said, frowning, "you look upset all of a sudden. I'll clean up this mess, I promise. I'm going to bake these babies, then start scrubbing. Okay?"

"Okay," Krista said, hearing the slight trembling in her voice. "The deal includes you taking the first bite of one of those things, though. I'll stand by the phone ready to dial 911."

"Oh, ye of little faith," Jesse said, plopping a spoonful of dough on a cookie sheet. "Hey, how did your lunch with Deedee go?"

"Thanks to your warning I was ready for her third-degree about us. She thinks she is losing her touch because she can't wiggle any information out of Teddy about Rosalie, either. She's the woman Teddy is working with in Italy, and Deedee is convinced there's something romantic going on between them."

"She mentioned that the other night," Jesse said, sliding the cookie sheet into the oven. "Shoot, I can't remember how long I'm supposed to bake these. I guess I'll start with twenty minutes, then see how they look." He paused and glanced at Krista. "Teddy, by the way, is on the same wavelength as his uncle Ted in regard to me. The two Teds believe I'm a phony."

"All those doubts will be settled soon, Jesse."

"Whatever," he said, then began to load the dishwasher with the pile of dishes.

The telephone rang and Krista answered the extension mounted on the kitchen wall. A moment later she held out the receiver to Jesse.

"It's for you," she said. "It's Robert MacAllister."

"*The* Robert MacAllister?" Jesse said, not taking the receiver. "The head of the entire MacAllister family? *That* Robert MacAllister?"

"The very one," Krista said, waggling the receiver. "Here. He wants to speak with you."

"Whew," Jesse said, then finally accepted the receiver. "Hello?"

"Hello, Jesse, this is Robert MacAllister. I think it's time we met, don't you?"

"Well, sir, wouldn't you prefer to wait until the DNA test results come back?"

"No, as a matter of fact, I wish to meet you before those results are known. Would you be free to come over this evening about eight o'clock?"

"Yes, all right. Sure. Eight o'clock, sir."

"Fine. Krista can give you directions to the house. Goodbye until then."

"Goodbye."

Jesse handed the receiver back to Krista, who wiped off a dusting of flour before replacing it.

"Man, I feel like a kid who has an appointment to see the principal at eight tonight," Jesse said. "I've heard so much about Robert MacAllister. He's loved and respected by everyone in the family, apparently, and no one likes to disappoint him in any way."

"Robert has well-thought-out reasons for everything he does, Jesse," Krista said. "He's a wise and wonderful, very loving man. His wife, Margaret, passed away last year, as you might have heard, but Robert refuses to move from the large home they shared. He says his memories of Margaret are there and he's not budging. He's remarkable. You'll like him, I'm sure of it."

"But why does he suddenly want to see me after all these weeks, Krista? And why the emphasis on the meeting being before the DNA results are back?"

"I guess you'll find out at eight o'clock tonight."
Krista frowned. "Jesse, there's smoke beginning to
come out of the oven. I have a feeling you just made
hockey pucks instead of biscuits."

"Oh well."

It would seem, Jesse thought, just before eight
o'clock that evening, that he was destined to spend a
great deal of time sitting in his vehicle in MacAllister
driveways, not wanting to enter MacAllister homes.

What a strange life he was leading these days, he
mused, as he walked slowly, very slowly, toward the
front door of the majestic home. There was a surreal
quality to his existence, with a minute portion of brain
wondering if he was asleep and dreaming, would
waken and once again put in long, tedious hours labor-
ing on the land at the ranch.

The only time he felt grounded, really alive and
solid, was when he was with Krista. Was he in love
with the enchanting Ms. Kelly? He didn't know. Or
possibly he was subconsciously refusing to address
the issue, because he was in the midst of a ridiculously
clichéd identity crisis and had no business exploring
the depths of his emotions for her.

Man, it had meant so much to him when she'd made
it clear that she finally trusted him enough to tell him
about the hurt she had suffered at the hands of self-
serving men who had been attempting to use her no-
toriety for their personal gain. What scums.

But Krista now trusted him—*him,* Jesse Burke, or

Jesse MacAllister, or whoever the hell he was. She trusted him not only with her innermost secret pain, but with the very essence of herself each time they made love, holding nothing back. And he trusted her. That mutual trust was good. It was very, very good.

Jesse reached the front door, rang the bell and drew a weary breath. He was running out of mental energy for these under-the-microscope encounters. And this one, geez, was with the king of the hill, the head of the entire MacAllister clan.

The door opened to reveal a tall, elderly man with silver hair, straight-as-a-stick posture and a welcoming smile on his still-handsome, albeit wrinkled-from-age face.

"Good evening, Jesse," Robert MacAllister said. "Come in. Welcome."

"Thank you, sir." Jesse entered the house and glanced around. "Another terrific house. MacAllisters have great taste."

"Let's go into my study, my den, my haven," Robert said. "I've had many important conversations in that room over the years. More than I could ever begin to count."

The den was definitely a man's room, with high-backed leather chairs flanking a stone fireplace, floor-to-ceiling bookshelves crammed to overflowing, and a massive desk with just enough clutter to indicate it was used regularly.

"Sit down," Robert said, gesturing to one of the chairs. "Would you care for a drink?"

"No thank you. I'm fine."

Robert settled onto the other chair and rubbed his knees. "I was tending to my Margaret's flowers today," he said. "My knees are telling me that at eighty-eight I'm a tad too old to be kneeling on the ground pulling weeds. I guess I'll hire a gardener to assure that nothing happens to those flowers. They were Margaret's pride and joy."

"You miss her very much, don't you," Jesse said, making it a definite statement, not a question.

"More than I could begin to tell you." Robert paused. "I'm sorry she isn't here to meet the grandson we knew nothing about until now. But I'd like to think she's smiling about the fact that you're finally here among us."

"How do you know I'm really your grandson?" Jesse said. "Not all the MacAllisters are convinced of that."

Robert looked at him for a long moment. "I know my own flesh and blood, a MacAllister, when I see one. But I knew before tonight, before actually meeting you, by listening to what members of the family are saying about you. I've heard enough to know you're a fine man, gentle, thoughtful, caring...a MacAllister. I wanted you to know that I acknowledge you as my grandson, Jesse, before the tests come back that will show it to be true."

An unexpected tightness gripped Jesse's throat and he looked away to gather his emotions.

Why had the approval of this man meant so much?

he wondered. Other members of the family had welcomed him, believed his story, and he'd thanked them
for that. But there was something different about knowing that Robert MacAllister viewed him as his grandson, had bestowed that honor upon him without DNA
proof.

Jesse shifted his gaze to meet Robert's again.
"Thank you, sir," he said, his voice gritty. "That means
a great deal to me. Thank you."

Robert nodded slowly, then frowned as he continued to look directly at Jesse. "You're going through a
very difficult time right now, aren't you?" The old man
waved one hand in the air. "Don't bother to answer that,
because I know it's a true statement. You were stripped
of your identity when you were told what took place
when you were born, and you're not comfortable with
the identity that is rightfully yours. You're no longer
Jesse Burke, but can't yet envision yourself as being
Jesse MacAllister. You're in limbo, and that has got to
be a living nightmare."

Jesse leaned slightly forward, listening to Robert intently, marveling at the older man's insight and intel-
ligence. No wonder the family held Robert MacAllister
in such high regard. He had the special ability of comforting with his understanding, knowing without asking, making it clear that he cared deeply by the words
he spoke, which came directly from his heart.

"I do believe, Jesse," Robert continued, "from bits
and pieces I have heard, that if it wasn't for your relationship with Krista you might very well have left Ven-

tura and this turmoil behind. Are you in love with Krista Kelly, Jesse?"

"Yes," he admitted, then sat bolt upward. "What I mean is, I…that is…how did you do that? I didn't know for certain if I loved Krista, because my life is such a mess I didn't feel prepared to look that closely at how I felt about her. But you ask me and—blam—there it is, popping right out of my mouth. How did you do that?"

Robert smiled. "Years of practice talking to people sitting in that very chair. So it's true? You are in love with our Krista?"

Jesse took a deep breath and let it out slowly, puffing his cheeks. "Yes, I guess I am," he said finally. "No, I *know* I am, which is a stupid thing to have gone and done."

"Why?"

"Why?" Jesse said, his voice rising. "Because I don't even know who I am, for crying out loud. I was lied to by the most important people in my world for thirty-two years. Who do I trust, believe in? Krista, yes, I trust her totally, absolutely, but…" He shook his head. "I have no business being in love with a wonderful woman like Krista when I don't even know what my future holds. Well, at least she won't know how I feel, because I won't tell her."

"Mmm," Robert said. "The wisdom of that is debatable, but we'll put that on the back burner for now and center on the topic of trust. You've met and spent time with your biological parents, your real mother and father, my son Ryan and his wife, Deedee. Correct?"

"Yes."

"But you don't trust their expressions of love for you, their joy that you are here, their desire to have you become a true member of the MacAllister family?"

"Not really," Jesse said. "Oh, I'm not saying they're lying to me the way Phyllis and Joe Burke did. I'm certain they believe that the emotions they're registering are real, but it all stems from titles. I'm their son, so they automatically are convinced they love me because of that title. In actuality I'm a stranger to them, to Sarah, to all the other members of the family I've met. How can they love me if they don't even know me?"

"You're underestimating the power of love, Jesse," Robert said, "the intensity and wisdom of it. The magic. I look at you and I don't see a stranger. I see a grandson who has a place in my heart just as all my other grandchildren do. Not because of a title, but because you are our Jesse and you've come to us at long last. I love you unconditionally, and I thank God you're home where you belong."

"I...I believe you," Jesse said. "I don't know why I believe that you truly love me, but I do. You stand apart and above the others somehow. I trust in you, sir, and I don't have a clue as to why it feels so right."

Robert smiled. "Love is powerful, magical and mysterious and wonderful. You know that to be true because you're in love with Krista. You opened your heart to her, now to me. Keep that door open for the rest of the family, Jesse. Give them a chance, won't you? Think about it. Will you do that? Think about it?"

"Yes. Yes, I will."

"Good. That's fine." Robert paused. "Over the past years I've given each of my grandchildren a gift, something special that I selected just for them. It's time to give you yours."

He reached into the pocket of the sweater he was wearing and withdrew a small, tissue-wrapped object.

"I bought this for my wife, Margaret, because she was forever rummaging through her purse in search of her keys. I thought if she had a key chain with something bigger, heavier on it she might find it easier. She used it for many years before she died. I'd like you to have it." He extended it toward Jesse.

"I can't accept something like that," Jesse said.

"Of course you can." Robert grasped one of Jesse's hands and placed the gift there, giving it a pat before releasing it again. "You can because you are Margaret's grandson, too, and she would approve of this, want you to have it."

With hands that were visibly unsteady, Jesse unwrapped the key chain, and his breath caught when he saw it. It was a two-inch-high, gold, block letter *M* attached to a short gold chain and ring for keys.

"The *M* was for Margaret at the time," Robert said, "but as of this moment it represents the name Mac-Allister. When you're ready, Jesse, use the key ring. When you are comfortable with your new identity, have accepted us all as your family, then claim this gift as your own. In the meantime, put it in a safe place and know it's waiting for you."

"And if I never feel I can use it?" Jesse said softly. "What then?"

"It's your gift. Do with it as you will."

"I don't know what to say, sir, except thank you."

"You're very welcome." Robert paused. "Now, at the risk of being rude, I'm going to send you on your way. I'm very tired and it's time for me to sleep."

Jesse got to his feet, rewrapped the key chain in the tissue and slid it into the pocket of his slacks.

"I'll see myself out," he said. "I won't forget this evening. It was very special. Good night, sir."

Robert smiled and nodded, then listened until he heard the front door close. Then he sighed and laced his hands on his stomach.

"He's a fine young man, Margaret," he said aloud, "this new grandson who has finally come home to the fold. He's troubled and confused, but I have every faith in his ability to set things to rights. After all, my darling, he's a MacAllister. Jesse…MacAllister. Yes."

With a decisive nod, Robert pushed himself to his feet, hesitated as he steadied, then walked slowly from the room, turning off the light as he went.

Chapter 11

Italy

Teddy MacAllister sat on a lawn chair beneath a large tree. A two-year-old named Carlo was taking a nap on Teddy's lap, plus two elderly men were snoozing in chairs on either side of him and his peacefully sleeping bundle. Teddy brushed the toddler's moist hair from his forehead, then stared at him for a long moment, marveling at his perfect features.

This one will break hearts, Teddy thought, but all the Cantelli clan were fine looking people, including his Rosalie, who was the most beautiful woman he had ever known.

Teddy swept his gaze over the multitude of people

in the distance, looking for her. The park where they had all spent the day was large, with lush green grass and towering trees that provided welcoming shade.

There had been enough delicious food, Teddy mused, to feed the Cantellis as well as the equally large family of MacAllisters, had they been there. Things were winding down from the fun-filled day, and he now saw Rosalie helping the others pack up the remaining food.

He'd had a fine time today, except when disturbing thoughts had inched into his mind—thoughts he'd attempted and failed to ignore. It had been over a month since he and Rosalie had squared off on the subject of where they would live once they were married—America or here in Italy. Neither one of them had addressed the issue again, and it was causing tension to slowly build between them.

He had told Rosalie that they'd find a solution to the problem, but every time he mentally broached the subject he hit a brick wall. He wanted to live in Ventura near his family, and Rosalie wanted to remain here near hers.

Neither of them was wrong in their thinking, Teddy mused. They came from large, loving families they didn't want to see only a few times a year. They also both had high-ranking positions in the companies they worked for, and neither wished to give up the career level they'd made many sacrifices to achieve.

There had to be a solution to this mess, he thought, frowning. He couldn't bear the prospect of losing Rosalie. No. No way. He loved her so damn much, wanted to spend the rest of his life with her, have oodles of kids like this nifty one snoozing on his lap right now.

But this picnic today, with so many Cantellis in attendance, had just emphasized how homesick he had become, how eager he was to see his own family.

Plus there was the bizarre business of this Jesse Burke guy showing up out of nowhere with his wild story. Burke was a MacAllister who had been kidnapped at birth? Was his and Sarah's long-lost brother? Deedee and Ryan's son his parents hadn't even known was one of a set of twins his mother had been carrying all those years ago?

"Give me a break," Teddy said, with a snort of disgust.

Carlo stirred but didn't waken.

Forget about Burke for now, Teddy told himself. The issue that needed his full attention was the one he and Rosalie were struggling with. They couldn't go on the way they were, not discussing the problem, because it was taking a toll, causing this underlying tension between them.

Yeah, they needed to talk about it again, but he had a sinking feeling in his gut that if they did it would be a rerun of the original argument on the subject. He hadn't changed his views, and he was certain that Rosalie hadn't, either.

Oh, man, what if there *wasn't* a solution to this mess? It could blow them apart, destroy what they had together, shatter all the hopes and dreams they had for the future. But, damn it, he didn't want to live permanently in Italy because…

Teddy's tormented thoughts were interrupted by the approach of an attractive woman, who smiled warmly at him.

"Thank you for taking care of Carlo while I helped clear up," she said. "He was so tired because he was operating at full tilt all day, having so much fun." She glanced at the men still sleeping on either side of Teddy. "More than the little ones have run out of energy. Did you enjoy the day, Teddy?"

"Very much, Maria," he said, smiling. "I ate too much, though, but it's hard to resist food that delicious. Do you think Rosalie is about ready to head out?"

"My little sister is packing up the last of the food. I need to round up my other four bambinos and get home in time to greet my husband. He was so disappointed that he had to work today. He loves these family gatherings."

"Everyone in my family likes this sort of thing, too," Teddy said. "We have get-togethers like this one as often as possible."

"You miss them, don't you?" Maria said. "Your family."

"Yeah, I do, I really do."

"Just as Rosalie would miss all of us if she lived in Ventura with you," Maria said. "She and I have talked, Teddy. I know you've hit a stumbling block in your relationship with my sister over this business of where you're to live and who's to give up their position in the company they work for. It will be so heartbreaking if you two can't find an answer to this."

"Your mother is on my side," Teddy said, getting to his feet with Carlo nestled in his arms.

"I know," Maria said, nodding, "but I'm afraid that Rosalie feels Mother isn't up with the times, the new way of thinking."

"And you? Where do you stand?"

"I don't really know," Maria said, "because I didn't have to face anything like that. Paulo and I grew up together because he lived two houses down from us. There was never a thought given to eventually leaving here. It's hard to project how I might feel, react, if he suddenly wanted to move us thousands of miles away, because I know it will never happen."

Teddy nodded. "That makes sense." He paused. "I don't want to lose Rosalie over this issue, Maria. I can't handle even thinking along those lines, but I don't know what the solution is. I really don't."

"Listen to your heart, Teddy," Maria said, then extended her arms. "Give me my sleepy boy. We must get home."

Teddy watched as she walked away with Carlo, who continued to sleep, then saw the four other children run to her after she called to them.

Maria and Paulo had it made, he thought. They had five fantastic kids, would spend the remainder of their days in a place where they both were contented. They had made a life together that was close to perfection, as far as he could tell.

But he and Rosalie? He shoved his hands into his pockets as he walked slowly to where she was waving goodbye to a number of family members. The two of them were in love with each other just as Maria and Paulo were, but there, the similarity stopped. There wouldn't be love and contentment, wouldn't be babies by the armload, wouldn't be forever and ever, if they couldn't reach an agreement on the problem. It was growing in strength and power, to the point where it could destroy them.

Teddy came up behind Rosalie, gripped her waist, then pulled her to him and kissed her on the neck. She gasped in shock, then wriggled out of his grasp and turned to face him with a smile.

"You startled me," she said. "The last time I glanced your way you still had a lapful of Carlo."

"Maria came and collected him. I don't think anything could wake that kid if he wasn't ready to surface. He sure is cute, you know? I'd like to place my order for a half dozen of those little people. Boys, girls, makes no difference to me as long as there are a whole bunch filling our house to overflowing with giggles."

"And squabbles," Rosalie said, laughing.

"Those, too," Teddy said, matching her smile. "It goes with the turf." He paused and his expression became serious. "I'd like to have the kind of happiness that Maria and Paulo do. They still look at each other like newlyweds when they're together, and they have those neat kids. I envy them—I really do."

"We could have a life together like that, Teddy,"

Rosalie said, placing her hands flat on his chest. "Our children could be running through this pretty grass in the future during a family picnic. Our youngest baby could be the one to take a nap on his daddy's lap beneath a shady tree. It's all there, waiting for us."

"Here. In Italy," Teddy said, frowning as he covered her hands with his.

"That's how I picture it in my mind, yes," Rosalie said, then sighed. "We've been dancing around the subject for a month and this isn't the time or place to bring it up again. But we know from the meeting we had at work the other day that the exchange program is winding down. The man from here who is at your firm in Ventura is more than ready to come home, and when fine-tuning the program to meet our needs to do background checks on people applying for a job is completed, that will be that. We can't play ostrich much longer about this problem we're facing."

"I know," Teddy said quietly. "I was talking to Maria. She said I should listen to my heart."

Rosalie nodded. "And I'll listen to mine. Perhaps the answer is waiting there for us."

"I hope so." Teddy glanced around. "I'll go volunteer to help carry things to the vehicles, then we'll go home. Okay?"

"Yes, fine."

As Rosalie watch Teddy walk away, a chill swept through her and she wrapped her hands around her elbows.

They would, she supposed, address the issue plaguing them once they were in the privacy of their own place. They were running out of time, had to find an answer to this dilemma that had the power to destroy them, rob them of all they hoped to have together in the future. There had to be an answer for them.

Rosalie gazed up at the gorgeous, crystal-clear blue sky dotted with fluffy white clouds. Did the sky look like this in Ventura? she wondered. Or was it true, as she had heard, that California was smoggy to the point that a person could actually taste the nasty air that shrouded the cities?

Oh, if only it was that simple. If all she had to do was get used to icky air when she moved to California with Teddy, she could be happy as a clam. Ta-da! End of the problem.

Sudden tears misted her eyes and she shook her head, knowing there was nothing even close to simple about what she and Teddy were facing. She loved him so much, would be devastated if she lost him, but he was asking far, far too much of her.

Dear heaven, what was to become of them? She would listen to her heart, as Maria had advised Teddy, and hope, pray, that the answer to all of this was there.

"Rosalie," Teddy yelled from across the park. "We're finished here. Let's rock and roll and head for home."

She waved and started forward, knowing she was dragging her feet, trying to postpone yet again the issue she and Teddy were facing. The drive home was made in total silence, with both of them focused on their own thoughts.

The telephone was ringing when they entered the apartment, and Teddy hurried to answer it. "Hello?"

"Teddy? It's Dad."

"Hey, how are you, Dad?" Teddy asked. "I hope you haven't been trying to reach me for hours. We were at a picnic with Rosalie's family all day. I think their number is close to the present count of the MacAllister clan."

"Well, that must have reminded you of home," Ryan said.

"It made me homesick," Teddy stated, sinking onto the chair next to the table where the telephone was sitting.

"We certainly miss you, Teddy." Ryan paused. "Listen, son, I have something important to tell you."

"Oh?"

"We just got the news from Kara about the DNA tests. The results came back, finally. Teddy, everything Jesse Burke told us is true. He's a MacAllister. He's Sarah's twin, your younger brother, a son that was stolen from your mother and me when he was born."

"You're kidding," Teddy said, hooking his free hand on the back of his neck.

"No."

"I'll be damned." He dropped his hand and leaned back in the chair. "I don't believe this. I mean, yeah, I believe it because you can't argue with DNA, but it's just so off the wall. What kind of person steals a newborn baby, for crying out loud?"

A noise caught Teddy's attention and he realized that Rosalie was running bathwater for one of her leisurely, bubbly soaks. He redirected his attention to what his father was saying.

"We're trying not to dwell on that," Ryan said, "because it serves no purpose other than to make me mad as hell. We were robbed of the first thirty-two years of our son's life and…see? Don't get me started."

"How is Mom taking the news?" Teddy said.

"She never doubted for one minute that Jesse was our son, but the actual test results have her smiling and crying at the same time. She isn't even going to attempt to speak to you during this call."

"And this Jesse guy?" Teddy said, frowning. "What did he have to say when Aunt Kara made her report?"

"He just nodded, because he knew all along that he was telling the truth," Ryan answered. "But, Teddy, he isn't *this Jesse guy*. He's your brother."

"That's going to take a while to sink in, I guess," he said. "It will probably be easier for me to accept once I get home and meet him, see him for myself, sit down and talk to him."

"When do you think that will be?"

"Sooner than I anticipated, Dad. We're wrapping things up here. I'd say another month maximum, but maybe not even that long."

"Your mother will be thrilled to hear that. She's indulging in one of her long bubble baths at the moment."

"Oh, yeah, so is Ros— What I mean is…ah, hell."

Ryan chuckled. "Rosalie is taking a bubble bath even as we speak? Don't worry, Teddy, you haven't shocked your old dad here. It didn't take a genius to figure out that you and Rosalie moved to that charming little village together.

"Your mother will shoot me dead as a post, though, if I don't attempt to discover what plans you two have. Just how serious is this relationship you're in?"

"I love her, Dad," Teddy said. "I'm in love with Rosalie."

"That's fantastic, son," Ryan said. "I assume she feels the same about you?"

"Yes, but…" Teddy glanced in the direction of the bathroom and lowered his voice. "Dad, we're in a helluva mess. I want to marry Rosalie and live in Ventura with her and our kids. She wants to marry me and live in Italy, raise our children here.

"Neither one of us wants to settle for seeing our families a few times a year, nor is either of us prepared to give up the position we've worked so hard for in our companies.

"This is scaring me to death because I don't see an answer, and I'm terrified that I'm going to lose Rosalie over this issue."

"Wow," Ryan said. "I had no idea you were facing something of this magnitude. I believe your fears are justified, son. Something like this could destroy what you and Rosalie have. Be certain that you think this through very carefully." He paused. "May I share this with your mother?"

"Sure, why not?" Teddy said wearily, as he squeezed the bridge of his nose. "But even her motherly wisdom isn't going to produce a magical answer that will solve this mess. Hey, enough about me. You're centered on Jesse right now and that's how it should be."

"Jesse is having a difficult time accepting his place in the family, Teddy," Ryan said. "Think how you'd feel if you suddenly found out you aren't who you thought you were, and are supposed to take on a new identity. He doesn't completely trust in us. After all, he was lied to for thirty-two years by people he loved unconditionally, only to discover they were not who they presented themselves to be. Now here we are, saying we're your parents, your mother and father—so love *us* now instead. Can you understand where he's coming from?"

"Yeah, I do. I really do. Why should he believe that your love is real, that you're who you present yourself to be?"

"Exactly. We're just praying he'll remain in Ventura long enough to allow us to prove to him that we're sincere. He's free to leave at any time, you know. Your mother and I aren't kidding ourselves that he has stayed this long because of us, even though he said he would wait until the test results were back. We think it's due to his relationship with Krista that he's still here."

"Ah, the plot thickens," Teddy said, chuckling. "The love bug bit." He glanced toward the bathroom again. "There's a lot of that going around."

"So it would seem," Ryan said. "Well, I think I'd better get off the line. I hope you and Rosalie work out a solution to your problem, son. Hell, you have to. You're in love with each other."

"I wish being in love was all it would take to be given a magic wand to fix this."

"Don't underestimate the power of love. I'm hanging up now, Teddy. Love from your mother and me, too, of course. Give Rosalie special wishes from us."

"I will. Oh, and greetings to Jesse. My...my brother. Whew. That is going to take some getting used to. Good night, Dad."

"Goodbye, son."

Teddy replaced the receiver, then dragged both hands down his face.

Incredible, he thought. That wild story Jesse Burke had told about being snatched at birth was true. He really was a MacAllister, a member of Teddy's own immediate family, his younger brother, Sarah's twin. Yeah, that was definitely incredible.

Teddy leaned back in the chair, folded his arms over his chest and stared into space.

It was hard to imagine, he mused, what it would be like to find out after thirty-two years that you're not who you believed yourself to be. Then, as a guy was trying to get used to the loss of his identity, he's handed a new one and told this was the real goods.

"Mmm," Teddy mumbled, narrowing his eyes.

That would definitely be a rough road to go. To top it off, Jesse had to deal with the cold hard facts that the people he had always believed to be his parents were really a man and woman who had taken part in a despicable act when he was born. Now he had a new mother and father in his face, telling him to trust them. Man, Jesse must be on mental overload.

Rosalie appeared in the room in a pink terry-cloth robe, her dark hair piled fetchingly on the top of her head. She crossed the room and wriggled onto Teddy's lap. He wrapped his arms around her hips.

"Well, my sweet," he said, "when I'm wrong, I'm wrong. Big time."

"Really?" She sat up straighter and looked at him intently. "I know that was your father on the phone. What did he have to say?"

"The DNA tests are back and Jesse Burke really is my brother. Everything he said about what happened when he and Sarah were born was true."

"Oh, I see," she said, her shoulders slumping. "Well, that's quite a bulletin, isn't it?"

"Yeah, it is, but why do you suddenly look so dejected?" Teddy paused. "Wait a minute. When I said I was wrong you thought my dad had read me the riot act, made me understand that I should stay here in Italy with you after we're married. Right? Is that what you thought?"

Rosalie sighed. "Yes. I had this flash of the older and wiser father telling his son that a man should do everything within his power to make the woman he loves happy. But why would he say that? My mother is from the same generation as your father, and she says I should go wherever my husband chooses."

"My father didn't offer an opinion," Teddy said, "other than to say that the problem had to be solved or it will destroy what we have together. That, however, is something I already know."

Rosalie nodded. "While I was in the bath I was thinking about it, Teddy, and it terrifies me because I can't see a solution for us. Suppose one of us gives in and agrees to live where the other one wishes. I'm so afraid that in time there will be resentment on the part of that person, a building anger that will damage our marriage beyond repair."

"I hear what you're saying."

"Oh, God, Teddy, what are we going to do? I love you so much, want to be your wife, the mother of your children. But you're asking too much of me, and I'm asking too much of you." Tears filled Rosalie's eyes. "There is no answer for us. Oh, Teddy, it's hopeless."

"Don't say that," he said, his voice rising. "Don't give up on us, Rosalie. There *is* an answer. We just haven't found it yet."

Rosalie shook her head and two tears slid down her cheeks.

"My father said not to underestimate the power of love," Teddy said, a near frantic edge to his voice. "Your sister said to listen to our hearts. Let's give this more time, think it through again. I love you and, God, Rosalie, don't give up on us. Please. Okay? Hey. Okay?"

"Okay," she said, managing to produce a trembling smile.

"Good. That's good." Teddy paused. "So, I have a brother I knew nothing about until now. How about that, huh? I sure didn't think that story would end up this way. I owe Jesse an apology, that's for sure. I'm eager to meet him now, get to know him, find out what makes him tick. I hope we have things in common, can grow close the way brothers should, you know? I sure hope he's still there when I…" Teddy's voice trailed off.

"When you go home?" Rosalie said. "When you go home to Ventura and have lots of time to establish a relationship with your new brother, because that's where you intend to stay?" She slid off his lap. "That's how you envision it, isn't it, Teddy?"

"I didn't say that. Even if I made the decision to live here in Italy I'd have to go home first to set things in motion to sell my house, ship the stuff I want to keep, dispose of the rest and…and say goodbye to everyone in…in my family. It would be a sort of hello, then see ya, thing with Jesse and…yeah, I'd have to connect with all of them because I wouldn't know when I'd be back to visit… Ah, man."

"Visiting a few times a year is a very bleak scenario, isn't it?" Rosalie said, taking one step backward, then another. "I can't handle that thought, either, when I think of my family. When we were first getting to know each other we thought it was so fine that we both came from large families, knew all the pros and cons of that type of lifestyle. Now? That oh-so-fine thing is creating a disaster. We'd be better off if one of us was an orphan and thrilled to have a huge clan to belong to, no matter what."

"There you go," Teddy said, attempting to produce a smile and failing miserably.

Rosalie pressed her fingertips to her temples. "I can't think about this anymore today," she said. "I'm tired and I'm going to bed."

"I'll come with you and we'll—"

"No, Teddy. I need to be alone right now." She dropped a quick kiss onto his lips. "Good night."

Teddy nodded, then watched Rosalie until she disappeared from view. With a weary sigh he got to his feet and went out onto the balcony, where he rested his forearms on the metal railing. He swept his gaze over the town square below where the old-fashioned streetlamps were glowing in the gathering dusk.

He knew for a fact that the square had been bustling with people most of the day, because it always was. Then when darkness fell people headed home to enjoy the remaining hours of the evening. He and Rosalie had stood on this balcony and watched the couples leave, two by two, making up fun and imaginary lives for them.

For the people they saw wander off alone they created happy tales of someone waiting eagerly for them to return, because they wanted all those they saw to be blissfully in love just as they were. No one, they declared, should be alone and lonely.

Teddy dropped his chin to his chest and drew a shuddering breath.

It could happen, he thought miserably. If a solution to his and Rosalie's problem wasn't found it could definitely happen.

He could spend the remainder of his days alone and so damn lonely.

Chapter 12

Jesse sank onto a lawn chair next to Krista in Jillian and Forrest MacAllister's backyard and chugalugged a bottle of water. "I am so out of shape," he said, placing one hand on his heart, "it's a crime. You'd think with all the hours I did physical labor on the ranch I'd be fit as a fiddle, but a touch football game with the MacAllister clan is a whole new experience. Whew."

Krista laughed. "They do give it their all. However, you will notice how many bodies are flopped on the grass. At least you made it back here to a chair." She paused. "Are you enjoying yourself, Jesse?"

"Yes, I am," he said. "In the week since the DNA results came in I've been warmly welcomed by so many MacAllisters I'll never get their names straight.

Once they realized I wasn't ticked because they were withholding judgment until the test results were known it has gone very smoothly. This gathering today is sort of like frosting on the cake."

"Do you feel as if these people are your family?" Krista asked. "That you're really a MacAllister?"

"It's coming slowly," he said, nodding. "I'm trying very hard to get rid of my it's-only-titles mind-set and drill into my brain the facts that Deedee is my mother, Ryan is my father, Sarah is my twin sister and on and on. I'm at least a little more comfortable with those truths."

"Do you believe now that they sincerely care about you?" Krista pressed, looking at him intently. "Unless you trust them… Never mind. I'm getting naggy." She paused. "Oh, look, Ted and Hannah just arrived. I wondered if they were going to come today."

"I'm surprised Ted is here," Jesse said. "I haven't heard word one from him since the test results came back. He was wrong about me and that has to be tough for a guy like him to admit. Man, he's headed right for me. This could get sticky."

Jesse set the empty water bottle on the grass and got to his feet as Ted approached. Hannah had veered off in another direction. Krista scooted out of her lawn chair and headed toward the dessert-laden table on the far side of the large yard.

Ted had no readable expression on his face when he stopped in front of Jesse.

"Ted," Jesse said, nodding slightly.

"I have only one question for you," Ted said.

"Oh?"

"Do I get to use ketchup when I eat my huge serving of crow?"

Jesse blinked in surprise, then laughed. "That is allowed," he said, smiling. "No hard feelings, Ted. I sincerely mean that. I would have felt the same way if the roles had been reversed. I had a pretty wild story to tell."

"Which proved to be true," Ted said. "I'm sorry I was such a hard case, Jesse. Welcome to the family. Hannah and I are sorry about what happened when you and Sarah were born, about your missing out on your rightful place in this family for so many years. It was a lousy thing to have been done back then, but you're here now and we hope you'll stay." He extended his hand toward Jesse.

"Thank you," Jesse said, shaking it warmly. "Thank you very much."

"What are your plans for the future?" Ted asked. "Do you know yet?"

"I'm looking into taking the bar exam so I can practice law here in California," Jesse said. "I could return to Nevada and avoid the hassle of taking the test again, but there's nothing there for me. Nothing at all. Here I…well, I have…"

"Krista," Ted said, grinning. "And a whole bunch of MacAllisters who will drive you nuts at times but who are damn fine people."

"Yeah," Jesse said, smiling. "I just hope I have

something to add to the family. That isn't clear to me at this point."

Ted frowned. "Nobody will be keeping score, Jesse."

"I don't know," he said, frowning in turn. "I have a completely different background than all of you and I sure don't have any experience being part of a large family. I'm not sure what's expected of me."

"Nothing," Ted said, shrugging. "Just, hell, I don't know, just be here."

"My turn," Hannah said, coming forward just then. "You two have settled your differences and I am butting in." She gave Jesse a peck on the cheek. "Welcome home, Jesse." She slid a smug look at Ted. "Of course, I believed you were a MacAllister from the beginning, unlike some stubborn people I know."

"Okay, okay," Ted said, laughing and raising both hands. "I was wrong, I'm sorry, I'll choke down my crow with ketchup, end of story."

"Fine," Hannah said. "Now come say hello to Robert. He's over there under that shady tree and you haven't paid your respects yet."

"See you later," Ted said to Jesse.

"Sure," Jesse said, then sat back down as Ted crossed the lawn with his wife.

Robert MacAllister, Jesse thought, watching as Ted and Hannah settled onto chairs next to the head of the MacAllister family. Everyone, including himself, had made a point of greeting Robert upon arriving at the picnic. He was held in the highest regard by them all.

Jesse somehow knew Robert would not say one word to him about the gift of the key chain. It would be up to him if he used it, considered himself a true MacAllister and, therefore, was comfortable with a key chain boasting the letter *M*. The gift was presently wrapped in the tissue and tucked carefully in the top drawer of his dresser at Krista's. Jesse wasn't ready to use it yet. Not yet.

"Everything okay?" Krista said, sitting down next to him and drawing him from his thoughts.

"Fine," he said, smiling at her. "Ted is going to add ketchup to his crow."

Krista laughed. "Yummy. You should go get some dessert, Jesse. I just had a piece of lemon pie that was to die for."

"Maybe later." Jesse paused. "I told Ted I didn't know if I had anything to add to the MacAllister family, and he said all I had to do was be here. That's kind of hard to buy into. I mean, hey, there are architects drawing up house plans for family members, and a construction company building the things, a doctor to pull strings like Kara did, police officers to... Anyone want an ear of corn? I can grow corn like a pro."

Krista frowned. "You're approaching this all wrong, Jesse. I mean, I'm considered a member of this family and what do I add, as you put it? Invade living rooms with the evening news? Whoopee. That's a big contribution. Ted's right. You just have to be here. It's like when I was taking care of the kids for Sarah and Barry so they could get away for a couple of days. You step up when someone needs something and you're capable of supplying it. It's very simple, really."

"Not if you've never been a part of anything like this," Jesse said.

"Uncle Jesse," little Jesse yelled, seeming to appear out of nowhere and flinging himself at his uncle.

"Hey, buddy," Jesse said, scooping the child onto his lap. "From the looks of your face you just had some chocolate cake."

"Yeah, I did, and it was great. I had to drink milk with it, though, 'cause my mom said. I don't think I should have to drink milk on a picnic, do you?"

"Sure, you should," Jesse said. "There is nothing finer than a cold glass of milk with a slice of chocolate cake. Your mother is a very wise lady."

"Oh. Well. Okay. You played football good, Uncle Jesse. I was watching you a lot."

"Yeah, right, I was great." Jesse laughed. "I fumbled the ball four times, sport."

"That's not so many," little Jesse said. "My dad dropped it six times. I counted 'em. Are you still my best friend, Uncle Jesse? All mine?"

"You bet I am."

"That's great 'cause it makes me feel okay about being the littlest kid in my family and not getting to do stuff that Emma and Rick can. I'm special now, too, 'cause you're my best friend. I gotta go check on my cars. 'Bye." He slid off Jesse's lap and dashed away.

Krista reached over and grasped Jesse's hand. "And

you think you have nothing to add to this family?" she said, smiling at him warmly. "Replay in your mind what little Jesse just said, and I think you'll come to a different conclusion."

"Food for thought," he said, nodding slowly. "Definitely food for thought." He paused. "Also on my mental agenda is the fact that I should stop mooching off of you, Krista."

"You're not," she said, dropping his hand and straightening in her chair. "You've insisted on buying the groceries for the meals we destroy as we cook them. You paid the utility bills that arrived last week. You're not mooching, Jesse."

"Well, I guess part of my problem is I'm getting antsy, sort of bored sitting around all day. I'm used to working long hours on the land, and long hours when I was an attorney. I was on hold, so to speak, waiting for the DNA test results, but that's finished business now. I'm going to take the California bar exam, but in the meantime I need a job of some sort."

"I can understand that," Krista said. "I did tell you how pleased I am that you plan to stay on in Ventura, didn't I?"

"I believe you mentioned that about ten times," he said, smiling at her. "Your reaction to that decision made me feel about ten feet tall, sweet lady." He frowned. "But back to the issue at hand. How to fill my days while I'm trudging through what it takes to be able to practice law here."

"Why don't you present the question to the entire

family?" Krista said. "That would set a lot of minds to working on the problem."

"No way," he said, shaking his head. "Someone would invent a job for me, make it sound like they're thrilled I'm available, and I probably wouldn't even be qualified to do whatever it is. No. I'm not approaching the MacAllisters about this."

"You still don't trust their sincerity, do you?" Krista said, then sighed. "They're your family, Jesse."

"Time," Jesse said. "I need more time, Krista."

And, he thought, he needed more time to gather the courage to tell her that he loved her, had fallen deeply and forever in love with her. He wasn't comfortable saying those words while he was—despite what she'd said—mooching off of her.

He'd sent for the paperwork necessary to get his name added to the list of those taking the bar exam when it was being given again. Until then he'd be studying, brushing up, so he'd be prepared.

He *wanted* to declare his love to Krista, shout it from the rooftops, ask her to marry him. But there was another problem. Ask her to marry who? Jesse Burke or Jesse MacAllister? He was still in limbo—no longer a Burke, but yet not ready to be a MacAllister.

"You look troubled, Jesse," Krista said.

"What? Oh, no, I'm fine. I was just doing some heavy-duty thinking there for a moment. You know, deciding whether I want some lemon pie you recommended, or the chocolate cake that little Jesse endorsed."

"There are even more choices on that table," Krista said, laughing. "It boggles the mind."

"I shall return," he said, getting to his feet. "The sweet stuff is calling my name."

Krista watched as Jesse headed for the desserts, stopping along the way to speak briefly with members of the family, which resulted in laughter floating through the air.

They're probably giving him a bad time about fumbling the football, Krista thought, smiling to herself. It had been a rough-and-ready game, but Jesse had held his own when he'd actually managed to hang on to the ball. He'd been right in there giving it his all, like the other boisterous MacAllisters.

Jesse MacAllister. In her mind that was who he was. Not Jesse Burke. No, he was a MacAllister. And she loved him. Oh, yes, she was irrevocably in love with him and she'd almost told him when he'd announced he was going to take the California bar exam and remain in Ventura.

But at the last second she'd kept silent. She knew he cared deeply for her, knew she was an important part of his life, but he hadn't even hinted at a future with her, a forever.

Well, what did she expect? He still had so much to deal with in the present. Granted, the DNA business being taken care of had lifted a great burden from his shoulders, but there remained the problem of his identity, his sense of self. He needed to know who he really was, was comfortable being, and she understood that.

Jesse MacAllister. Maybe—oh, please, yes—
maybe when he was finally secure in the knowledge
that he'd come home where he belonged, was truly
an accepted member of this wonderful family, when
he had achieved an inner peace, then he, Jesse Mac-
Allister, would be ready to look deep within himself
and discover how he felt about her. Maybe then he
would realize he loved her as she loved him, and
wanted to spend the remainder of his days with her.
Maybe.

A piercing scream jolted Krista from her dreamy
thoughts and she jumped to her feet as she saw everyone running toward the far side of the yard.

Dear heaven, she thought, her heart beating wildly
with fear as she rushed forward in turn. What had happened?

When Krista reached the gathered crowd she
couldn't see what was taking place beyond them. She
saw Forrest dash in the direction of the house.

"What's wrong?" she cried, moving next to Sarah.
"What's going on?"

"It's Grandpa," Sarah said, tears spilling onto her
cheeks.

"Robert?" Krista said, feeling the color drain from
her face. "What about him? Sarah?"

"Oh, Grandpa," Sarah moaned, pressing trembling
fingertips to her lips. "No."

Krista looked around frantically, then Jesse appeared at her side.

"Robert collapsed," he said quietly. "Ryan is giving

him CPR and Forrest is calling 911. They think he had a heart attack."

"Oh, dear God, no," Krista said. "He had a heart attack years ago, but he's been fine, Jesse. Fine. We were all worried about him when Margaret died, but he was strong despite missing her so very much and…" She shook her head. "He'll be all right. He's Robert Mac-Allister, for heaven's sake. He's indestructible and…oh, God, Jesse."

Jesse circled her shoulders with his arm and pulled her close to his side. She splayed one hand on his chest and could feel his heart beating in a tempo as rapid as her own. She was vaguely aware of Jillian, Emily and Andrea rounding up the children and ushering them toward the house.

"Move back," Ryan yelled. "Give him some air. Everybody move back."

The family spread out, faces pale, tears streaking many cheeks, hands holding other hands for comfort. As the group shifted, Krista was able to see Ryan continuing the CPR on Robert, who lay still, so very still, on the lush grass, his skin a sickly gray.

"Oh, God," she whispered.

Jesse tightened his hold on her as the wail of a siren in the distance came closer and closer.

Hang on, Robert, he thought frantically. Hang on, Grandpa. This family needs you. I need you. Your wisdom, your love and unconditional acceptance. You're my grandfather and I just found you. I don't want to lose you. I want you to see me use the key chain, that special and wonderful gift you gave me. I'm…ah, yeah, Grandpa, I'm ready to use the key chain. Standing here right now I know that. I do. I'm Jesse MacAllister, grandson of Robert MacAllister. Don't leave your MacAllisters. Don't leave me. Hang on, Grandpa.

Michael ran to the gate of the yard, and moments later paramedics entered with their equipment. Ryan moved out of the way and Deedee wrapped her arms around his waist. No one spoke, nor hardly breathed. Krista trembled in Jesse's arms and he swallowed heavily as an achy sensation seized his throat. After what seemed like an eternity, a stretcher was brought in and Robert was lifted carefully onto it.

"Mr. MacAllister has suffered a heart attack," one of the paramedics said, sweeping his gaze over the throng. "We're transporting him to Mercy Hospital. We know you want to be there and we urge you to drive carefully despite being upset." He shifted his attention to the other medics. "Okay, guys, let's hustle."

Even though Michael was the oldest of Margaret and Robert MacAllister's four children, everyone turned to Ryan for instructions as to what should be done next.

"We all want to be at the hospital," Ryan said, "but we have the children to think about. Decide among yourselves how you're going to tend to your kids, and come to Mercy as soon as you can. We don't know what we're facing yet. Pray. Don't forget to pray. Come on, Deedee, let's go."

A buzz of voices erupted as Ryan's instructions were followed regarding the children. Barry came to where

Jesse was standing with Krista still tucked close to his side.

"Jesse," he said, "will you take Sarah to the hospital? I'm going to get the kids home and see if I can find a sitter to come over. I'll be at Mercy as quickly as I can. I want to be certain the kids are all right first, though. They adore their great-grandfather and are no doubt very upset. Sarah is falling apart, so I'd feel better knowing she's with you."

"Of course," Jesse said. "Sure."

"I'll stay here for now," Krista said, "so Jillian can go with Forrest. I'll see that all this food gets inside and put away. If anyone needs me to take care of their children, I will. If not, I'll come to the hospital as soon as I clean up here. I don't work tonight, so I'm free to do whatever is needed."

She paused. "This is so terrifying. I think we're all guilty of believing that Robert would always be there as head of the family."

"You're right about that," Barry said, nodding. "He's the anchor, the... Well, we're wasting time. Let's get moving. Jesse, Sarah knows you're taking her to the hospital." Barry turned and jogged toward the house.

Krista drew a steadying breath and looked up at Jesse. "I'll see you at the hospital when I can get there, Jesse," she said. "Take good care of Sarah."

"I will," he promised, then gave Krista a quick kiss on the lips, not caring who saw him. "I'll be waiting for you, Krista."

Agreements were made among the group for sharing rides, so everyone would have a vehicle. Jesse was to use his car, while Krista borrowed Jillian and Forrest's extra one, leaving the Barstow vehicle free for Barry to take the children home.

The others made similar arrangements, and as quickly as possible, everyone rushed off to their assigned tasks, a sense of urgency, worry and tension becoming a nearly tangible entity hovering over them like a dark, menacing cloud.

Krista found herself abruptly alone in the huge backyard, and a shiver coursed through her. What Jesse had said suddenly echoed in her mind.

I'll be waiting for you, Krista.

She was going to cling to those words like a lifeline, she thought, as she started toward the food-laden tables. It gave her comfort and strength to know that Jesse was waiting for her, ready to take her in his arms as he had done here in this yard, and just be there for her through this frightening ordeal.

She wasn't alone, not anymore, because Jesse was waiting for her. And she knew in the very center of her heart that she had been waiting for him all of her life.

Krista picked up a plate of chocolate chip cookies and made no attempt to blink away the tears that filled her eyes as she stared at the dessert.

"Robert's favorite cookies," she whispered. "At every family gathering someone sees to it there are chocolate chip cookies for Robert."

She looked up at the crystal blue sky as tears spilled onto her cheeks.

"Oh, Robert, are you just so very tired? Is it time for you—" A sob caught in her throat. "—for you to join your beloved Margaret? Is Margaret waiting for you?"

Chapter 13

The vigil began.

The MacAllisters were shown to a large, private waiting room on the cardiac-care floor at Mercy Hospital due to their vast numbers and also because of the fact they were the MacAllisters.

Newspaper and television reporters who had picked up the 911 call on their scanners and cross-referenced the address to a name, descended upon the hospital for information on which MacAllister had been rushed there and why. A MacAllister in crisis was definitely an important story to be told in Ventura.

The hospital security guard kept the press corralled in the lobby and informed them in no uncertain terms that he had no idea what was taking place beyond where he stood.

When Krista arrived at the hospital over an hour after Robert had been whisked away from Jillian and Forrest's home, she mentally groaned when she saw the gauntlet she would have to run through to reach the family.

The minute she entered the hospital she was literally pounced upon by a man in his late thirties who reported for the television station where she worked.

"Hey, Krista, great," the man said. "I forgot that you've got an in with the MacAllister clan. What's the scoop? Who's sick, hurt, whatever?"

Krista frowned. "No comment, Curtis. I'm here as a family friend, not as a news reporter."

"Where's your loyalty to the station?" Curtis demanded. "Don't you see? We can have the breaking news bulletin about whatever has happened to one of the MacAllisters while everyone else is standing around fumbling for something to report.

"This is no sprained ankle or some dumb thing, because the MacAllisters are here en masse and are obviously very upset. None of us got here in time to see them unload the ambulance, but you know what's going on. Come on. Give."

"No, Curtis," Krista said. "Now get out of my way."

"The big brass at the station aren't going to like this," Curtis said. "Hey, what are you doing? Keeping the info for yourself so you can break it on the air? You've already got the cushy anchor job, for Pete's sake, while I'm stuck on the street chasing ambulances and cop cars. This story is mine, damn it."

Krista glared at Curtis and moved on, making her way through the other reporters, who were shouting questions at her. She spoke quietly to the security guard, who looked at a clipboard he was holding and nodded. He whispered something close to her ear and she rushed to the bank of elevators.

When she entered the private waiting room, Jesse hurried forward and gave her a quick hug.

"Is there any news?" Krista asked, her voice trembling slightly.

"Robert had a massive heart attack," Jesse said. "They're running tests now to determine the extent of the damage."

"Oh, God." She shook her head. "Jesse, we all have to remember that Robert is eighty-eight years old and has had a heart attack in the past. There's just so much the human body can take. There's also the fact that…" She glanced around and lowered her voice even more. "…that he misses Margaret so much. I've heard him say that he's looking forward to when they'll be together again. I think he's tired. Jesse, I think he's ready to go, to be with her."

Jesse nodded slowly. "Deedee said something like that, too, but when she did Sarah got hysterical and told her not to say such a thing."

"How do you feel about what's happened?" Krista asked, searching his face for an answer.

"My first reaction was that I didn't want to lose such a terrific grandfather I just discovered I had,"

Jesse said, "but I've been sitting here thinking about what a dynamic man Robert has always been. Would he want to be dependent on others for his care if there is extensive damage to his heart? I don't think so."

"Well, all we can do now is wait, I guess, and see what the verdict is," Krista said. "Where's Ryan?"

"He went to call Teddy in Italy. Forrest is phoning that royal family those MacAllisters married into. From what I heard Ryan and Forrest say, they're going to tell those they talk to to get here as quickly as possible. That says something right there, Krista. It doesn't look good for Robert, for Grandpa."

Krista sighed. "No, it doesn't. Let's sit down." She paused. "The lobby downstairs is jammed with reporters, including an obnoxious guy from my station I have never cared for. He's very ambitious, wants to have his own spot on the news at the station instead of racing around doing stand-ups all over town. None of them down there know which MacAllister is in trouble, and I refused to tell Curtis, who is, I'm sure, going to run to the powers-that-be at the station and tell them I had the ability to give us an edge and refused to do it."

"Will that create problems for you?" Jesse said, frowning.

"I don't care if it does. Family comes first, Jesse."

They settled onto one of the many sofas in the room, sitting close together, gaining comfort and strength from the other.

"This is going to be so difficult for those who are far away," Krista said, after several minutes of silence.

"Those plane trips home are going to seem endless. The royal family has their own plane, so that will help, but Teddy will have to scramble to get an empty seat on the first available flight. Teddy—well, everyone— loves Robert so very much."

"Yeah," Jesse said, reaching for Krista's hand. "I don't envy Forrest and Ryan having to make those calls. Teddy is going to be especially upset and frustrated, I think, because he'll be struggling to make connections on commercial flights. I've never met him but I have a feeling I wouldn't want to get in his way right now. He's going to be right at the edge."

"I totally agree," Krista said, nodding. "I doubt if it would do any good for someone to tell Teddy Mac-Allister to calm down at the moment."

Italy

"Teddy, calm down," Ryan said into his cell phone, as he paced around a small room at the end of the hospital corridor.

"Calm down?" Teddy yelled. "My grandfather might be dying, I'm halfway around the world and you're telling me to calm down?" He sighed. "I'm sorry, Dad. I'm taking this out on you and that's not fair. I'll get off the line and start calling airlines and see what I can book."

"All right," Ryan said. "Son, listen to me. You must remember that your grandfather had some damage to his heart from that attack years ago. Also keep in mind that he's eighty-eight years old and has been struggling for a year now to accept your grandmother's death."

"What are you saying?" Teddy asked. "That Grandpa won't fight to live? That he'll just give up? No way. Not Robert MacAllister. How can you even suggest such a thing, Dad?"

"Because I'm his son," Ryan said quietly. "Because I saw the light go out of his eyes after my mother died. Because I know how I'd feel if something happened to your mother. Because I love my father, Teddy, and I'd understand if he just didn't want to take on this battle. Are you listening to me? Please think about that as you're coming home."

"No. Yeah, okay. Hell, I don't know. I've got to get on the phone to the airlines, Dad."

"We'll see you when you get here, Teddy. We love you."

"Yeah. 'Bye."

Teddy slammed the receiver into place, then reached in a drawer of the table where the telephone sat, and yanked out a phone book.

"Teddy?" Rosalie said. "I'm trying to piece together what I heard. Your father feels your grandfather might be ready to…"

"Yeah," Teddy said, flipping through the pages.

"I can understand that," Rosalie said, nodding. "Robert misses his Margaret beyond measure. From what you've told me they had a marriage like something out of a fairy tale."

"They did," Teddy said. "Okay, airlines. Here we go.

Rosalie, get packed. If I get stuck on hold listening to stupid music, throw some clothes in a suitcase for me, too, would you? Then if I'm still tied up here, go downstairs and use the Murrettis' phone to call your parents and tell them you're going with me, then leave a message on the voice mail at work. Ah, damn, I've been put on hold."

"What?" Rosalie said. "Teddy, I can't go with you. You and I are in charge of the project at work. I'll be pressed as it is to do your part as well as mine, but we both certainly can't just up and leave, with where the program stands now. That would cause all kinds of problems that… No, I can't go with you and you know it."

"What I know is that my grandfather might be dying," Teddy yelled, "and I've told you what that man means to me. I need you with me, Rosalie. This is the kind of crisis where a man and woman who are in love with each other stand together. I don't have to make that god-awful flight home alone because, supposedly, I have a partner in life who will be sitting right next to me, helping me get through those hellish hours. I need you to come to Ventura with me, damn it."

"And I need to stay here and do what you normally would be doing at work," Rosalie said, matching his volume. "That's being your partner in life in a way that is just as important."

"No, it's not. I don't give a flying flip about work right now," Teddy said. "We are going to Ventura, Rosalie."

"I am not going to Ventura, Teddy," she said, planting her hands on her hips. "Not now, not…" Her voice trailed off.

Teddy stared at her for a long moment and his voice was raspy when he spoke again. "Not ever?" he said finally. "Is that what you're saying?"

"I…"

A voice suddenly spoke in Teddy's ear and he jerked his gaze from Rosalie.

"Yes, you can assist me," he said into the receiver. "I need to get to Ventura, California, as quickly as possible. This is a medical emergency, so bump somebody off a flight, do whatever you have to to get me home…what?" He looked again at Rosalie, who had tears shimmering in her eyes. "One. I'm just booking a ticket for one person. Return flight to Italy? No, that won't be necessary. I won't be coming back here."

Rosalie's eyes widened for a second, then she spun around and ran from the apartment, nearly falling as tears blurred her vision. Teddy watched her go, then slammed his fist onto the table.

"What?" he said into the receiver. "I'm sorry. I didn't catch what you said. What time is the flight?"

In Ventura, day turned into dusk, then darkness settled like a heavy curtain. In the waiting room at the hospital time lost meaning. A volunteer arrived with a platter of sandwiches, a pot of coffee and a pitcher of orange juice. MacAllister mothers left to change places with fathers who were home with children, and vice versa.

Sporadic conversations took place in the room, then silence would descend again, with everyone's attention riveted on the door as they waited for the doctor to appear with some word of Robert's condition. The more time that passed, the greater the tension became until it was a nearly palpable entity taunting the group.

After more than four hours that seemed closer to four days, the door opened and a man in his early sixties, wearing a white coat, entered. Everyone got to their feet.

"I'm sorry it's taken so long to get back to you," the man said.

"What is going on, Dr. Eastman?" Ryan asked.

"We've been attempting to run tests to determine the damage to Robert's heart, but had to continually stop because his heartbeat is so erratic. We had to go very slowly so as not to aggravate his condition."

Ryan nodded. Deedee slipped her hand into his and he squeezed it.

"I wish I had better news," the doctor said. "There has been extensive damage to Robert's heart and there's no way to repair what is no longer functioning. There is simply not enough heart left to maintain the human body. I'm sorry. I'm very, very sorry. I've known Robert for many years and he is one of the finest men I've have the pleasure and honor to call my friend. I…" He pressed his thumbs against his eyes for a moment. "I am just so damn sorry."

"What are you saying?" Sarah said, stepping forward. "That my grandpa is going to die? You're just giving up? You can't do that. You have all kinds of fancy equipment here. I know you do because Mac-Allister money paid for a lot of it. You're sorry? Well, sorry isn't good enough. You've got to do something."

"Sarah, honey," Deedee said, going to where she stood. "We must accept the truth."

"No," Sarah said, shaking her head. "No, no, no."

"Sarah," Dr. Eastman said gently, "there's something you should know. A few months after your grandmother died, Robert came to me and signed a Do Not Resuscitate form, which is on file here. He made it very clear that if something like this should happen he wanted no extraordinary measures taken. Those wishes will be followed by me and my staff."

"Oh, God," Sarah said, covering her face with her hands.

"We have to let him go, sweetheart," Deedee said, tears spilling onto her cheeks as she led Sarah back to a sofa.

"Your grandmother…" Krista said, a soft sob catching in her throat "…is waiting for him, Sarah. Think about how wondrous it will be for them to be together again."

Sarah nodded jerkily.

"You may go to Robert's bedside a few at a time," Dr. Eastman said quietly. "Short visits, please, so everyone will have a chance to say goodbye." He paused. "Bless you all." He turned and left the room, his shoulders slumping as though they carried the weight of the world.

* * *

At eight minutes before midnight, with his four children standing around his bed, Robert MacAllister slipped gently and peacefully away. He was gone. He would never be forgotten.

An hour later Krista cried herself to sleep, while Jesse held her where they lay in Krista's bed. Jesse's tears dropped silently and steadily onto her silky hair.

At thirty thousand feet above the ground in the rumbling airplane, Teddy jerked awake from a fitful sleep…and knew.

Goodbye, Grandpa, he thought, blinking back his tears. I'll miss you. You were the best grandfather any kid ever had. The very best. Say hello to Grandma for me, huh?

God, he thought, dragging his hands down his face. Within a handful of hours he'd lost one of the finest men he'd ever known, as well as the only woman he had ever loved. There he sat in a metal capsule being flung through the skies, surrounded by close to two hundred people, and he had never felt so incredibly alone.

And lonely.

Ah, Rosalie.

Teddy opened the shade covering the small window, and stared out at the inky darkness beyond, which stretched into infinity like a vast sea of…nothing.

Chapter 14

" . . . And following the moving eulogy by the governor of California," Krista said, looking directly into the camera, "the mayor of Ventura also spoke at the funeral of the endless contributions to our city that Robert MacAllister had made.

"As you could see by the footage we showed earlier in this report, St. Luke's Catholic Church was filled to overflowing for the service, which was held this morning. A multitude of reporters, including our own from this station, were there as well.

"Robert MacAllister and his wife, Margaret, who passed away last year, were household names in our city, as is the entire MacAllister family. They have given so much, not only monetarily, but also in volunteer hours to many causes close to their hearts.

"Robert will be greatly missed, as is Margaret. Yet we know that the large number of remaining MacAllisters will follow in their footsteps. Farewell, Robert…and thank you for everything.

"We'll be back to learn about the weather we can expect in the next few days after these messages."

Teddy pressed the remote and turned off the television set in his living room, silencing the commercials on the ten o'clock news.

"Well," he said, "they gave Grandpa the send-off he deserved, although I doubt if he would have liked all that hoopla." He paused. "Some of the family thought I might be really upset because I didn't get here before Grandpa died, but I'm all right with that. I said my goodbye to him while I was on the plane. The service today should give all of us the closure we need. Krista just did a really nice job reporting the funeral, too."

"Yeah, she did," Jesse said. "I heard the emotional catch in her voice, but I don't think the general public would have been aware of it."

"I didn't hear it," Teddy said. "But then you and Krista have something special going, so it stands to reason. You're a lucky man, Jesse." He paused again. "I appreciate your coming over here tonight. I haven't had a chance to talk with you privately since I arrived home from Italy four days ago. I thought it was time to have a conversation with…my brother. Man, that really sounds weird."

"No joke," Jesse said. "Turn it around a minute. You have to get used to the idea there is one more MacAllister, your brother, in the family. Think about what I'm attempting to adjust to."

Teddy laughed. "I wouldn't change places with you, buddy. No way. There's a helluva lot of us and the majority are not shy and retiring types. Hey, have you been in a touch football game yet?"

"Yep, and lived to tell about it," Jesse said, chuckling. "Sort of. I was battered and bruised, that's for sure. As for how many of you there are? That's still overwhelming, because I was raised as an only child."

"Whew. Well, being part of this clan made it easy for me to feel comfortable with Rosalie's large family in Italy when they all got together. They…ah, hell, I don't want to go there. I'll just thoroughly depress myself. I'm already bummed out, because no matter how 'appropriate' a funeral is, it's still not a whole lot of fun."

"I'm very grateful I had a chance to meet our grandfather," Jesse said quietly. He shifted and pulled the key chain with the *M* out of his pocket. "He gave me this. It belonged to your—our—grandmother and the *M* was for Margaret. Robert…Grandpa said I should consider it an *M* for MacAllister and to use it when and if I was ever comfortable being a real MacAllister. I put my keys on it this morning before Krista and I went to the funeral. After all these weeks I finally have an identity again, trust and believe in the welcome I've received into the family, and I owe a great deal of my inner peace about that to our grandfather."

Teddy held his hands up as though making a frame. "Jesse MacAllister," he said. "Works for me, little brother, even if I thought you were a scummy con man at first. Hey, when I'm wrong, I'm wrong, just like Uncle Ted was about you. I'm sorry about that."

"No problem," Jesse said. "I wouldn't have believed my story, either, if someone was trying to sell it to me." He paused. "Have you talked to Deedee about Rosalie? She is eager for details, believe me. Has she nailed you yet?"

"No," Teddy said, frowning. "I've been dodging Mom because I'm not ready to talk about what happened between me and Rosalie. Mom knows what the problem is but she isn't aware that it all blew apart before I left Italy. I lost Rosalie, Jesse. I love her so damn much and I've lost her forever."

"Hey, I am no expert on the subject of love, believe me," Jesse said, "but the MacAllister theory is that it is very powerful and shouldn't be underestimated, or however that goes."

"So I've been told," Teddy said, a slight edge to his voice.

"Hey, before I met Krista I would have said, 'Yeah, right,' but now… Are you certain you can't fix things with your Rosalie?"

"Very certain," Teddy said wearily. "I want her to leave her family and live here in the States with me. She wants me to leave my family and live with her in

Italy. There it is in a nutshell. Neither one of us can imagine seeing our families only a few times a year for quick visits. And that, as they say, is that."

"Oh," Jesse said, nodding. He glanced around the large living room. "This sure is a nice house you have here, Teddy. The thing is…never mind. I'm overstepping."

"No, you're not, Jesse. Say whatever it is you're thinking."

"Well," Jesse said, looking directly at his brother, "you can fill this place to overflowing with MacAllisters for one of your—our—get-togethers, have a great time, play some football, the whole bit."

"And?" Teddy said.

"And when the event is over, everyone goes home…two by two, in couples. You'll wave goodbye to the clan, shut the door and then what? You're alone. Here. In this big, fancy house that's meant for a family, you'll be all alone. The MacAllisters are a fantastic, really sensational family, close, willing to go the extra mile for one of their own, but not one of them is capable of filling the void in your life, Teddy. Only the woman you love—only Rosalie—can do that. Are you really willing to lose her so you can barbecue a bunch of hamburgers in your backyard, then toss a football around?"

"It's not that simple," Teddy said, none too quietly.

"Isn't it?" Jesse said, raising his eyebrows. "Think about it." He got to his feet. "I'd better shove off. I want to be there when Krista gets home from the station. I'm leaving now, Teddy, and here you'll sit. Alone. I'll let myself out. Thanks for inviting me over so we could get to know each other better. See ya."

"Yeah," Teddy said, staring into space. "See ya."

A heavy silence fell after Jesse closed the front door behind him with a click, and Teddy got to his feet. He began to wander around the large room, glancing at the expensive furniture, the plush carpeting, the framed pictures on the walls.

It looked like a model home, he thought. Like nobody lived here. There was no fluffy sweater of Rosalie's tossed on a chair, no shoes in front of the sofa where she'd slipped them off her feet and wiggled her pretty toes, no tangled ball of yarn that she needed his help once again to unravel as she struggled to learn how to knit.

MacAllister couples, two by two, Jesse had said. When the hamburgers were eaten and the football game played, they all went home. Together. Two by two. They closed the door on the world and focused on the one they loved, their soul mate, their partner in life.

They were not, nor should they be, giving one thought to ol' Teddy at that point, and what he'd lost so he could take his turn having the family gather in his backyard.

"My God," he said, dragging his hands down his face. "What have I done?"

When Jesse arrived at Krista's apartment he stood statue still in the middle of the living room and listened intently for any sound.

Nothing, he thought. Just silence. That's how it was when a person was alone. Just chilling silence. That's what he'd been trying to get across to Teddy. Families were great, wonderful, but the bottom line of a person's life was what do you have when they all go home?

Man, he'd been pretty cocky, whipping out all that stuff for Teddy like the guru of love, the man who had all the answers, which was definitely a crock.

He was going to end up just as alone and lonely as his brother if he didn't declare his love to Krista, tell her exactly how he felt about her and ask her to become his wife when he was once again employed.

And he was going to end up just as alone and lonely as Teddy if Krista refused his proposal and said that while she cared deeply for him, she didn't love him and, therefore, couldn't marry him. Talk about a depressing scenario, Jesse thought, slouching on the sofa.

If Teddy quit being so stubborn and put his love for Rosalie on top of the list where it belonged, he would have a fighting chance of mending fences with her, have his dreams come true and ride off into the sunset with the woman of his heart. Which was corny as hell, but feasible.

But if Krista didn't love Jesse, that would be the end of the story. A bleak future, alone and lonely. Filled with silence.

So? So, okay, he was going to gather his courage and lay it all on the line. The time had come. Tonight was it. No, maybe next week would be better. They were all on emotional overload because of Robert. Two weeks. Waiting two weeks was good. Maybe three weeks would be better because…

"Man oh man," Jesse said, lunging to his feet. "I am such a wuss."

He slid his hand into his pocket and wrapped it around the key chain.

It was now his talisman, he decided, a gift from a wise and wonderful man. It would give him the strength and courage he needed to tell Krista that he loved her, and would hopefully bring him good luck, or whatever it would take for her to say she loved him in return.

"Okay. I'm ready," Jesse said aloud. "I'm calm, cool and collected. I'm going to do this—in two weeks. No, damn it, tonight. This is it. My entire future happiness depends on…oh, geez."

The sound of a key being jiggled in the lock on the door caused Jesse to spin around, the sudden wild beating of his heart echoing in his ears. Krista entered the apartment and smiled at him as she pushed the door closed behind her.

"Hi," she said brightly. "You're so nice to come home to." She laughed. "Good grief, now I'm quoting lines from songs." Her smile disappeared and she cocked her head slightly to one side. "Is something wrong, Jesse? You look, I don't know, tense or something. Didn't your evening with Teddy go well?"

"Who? Oh. Teddy." Jesse said it a tad too loudly. "The visit was good, great, just fine. We hit it off like brothers. There was an instant bond. It went fine. Yep. Just fine."

"Definitely acting weird," Krista said, narrowing her eyes as she dropped her purse onto a chair. "Talk to me, Jesse."

"You bet," he said, nodding. "I'm going to do exactly that. In two weeks."

"What? You're not making any sense."

"I know," he said, his shoulders slumping. "Give me a second here."

He drew a steadying breath, placed one hand on his chest to check his heart rate, shoved his other hand into his pocket to grasp the key chain one more time, then withdrew his hand and extended it toward Krista.

"Okay," he said. "Let's sit down, shall we?"

"Shall we?" She eyed him warily. "Well, yes, we shall if that's what you want."

Jesse took her hand, led her to the sofa, then shifted to face her after they were seated.

"Krista," he said, "after the hamburgers are eaten and the football game is played, everyone goes home."

"Pardon me?" she said, an expression of total confusion on her face.

"Ah, damn," he said, shaking his head.

"Jesse, what on earth...?"

"Krista Kelly," he said, nearly shouting, "I love you. I am deeply and forever in love with you. I want to marry you, and spend the rest of my life with you, and have babies with you, and have you by my side when the hamburgers are gone."

"Oh, I—"

"We can't get married until I pass the California bar exam and get a decent job, because a man has his pride, you know. But we could get engaged for now and talk about our plans, and hopes and dreams."

"Jesse, I—"

"Of course, we can't get married at all if you don't love me as I love you, and you don't want to be with me forever, and have babies and—"

"Jesse!"

"What?"

"I love you," she said, her eyes misting with tears. "Oh, Jesse, I love you with my whole heart. Yes, I want to marry you, and have babies with you, and do whatever it is we're supposed to do with the hamburgers. Yes. Yes, yes, yes."

"Oh, thank God," Jesse said, then gathered her into his arms and kissed her.

The kiss was rough and urgent, born of Jesse's stressed-out state, but then it gentled as the realization of what Krista had said caused a warmth to consume him, a sense of joy like nothing he had ever known.

Krista loved him. She'd agreed to marry him, spend the rest of her life with him, have their babies. They'd be one of the MacAllister couples. Two by two. Oh, God, how he loved his woman.

Jesse broke the kiss to draw a much-needed breath, then spoke close to Krista's moist lips. "I love you so much," he said. "We're going to be so happy together, have it all. If I'm dreaming, don't wake me up."

"I love you, too, Jesse," Krista said. "I've fantasized about what it would be like to be your wife, spend my life with you, but I wasn't certain how you really felt about me."

She paused. "I really should call my parents. This is the kind of news a person is supposed to share immediately with her mother and father, but tomorrow is soon enough. This night, this memory-making night, is ours. Make love with me, Jesse. Please?"

"Yes, ma'am," he said, getting to his feet and pulling her up to nestle against him. "Tricky part will be to make it all the way to the bedroom. I want you so much."

Krista smiled and slipped her arm through his. "Let's hurry, really rush down the hallway," she said. "I don't care how immature that might appear. In our private world we can do anything we want to."

Laughing with delight, they burst into the bedroom, then Krista swept back the blankets on the bed. They removed their clothes, tossing them here, there, everywhere, then moved onto the cool sheets and lay close, gazing into each other's eyes, seeing the sparkle of laughter change to smoky hues of desire.

"I love you and always will," Jesse said, his voice husky with emotion. "I respect you, and even more, Krista, I trust you with an intensity I didn't think I would ever be capable of again. Robert MacAllister told me not to underestimate the power of love, and he was so very, very right."

"Yes," Krista said. "He was so wise, so loving and giving of that wisdom. Oh, Jesse, the future is ours, together, and it's going to be glorious."

His mouth melted over hers and heat exploded within them, churning, swirling, tightening. They were sealing their commitment to each other by sharing the most intimate act there was between a man and a woman, and it was so special, so incredibly beautiful.

They caressed and explored as though making love for the first time, yet rejoicing at the same moment at the wondrous familiarity of what they found. Theirs. Given in love, received in kind.

Hearts quickened and passions soared along with the heat, the want and need.

"Come to me, Jesse," Krista whispered. "My husband."

"My wife."

They became one. It was more, far more, than just a physical joining, it was an intertwining of emotions as well, perfectly matched, the hopes and dreams for the tomorrows meshing just as their bodies were.

The rocking rhythm began, intensified, carried them up and away as they sought—then found—the vibrant dancing colors that belonged only to them. They hovered there, not wishing to leave, then realized the reality they would return to was just as splendid.

Jesse moved off of Krista, then they snuggled, not wanting even inches to separate them. He kissed her moist forehead.

"My wife," he said. "That sounds so right, so good. My wife."

"Yes," she said, her head resting on his shoulder. "I'll be Mrs. Jesse…oh. Wait. I think of you in my mind as Jesse MacAllister, but I guess you're legally Jesse Burke, aren't you?"

"I suppose," he said, frowning. "Yet as an attorney I want to cover the bases. There may be a technicality that makes me a MacAllister already, because I was born a MacAllister, but I'd rather change my name in the courts so there's never any question about it. You'll be Mrs. Jesse MacAllister. Krista Kelly MacAllister."

"Lovely."

"Except…"

"What?"

"I've noticed that court actions are listed in the newspaper here. If it's printed there for all to see that Jesse Burke changed his name to Jesse MacAllister, the press is going to pounce. Big time."

"Oh, they certainly will," Krista said. "MacAllisters are news if they attend an opening of a play. Imagine what will happen if reporters sniff out a mystery, a potential scandal or whatever, surrounding the family. Goodness, Jesse, what are we going to do?"

"I'll talk to my father." Jesse smiled. "It's getting easier and easier to call Ryan that. Anyway, let's hope that with all his connections in Ventura we can accomplish the name change and keep it under wraps."

"Good plan." Krista paused. "I saw you hug Deedee

after the service for Robert. Was that difficult for you to do?"

"No, it felt very natural now. My mother was mourning her father-in-law and I wanted her to know I understood and was there for her. She said she had lost a father but gained a son, and wasn't God something the way he balanced things out? She's a remarkable woman."

"Yes, she is." Krista yawned. "So, tomorrow you'll talk to Ryan about the name change dilemma?"

"Count on it."

"'Kay. Oh, I'm so sleepy."

"Then sleep and I'll hold you right here in my arms. My wife."

"My husband," Krista murmured, then drifted off into blissful slumber.

"Ryan…my father will have the answer to the name thing," Jesse said, his eyes beginning to close. "No problem."

And then he slept with Krista nestled at his side.

"No problem," Ryan said.

Ryan, Deedee, Jesse and Krista were sitting in the sunny breakfast nook at Ryan and Deedee's home the next morning.

"No?" Jesse said.

"I have a good friend, Ron Spencer, who is a judge," Ryan said. "We play golf together sometimes—Ted, too—because we're all awful at the game and we don't feel badly about our scores when it's the three of us.

I'll explain the situation to Ron, and we'll arrange for the documents to change your name to be signed in his chambers. And most importantly, for the information not to be given to the clerk who submits data to the newspaper."

"Great," Jesse said, nodding. "Thank you."

"I'm so thrilled that you're officially changing your name to MacAllister," Deedee said, "and about you and Krista getting engaged. Krista, did you phone your parents?"

"Yes," she said, laughing. "My mother is on cloud nine. I think she had just about given up on me ever marrying. She was talking about grandchildren before I could get off the line."

"Halt," Jesse said, raising one hand. "Before you go off on a tangent about flowers and colors and who will wear what and all that stuff about the wedding, we have to back up here. The wedding has to be private and small, family only. Krista and I talked about this before we came over this morning."

"Oh, Krista," Deedee said, "don't you want a big wedding with a gorgeous dress and—"

"Whoa," Jesse said. "Think about it. A wedding like that, a MacAllister wedding, would get press coverage. Jesse MacAllister, son of Ryan and Deedee MacAllister? Where did this kid come from? Everything ever written about the family says that Deedee and Ryan have two children, not three. Get it?"

"Well, phooey," Deedee said. "I love to help plan big weddings."

"As time goes on I'll just be another MacAllister in the clan," Jesse said, "as long as there isn't major emphasis on who my parents are. I feel confident that will work in the future. It's the present we have to be concerned about. If pushed about which MacAllister she married, Krista will just say breezily that I'm a distant cousin who moved to Ventura."

"Good," Ryan said, nodding. "That's good."

"I hate this," Deedee said, sighing. "I want the world to know that you're my son, but I'll just count my blessings that you're here, and not pout about having to keep silent about what happened when you and Sarah were born. I get chills just thinking about what the press would do with that information."

"It would be the story of the year," Krista said. "An award winner for whichever reporter broke it first. I wouldn't be surprised if there was a book deal in the soup, too. That reporter could write his, or her, own ticket from there on out."

"You sound a little wistful," Jesse said, frowning.

"As a reporter, a journalist?" Krista said. "Sure I am. Incredible stories like this don't come down the pike very often. But as a future MacAllister?" She waved her hands in the air. "No, no, no. Not one word of this can leak out. Nothing."

Jesse studied Krista for another long moment, then nodded. "Right," he said, forcing the sudden unease he'd registered out of his mind. "You just threw me for a second there. So. Ryan—Dad—you'll contact this Judge Spencer?"

"Consider it done," Ryan said. "Isn't this something, Deedee? Now we're getting another daughter, too. Wouldn't my father be pleased?"

"Robert and Margaret are smiling, my darling," Deedee said, covering one of Ryan's hands with her own. "They're together again, and they're smiling." She stared into space. "Now if I could just figure out what's what with Teddy. That boy is avoiding me. Surely this business about where he and Rosalie should live hasn't caused them to end their relationship, has it? Ryan?"

"You'll have to talk to Teddy about that," he said, raising both hands.

"Oh, I can't believe he would be so foolish to allow something like that to destroy what he has with the woman he loves," Deedee said. "He does love Rosalie, doesn't he? Yes, of course he does. A mother knows these things. Hmm. The fact that he doesn't want to speak to me says he's done something dumb. Why doesn't he come to me for advice?"

"Because, Mom," Jesse said quietly, "there are some things in life that a guy just has to figure out on his own. Been there, done that. What Teddy needs now is time and space, just as I did. You did it for me, now you have to do it for him."

"Oh, phooey," Deedee said. "All right. I hear you, Jesse, and I'll do as you say but...phooey."

Chapter 15

In the late afternoon three days later, Jesse shook hands with Judge Ronald Spencer in his nicely furnished chambers at the courthouse.

"I really appreciate this, sir," Jesse said. "Thank you very much."

"It's my pleasure," Ron Spencer said, then looked at Ryan. "Congratulations on your new son, Ryan. I think that's the best way to look at it. If you dwell on all the years you missed out on having Jesse with you, you'll just chase your own thoughts in circles. Better to be grateful that the wrong was set to rights at long last." He furrowed his brow. "It's hard to imagine that people would steal a newborn baby, but enough of that."

"You're right," Ryan said. "We're just glad that Jesse

is home now. As I said, though, Ron, it's vitally important that this story doesn't get sniffed out by the press."

"I'll make certain of that," he promised. "I'll have my secretary walk it through the recording process, then file it away. It won't go into the stack of court business the reporters have access to each day." He paused. "Are you and Ted up for some golf soon?"

"Anytime you're free," Ryan said. "Winner buys lunch. I like that bet. I can't remember when I've had to pick up the tab for that meal. Of the three of us, I always have the score from hell."

Judge Spencer laughed, then saw Ryan and Jesse to the door. A few minutes later he picked up the document to change Jesse's name and stepped out of his chambers to speak to his secretary.

"Sharon," he said. "I'd like you to take this to the recording office, see that it's tended to properly, then bring it back and file it, please. Tell the clerk over there that this is highly confidential and not to be discussed with anyone."

"Yes, sir," Sharon said, getting to her feet and accepting the paper.

"Good. I'm gone for today. See you tomorrow. Have a nice evening."

"You, too, Judge Spencer," Sharon said, smiling. "Oh, are the other court-proceeding documents signed? I should get them to the secretary who types them up for the newspaper and has to deal with the hovering reporters."

"Yes, they're on my desk."

"Fine. I'll drop them off on my way to get this one recorded."

Ron nodded, then left her outer office, emerging into the busy corridor beyond. Sharon set the paper Jesse and the judge had signed on her desk and went into the judge's chambers.

The moment she disappeared from view, Curtis Cushman, the reporter from the television station where Krista worked, slipped into Sharon's office. He had stopped outside her office to tie his shoe, and overheard Judge Spencer's instructions to his secretary. Curtis grabbed the document Sharon had left on her desk, his eyes widening as he read it as quickly as possible.

"Unreal," he whispered, then set the paper back on the desk exactly the way it had been. He hurried toward the door. "Pay dirt. Big time."

When Ryan drove Jesse back to Krista's apartment building, he agreed to come up and have a cool drink before heading home.

"Krista already left for work," Jesse said, as they stepped out of the elevator on her floor. "She's going to call me later and see if things went smoothly at the courthouse."

"It's a done deal," Ryan said, patting Jesse on the back. "You're officially Jesse MacAllister now. I'd better have tissues ready for Deedee when she returns from her volunteer-group meeting at the hospital. She'll be all weepy when I tell her the document has been filed."

Jesse nodded and chuckled, then looked up and quickened his step.

"There's Teddy leaning against the wall next to Krista's door. Hey, brother, we didn't expect to find you here."

Teddy straightened and greeted the pair. "I couldn't find anyone home anywhere," he said. "So I decided to wait here."

"Come on in," Jesse said, unlocking the door. "Want some iced tea? Soda? Beer?"

"No, I don't have time," Teddy said, as Jesse closed the door. "I'm glad you're here, Dad. You and Mom weren't home and I didn't want to leave this news on your answering machine."

"That sounds rather ominous," Ryan said, frowning. "What's going on?"

"I'm leaving for Italy in a few hours," Teddy said. "Thanks to a discussion I had with Jesse on the subject the other night, I now know I've been a real jerk, a fool, who had his priorities wrong in regard to Rosalie."

Jesse grinned. "The hamburgers and the football game."

"Yeah," his brother said, matching the smile.

"The what?" Ryan asked, totally confused.

"Dad," Teddy said, serious again. "I'm going to Italy to beg Rosalie to forgive me for being so selfish. I'd made up my mind how things should be, and didn't take her feelings into consideration. I'm planning to tell her that I'll live in Italy with her so she can be near her family. One of us has to give on the topic, and it's going to be me. I just hope I'm not too late, haven't hurt her too much."

"I'm proud of you, son," Ryan said. "Heaven knows we'll miss you, but you're doing the right thing. Rosalie must come first with you, not the MacAllister clan."

"I realize that now," Teddy said. "If things go with Rosalie as I hope and pray, I'll be back soon to take care of getting my house on the market and what have you. If I don't connect with Mom before my flight tonight, tell her what is going on and let her know I'll call her." He sighed. "Or show up on your doorstep with a heart that's smashed to smithereens."

"Think positive," Ryan said, giving him a quick hug. "Remember, never underestimate—"

"The power of love," Teddy and Jesse chimed in unison.

"Right," Ryan said.

"Thanks, brother," Teddy said, shaking Jesse's hand. "You really made me come out of the ether. Well, wish me luck."

"You've got it," Jesse said, then Teddy left the apartment.

"I hope Rosalie loves him enough to forgive him," Ryan murmured, frowning.

"Yeah," Jesse said. "I wonder if she will forgive him."

"Son," Ryan said, "if we knew the answer to that one it would mean we understand how women's minds work. That will never happen. We'll just have to wait to hear from Teddy to learn how this scenario ended up." He paused. "Now, what's this about hamburgers and a football game?"

Jesse laughed. "Let's get a soda and I'll explain the great theory of Jesse MacAllister. Jesse MacAllister...I really like the sound of that."

Teddy frowned as he had to wait at the end of his driveway for a taxi to pull out before he could get in.

"Unexpected company?" he said aloud, unable to see the front porch as he finally drove forward, due to the tall trees in the front yard. "Not now, whoever you are, because I'm on my way to my future...I hope."

As Teddy strode across the lawn, he wondered who had just decided to pay him a visit with no warning, and an edgy anger began to build within him. When the porch finally came into view, he stopped so suddenly, he staggered slightly.

"Rosalie?" he cried, starting off again slowly. "No, I'm dreaming, totally losing it."

"Hello, Teddy," Rosalie said, stepping between two suitcases.

They stopped about two feet apart, each drinking in the sight of the other.

"I was going—"

"I came—" Rosalie said at the same time.

"You first," Teddy said.

"No, you."

"Yeah, okay." Teddy drew a steadying breath. "I have reservations on a flight to Italy tonight, Rosalie.

I was going over there to beg you to forgive me for being such a selfish jerk. I'll live in Italy with you. Hell, I'll live at the North Pole if that's what you want, just as long as we're together. I got my priorities wrong and I'm so damn sorry. Will you, Rosalie? Forgive me? Please? And marry me and—"

Rosalie burst into tears.

"Oh, no, no, don't cry," Teddy said, stepping forward and wrapping his arms around her. "I blew it, didn't I? What did I say wrong just now? I love you. I forgot to tell you that I love you. I'm a little shook up here, you know. Rosalie, I love you.

"I don't want to go through life without you. I'd be so alone and lonely. I want us to be one of the two by two couples, and I'll explain later about the hamburgers. Don't cry. Okay? And…wait a minute. Rosalie, why are you here?"

Rosalie eased out of his embrace and dashed tears from her cheeks. She sniffed and he whipped a pristine white handkerchief from his back pocket and gave it to her.

"I'm here," she said, then dabbed at her nose, "because I couldn't bear being there without you. I missed you so much. I was performing like a spoiled baby who wanted everything her way or forget it. I love you, Teddy. I'll go wherever you are and stand proudly by your side as your wife. I love my family, but they don't come first, not anymore, not when I'm a woman in love with a wonderful man I want to spend the rest of my life with, have babies with. I'm so sorry I acted the way I did. I'm here to ask you to forgive me."

Teddy whooped with joy, grasped Rosalie by the waist and swung her around until she begged for mercy. He set her on her feet again and kissed her deeply.

"I love you, I love you, I love you," he said, when he finally ended the kiss. "We're going to have a fantastic life together. Oh, man, this is so great. Listen, how's this plan? We'll live six months here, six months in Italy. I bet the companies we work for will go for that. If not, we'll start our own company.

"Then, my sweet, when it's time for our firstborn child—the first of many—to start school, we'll settle in Italy. I want our kids to speak both languages of their heritage, really understand who they are, their roots, and Italy is the place to do that, with frequent visits back here, of course. Okay? Say yes? Please? Rosalie? Oh, God, you're crying again. What did I mess up?"

"Nothing, nothing," Rosalie said, smiling through her tears. "And yes, yes, *sì, sì,* yes, I will marry you and we'll have oodles of babies, and I think your plan is splendid.

"Oh, my darling Teddy, I love you with my whole heart, soul and mind. And, Teddy? The lady next door is standing on her porch watching the whole thing we're doing here, and she has a cell phone pressed to her ear to share it with someone else."

Teddy laughed, swept Rosalie up in his arms, then turned and bowed to the woman next door, who smiled and blew them a kiss.

"The next act in this play, however," he said, close to Rosalie's ear, "is not for public view. I'm going to take you inside and make slow, sweet love with you for hours. How does that sound, Ms. Cantelli?"

"Perfect, Mr. MacAllister," she said. "Absolutely perfect."

During the next week MacAllister gatherings were held so that everyone could get to know Rosalie. It was love at first sight. The MacAllisters welcomed Teddy's bride-to-be to the family with warmth and sincerity, and Rosalie wore a constant smile as she attempted to remember names. Time after time she reached out eagerly to hold yet another MacAllister baby, which caused Deedee to beam.

Congratulations and best wishes were also extended to Krista and Jesse on their future marriage. Everyone understood the need for secrecy as far as not revealing that Jesse was Deedee and Ryan's son.

"I bet someone would make a movie out of Jesse's story," Forrest said, at one of the backyard barbecues.

"Could they do that without his permission?" Michael asked.

"Sure," Forrest said. "They'd change the names, but add enough stuff that there would be no doubt in anyone's mind that it was about the MacAllisters. We wouldn't have a legal leg to stand on. It's enough to give me cold chills."

"Don't even think about the press getting wind of this," Deedee said with a shudder. "What a nightmare that would be. The reporters would hound all of us day and night. I feel badly for Krista that she can't have a big, fancy wedding, which is every girl's dream, but it just isn't possible under the circumstances."

"I don't mind at all," Krista said. "Just concentrate on the coming wedding of Teddy and Rosalie and the trip to Italy that's on the agenda in a couple of months for everyone who is able to go to the gala event."

"An Italian wedding. That is going to be one fine celebration," Forrest said. "Jillian and I will be there with bells on."

"Me, too," Teddy said, smiling at Rosalie.

Teddy took Rosalie to Disneyland and she was enchanted with the magical kingdom. Two weeks after Rosalie had arrived in Ventura, Deedee and Ryan drove the couple to the airport to catch their plane for Italy.

"Call soon," Deedee said, sniffling.

"We will, Mom," Teddy promised, smiling. "You won't even miss us, though. You have lots of shopping to do for the trip to Italy for the wedding."

"Oh," Deedee said, brightening. "That's true, isn't it? Rosalie, let me know the minute you decide on your color scheme for the wedding so I can find the perfect mother-of-the-groom dress. Hmm. I'd best speak with your mother at that point so we don't show up in the same shade of whatever. I'll need matching shoes, of course. Goodness, so much to do."

"And she's off and running, folks," Ryan said, laughing. "Just keep out of her way."

Deedee smiled through happy tears as she and Ryan watched the airplane carrying Teddy and Rosalie disappear into the clouds.

"All three of our children have found true love, Ryan," she said, then dabbed at her nose with a tissue. "That is so wonderful."

"They take after their parents," he said, tucking her close to his side and dropping a kiss on the top of her head. "Come on, my sweet. Let's go home."

Later that same day Curtis Cushman arrived at the Ventura airport after a trip to Nevada. He held tightly to a briefcase as he strode through the crowds in the terminal, making no attempt to hide the smug smile on his face. After a series of lies to some and bribes to others, he had discovered the truth about Jesse Burke, who had so quietly changed his name to Jesse MacAllister.

"This is my ticket to the top," Curtis said under his breath as he took his place in line for a taxi after collecting his suitcase.

When Krista arrived at the television station the next afternoon she was told that the producer of the news programs, Milton Jones, wanted to see her. She entered his office to find Curtis Cushman sitting in one of the chairs opposite Milton's desk. She greeted Curtis coolly, then sat in the other chair, which Milton gestured to.

"We're changing the format for the six and ten news

today, Krista," Milton said. "We'll flash the breaking news logo on the screen as soon as we go on the air, then you introduce Curtis, who will be sitting next to you at the anchor desk. It's his story and he's going to report it, ending with the statement that he'll be approaching the MacAllisters for their reactions and comments and blah, blah, blah. Got that?"

"The MacAllisters?" Krista said, feeling the color drain from her face.

Milton frowned. "We all know that you're friends with the MacAllisters, Krista. I would not be a happy man if I learned that you knew about this and didn't give it to this station as an exclusive. I'm giving you the benefit of the doubt here because Curtis has done a helluva job of discovering the truth. This is going to put him and this station on the map."

"What are you talking about?" Krista asked, gripping the arms of the chair.

"Jesse Burke," Curtis said. "Also known as Jesse MacAllister. I have it all." He splayed one hand on his heart. "It's beautiful. The infant snatched at birth, ripped away from his parents and twin sister, only to show up thirty-odd years later. I'm telling you, I couldn't have fantasized about a story this great. I did one fine job of investigating to get this stuff and it's mine. All mine, cute Krista. The camera will be on me when this beauty breaks."

"Oh, my God," Krista said. "No. No. You can't report that. Milton, listen to me. Think about what you're doing. This is a gross invasion of personal privacy. Reporters will flock from around the country to cover this. You'll be forcing the MacAllister family into a living nightmare. You can't do this to them. Please. It's not right."

"It's big news," Milton said, leaning forward, "and we're going to be the first to report it, thanks to Curtis. You'll do the lead-in to it, then the camera will switch to him."

"No. Absolutely not. I won't take part in this travesty in any manner," Krista said. "What you're doing is wrong, terribly wrong."

Milton pointed a chubby finger at her. "You'll do as you're told. You're under contract, remember? You don't pick and choose what you report, you do as I decide, follow my orders. People are accustomed to seeing your face first when they tune in the news and that's what I want before Curtis gets the mike."

Krista jumped to her feet. "No. I won't do it. I refuse, Milton."

"You will if you want to keep your job here, miss," Milton said, nearly yelling.

"Then I quit," Krista said, planting her hands flat on the producer's desk. "Do you hear me, Milton? This is not a threat, it's a promise. If you allow Curtis to disrupt the lives of that wonderful family for his own gain I will walk out of here and never come back."

"Go ahead and quit," Curtis said. "I'm very prepared to take your spot as anchor, Krista, and with this story I will have earned it."

"You'd better read the fine print in your contract,

Krista," Milton said. "Oh, you can quit, but you have to stay on the air for two weeks after giving notice. You can't take any yet unreported news with you, either, once you've given notice you're terminating. In other words, if you warn the MacAllisters between now and six o'clock about this story breaking, or walk off the set now, I will sue you, tie you up in court so long you won't have a penny to your name, or a reputation left that will get you even a job as a stringer on a crummy little newspaper somewhere."

"My God," Krista said, sinking back onto her chair as her trembling legs refused to support her another second.

"Hey, maybe the rich and oh-so-wonderful MacAllisters will support you, toss you a crust of bread from time to time," Curtis said, a nasty edge to his voice, "for being so noble. That will be your only hope of eating, cocky Krista. Mooch off the MacAllisters. Hey, latch on to this Jesse guy, why don't you?" he added. "I found out the California bar exam is being given in a month and his name is on the list to take it. He can be your meal ticket down the line. No, forget that. The MacAllisters are movers and shakers. They don't mess with people who are washed up, are looking for hand-outs. Nope, ol' Jesse wouldn't be interested in you. You'd just drag him down as he's attempting to start a new career in Ventura."

Milton leaned back in his chair and laced his hands over his bulging belly. "Think about it, Krista," he said. "The MacAllisters are going to have a lot to deal with as of six o'clock tonight. Do you want to add to their problems by having us continually report your personal connection to them as we drag you through the courts?"

"No, I…no," Krista whispered. "I don't want to be the cause of more trouble."

"Then be a good little girl. Keep your mouth shut between now and six," Milton said, "and put in your two weeks as the anchor per the terms of your contract. To do otherwise will only increase the fodder the press will have to bombard the MacAllisters with."

"You're despicable," Krista said, getting to her feet. "Both of you. You leave me no choice but to comply to the terms of my contract, because the MacAllisters are like family to me. But I hope you both rot in hell."

"Oh, my," Curtis said, clapping his hands slowly. "How very dramatic and corny, my dear. I'll see you on the set at six. I suggest you spend some extra time in makeup, sweetness, because you're a tad pale around the edges. You're just not looking like your usual perky, pretty self, Ms. Kelly."

Krista rushed from the room, nearly stumbling as tears filled her eyes and blurred her vision. She ran to her dressing room, snatched up the receiver to the telephone to call Jesse, to warn him, then replaced it, her shoulders slumping in defeat.

She sank onto a chair, buried her face in her hands and wept.

Chapter 16

Jesse placed the letter carefully on the coffee table and read it for the umpteenth time since it had arrived in the mail that afternoon.

He would leave it right there, he decided, and Krista would see it when she got home from work, read the words that said he was scheduled to take the California bar exam. Words that meant they would be one step closer to being married and officially starting their life together.

"Fantastic," he said, then glanced at his watch. "Whoa. My lady is about to smile at me from the tube."

He pressed the remote and the television hummed to life on the proper station. The theme music played, the station logo materialized, then the announcement of "Breaking News" filled the screen.

Jesse crossed his sock-clad feet on top of the coffee table and settled back to watch his Krista report the six o'clock news, breaking bulletins and otherwise.

"Good evening, Ven...Ventura," Krista said, no hint of a smile on her face. "I'm...Krista Kelly."

Jesse frowned.

Something was wrong, he thought. Something was wrong with Krista.

"We're starting our broadcast tonight," she continued, "with a breaking story that I don't... What I mean is, I'm going to turn the microphone over to Curtis Cushman, who is here on the anchor desk with me. Curtis?"

The camera shifted to Curtis, who smiled, then became serious in the next instant.

"Thank you, Krista. Ladies and gentlemen, the story I am about to tell you will sound unbelievable, almost beyond anyone's imagination, but I assure you that it is true." He paused. "Everyone here in Ventura is familiar with the larger-than-life MacAllister family. We did, in fact, recently devote a great deal of airtime to cover the funeral of Robert MacAllister, the head of this highly respected group of people."

Jesse pulled his feet to the floor and leaned forward, his elbows propped on his knees as he riveted his gaze on the television screen.

"But the MacAllisters have a secret," Curtis said, "a dark, ominous event that took place over thirty-two years ago and has just come to light.

"Picture if you will a raging storm in the dead of

night in rural Nevada. This is farm country, small ranches they are called, with the homes miles apart, and dirt roads turning to unpassable trenches of mud from the pounding rain.

"Picture a young couple whose vehicle is stuck in that mud. That couple is Ryan and Deedee MacAllister, and they are expecting their second child in a few weeks. What they aren't aware of at that point is that Deedee MacAllister is carrying twins—a girl and a boy. Two babies. Not one. Two.

"Picture Deedee and Ryan's joy and relief as they see the lights of a small cabin in the distance, a refuge from the storm. But what takes place within that cabin is a horror story that is hard to comprehend."

As Curtis continued speaking, a strange buzzing noise in Jesse's head was louder than the broadcaster's voice.

"No," he said, getting to his feet, then swaying slightly. "No, Krista, tell me you didn't do this. But you did, didn't you? All of Ventura is hearing what you've done. Oh, God, why? Why, Krista?"

It would be the story of the year. An award winner for whichever reporter broke it first. I wouldn't be surprised if there was a book deal in the soup, too. That reporter could write his, or her, own ticket from there on out.

Jesse's heart began to race as he recalled what Krista had said in that wistful voice at his parents' house.

The temptation had been too great, the lure of fame and fortune bigger, stronger than her love for him and her loyalty to the MacAllister family.

They were going for the maximum dramatic presentation at the television station. That Curtis guy was telling the story, then Krista would announce that she was the one to discover the truth of it. But, dear viewers, it was too difficult for her to report because of her close relationship with the MacAllister family, too emotional for her to tell the sordid tale.

"No, no, no," Jesse said, striding to the television set and smacking the off button. "Shut up. Just shut the hell up."

He dragged shaking hands through his hair, then began to pace around the room with jerky steps.

It had happened again, he thought incredulously. He'd been betrayed by someone he loved unconditionally, had come to trust with every fiber of his being. Krista was not who she had presented herself to be. She didn't love him. Hell no. He was a stepping-stone to where she intended to rise to in her career. He was the walking, talking story of the year.

Krista was Phyllis Burke, and Joe Burke, and Maddie Clemens. Evil. Conniving. Self-centered, selfish, not caring who she hurt as long as her goals were achieved.

Lies. So many lies had flowed like a never-ending stream from Krista's enticing lips. *I love you so much, Jesse, my husband.*

I love you to pieces, my precious son, Phyllis had said over and over.

I'm so proud to be your father, Joe had declared through the years.

You're like the son I never had, Maddie had told him, even producing glistening tears.

I love you so much, Jesse, my husband.

Words based on dark, evil lies. A secret agenda. Betrayed. Again. A fool. Again. His heart shattered once again. Because he had loved, believed in, trusted, the wrong person. Again.

He had to get out of here, Jesse thought frantically, his eyes darting around the room. He had to leave this place of lies and betrayal. He was being crushed under the weight of it, couldn't breathe, could hardly see past the red haze swirling before his eyes.

Go. He had to go.

Jesse staggered down the hall to the bedroom. He grabbed his suitcase from the closet in Krista's room, then scooped an armload of clothes from the dresser drawer, stuffing them into the luggage. He snatched his shaving kit from the bathroom and threw that on top of the rumpled clothing. He swept his gaze over the room, seeing a pair of his shoes on the floor and tugging them onto his feet.

There was a book he was in the middle of reading, clean handkerchiefs in a stack on the dressertop, his change in a shell dish next to them, but he didn't have time to gather all his belongings.

No more time. No more air in this room. No more strength to bear the weight of deception that was a nearly living entity determined to drain the very life from his body.

He closed and latched the suitcase and swung it off

the bed, knocking a lamp from the nightstand onto the floor in the process. He ignored it and hurried back down the hall, then across the living room and out the door, leaving it standing open behind him.

He had to go. Run from the lies.

Run, Jesse, run, his mind screamed. Run.

The next thing that Jesse was consciously aware of was turning onto the street where Deedee and Ryan lived. He slammed on the brakes and leaned over the steering wheel as he looked down the block, seeing the cars in front of his parents' home, the van with the transmitting saucer on top, the milling people.

The vultures, the reporters, were already here, he realized, fury building within him. This was Krista's doing. It would be the same at the home of every Mac-Allister in Ventura. He had nowhere to go, nowhere to hide from those who would push the microphones in his face and demand he bare his soul to them. His entire family would be hounded because of Krista Kelly and her lies and betrayal.

Jesse spun the car around on screeching tires and drove away into the night.

Between the six and ten o'clock newscasts Krista tried desperately to reach Jesse by telephone at her apartment, only to hear her own voice on the answering machine time and again.

She called every MacAllister in the family, but no one was picking up the phone, no one was allowing her the chance to tell them how sorry she was, that it wasn't her fault, that she hadn't done this horrendous thing. No one would talk to her.

Milton had ordered that she was not to leave the station between the six and ten news, and she'd nodded obediently, totally defeated by the powerful man. He had made it chillingly clear that the lawsuit he would launch against her would cause further grief for the MacAllisters, and she couldn't bear the thought of that.

She tried once more to find Jesse and once again heard her own cheerful voice urging the caller to leave a message and she'd phone back as soon as possible.

Sitting in her dressing room, she wrapped her hands around her elbows and rocked back and forth.

Jesse, she thought desperately. I didn't do this, my darling, I swear to you I didn't. I love you, Jesse. I didn't betray you, your trust in me, your love for me. I didn't. Oh, please, Jesse, hear me, somehow hear me. Jesse?

But there was no answering message from Jesse in the small room. Krista was convinced there was just the haunting echo of her heart breaking into a million pieces.

Somehow, Krista managed to make it through the ten o'clock news and Curtis's repeat performance of revealing the incredible story about the MacAllisters.

After the newscast she drove above the speed limit to her apartment, her heart sinking when she saw the open door, then the chilling evidence inside of Jesse's obvious rush to leave.

She cleaned up the broken pottery from the lamp in the bedroom, smoothed and straightened the clothes Jesse didn't take with him, then closed the dresser drawers. It was only when she sank onto the sofa in the living room that she realized tears were streaking her cheeks. With a shaking hand she picked up the letter regarding the scheduling of the bar exam and cradled it to her chest, allowing fresh tears to flow.

God, she thought, carefully placing the letter back on the coffee table, then pressing fingertips to her throbbing temples, she couldn't stand the silence in this room. She couldn't bear the image in her mind of what Jesse must be thinking about her. He was obviously convinced that she had planned all along to further her career by betraying his trust, his love for her, and revealing the truth about what had taken place when he and Sarah were born.

Oh, she wished she could get angry at Jesse, decide that if he truly loved her he would know, in his heart, his mind and soul, that she was innocent of any wrongdoing. That what had happened had been beyond her control, beyond her ability to stop it from taking place.

But there was no anger within her to reach for because everything, *everything* pointed to her guilt. She had sat right next to Curtis on that anchor desk and listened without interruption as he destroyed the peaceful lives of the entire MacAllister family.

The only chance, the very slim chance she had to convince Jesse of her innocence, to make him realize he had not been wrong to love and trust in her, was to see him, talk to him, tell him exactly what Curtis and Milton had done.

But she didn't know where Jesse was.

He was gone.

"So, damn it, Krista Kelly," she said, getting to her feet. "Find him. Don't give up without a fight on the wondrous future you could have with him."

Dashing the lingering tears from her cheeks, Krista picked up the phone on the end table, sat back down on the sofa and punched in Deedee and Ryan's number. She once again got the answering machine after four rings, with Ryan's cheerful voice telling the caller to leave a message.

"Deedee, Ryan," she said, "this is Krista. I know it's terribly late for me to be calling, but please pick up. I need to talk to you. Please."

"Krista?" Deedee said, coming on the line. "Oh, my darling girl, where are you?"

"I'm at home and, Deedee, you called me darling girl. You're not angry at me? I was prepared to beg you to listen to me, allow me to explain what happened, why the story was on the news and—"

"Krista, Krista," Deedee said, "slow down, calm down. Ryan and I don't believe for one minute that you had anything to do with what took place on the news tonight. It was that sleazy Curtis person, wasn't it? Oh, he gives me the creeps. Heaven knows how he discovered the truth about Jesse, the Burkes, the whole sordid tale.

"The reporters pounced on us right after the six

o'clock news and we just closed the drapes and refused to answer the phone or the insistent pounding on the door. I've spoken to Sarah and the press is there, too, but she and Barry are ignoring them. I'd hate to be in one of those reporters' shoes if they attempt to approach those kids tomorrow. Color that reporter dead as a post.

"I'm sure Jesse is upset about this," Deedee rambled on in a distressed voice. "Well, we all are, but we'll just have to weather the storm. It will be old news once something more exciting happens in Ventura. We've been MacAllisters for a long time, sweetie, and this people-on-our-lawn nonsense has happened before for various reasons. It's new to Jesse, though. How is he holding up?"

"He's gone, Deedee," Krista said, a sob catching in her throat. "I'm so grateful to you, all of you, for trusting in me, knowing I didn't do this, but Jesse believes I did. He grabbed some of his clothes and he's gone. I have no idea where he is."

"Oh, my goodness, what on earth is the matter with him?" Deedee said. "He shouldn't have doubted for one second that you love him. No, now wait a minute, Krista, let's be fair about this. Jesse's world as he had known it all of his life was destroyed when he learned the truth about what Maddie Clemens and the Burkes did all those years ago. He came to Ventura feeling betrayed, disillusioned, not trusting anyone, which is understandable. Are you with me here?"

"Yes," Krista said, then sniffled.

"It's taken Jesse all these weeks to take down that wall he built around himself, but he did it, brick by emotional brick. He fell in love with you, trusted and believed in you. He accepted me and Ryan as his parents and took his rightful place among us as a MacAllister. It was a difficult journey for him to make, yet he did it, thank God. But he's still fragile, Krista. His wounds are just barely healed and are still tender and painful. Understand?"

"I guess so. Yes. Okay."

"What happened tonight must have ripped those wounds wide open again," Deedee said. "Brought back all the painful memories in full force. He's not thinking straight right now, Krista. He's been thrown for a loop, doesn't know how to deal with the shock of what he saw and heard on the newscast.

"Oh, honey, don't you see? It's not you he's upset with, not really, even though he believes he is. It's himself. He's raging in anger at himself. He thinks he trusted and loved the wrong person again. He thinks you betrayed him, but his pain is *his* fault, he's convinced, because he let down his guard and allowed himself to fall in love with you."

"But I didn't betray him, Deedee."

"I know that. All the MacAllisters know that. Jesse will come to realize that, too, once he's had time to calm down and think things through. He believes the worst of you at the moment, which makes him so angry at himself he could spit nails.

"Give him some time and space, Krista. You love

him, so wait for him. I waited thirty-two years for him, although I didn't know I was, and he's worth it. Just center your thoughts on how much you love him, how much he loves you, the power of that love…and wait."

"But what if he never comes to trust and believe in me again, Deedee?"

"Remember what Robert taught all of us. Never underestimate the power of love. Be patient. Ryan and I will attempt to get through to Jesse if he contacts us, make him realize he jumped to the wrong conclusions, but it may be something he has to figure out on his own."

"But where is he? Where has he disappeared to?"

"I don't know, Krista." Deedee laughed softly. "But more power to him. Wherever he is, the reporters don't know, either, and he isn't being bugged to pieces the way we are. Goodness, look at the bright side. The truth is out about who Jesse is. So if you want a big wedding—every-girl's-dream wedding—you can have it."

"Not if there's no groom," Krista said miserably.

"Phooey on that thought. Go to bed and get some sleep. Everything will look better in the morning. Those yo-yos better not tromp through my flower beds out front if they know what's good for them. Their morning isn't going to be better if they do that, by gum. Good night. Sleep tight. We love you."

"Good night, Deedee, and thank you so much, so very much."

Deedee replaced the phone receiver on the nightstand, then looked at Ryan, who was next to her in the bed.

"Nicely done, my lovely wife," he said. "You are a wise, wonderful and loving woman." He frowned. "I take it Jesse believes that Krista revealed the truth about him and what happened that night in Nevada?"

"Yes, he does," Deedee said, sighing. "But it's understandable under the circumstances. He's not that steady on his emotional feet yet to be able to deal with this right off the bat. He needs time and space."

"And the power of love."

"And the power of love, yes. Our son had better come to his senses, Ryan, or he's going to lose Krista, and that would be heartbreaking, just devastating. Heavens, he will calm down and realize that Krista is innocent of any wrongdoing, won't he?"

"I certainly hope so," Ryan said. "The problem is he's a man, and men have been messing things up in this world since the beginning of time."

"Ah, yes, but said man is loved by a fantastic woman, and women have been sweeping away those messes for as long as they have been made by the male species."

"'Tis true. Jesse and Krista are meant to be together. We'll just have to believe that will be the ultimate outcome of this particular mess. Now then, let's get some sleep. Tomorrow is going to be a long day because those nasties outside have staying power, as we know from past experience, and it's going to take a great amount of patience to deal with them. Good night, my darling Deedee. I love you."

"Good night, Ryan. I love you, too."

* * *

Far into the night Jesse lay on the lumpy bed in the dingy motel where he'd registered under the name of James Jones. He stared up into the darkness, knowing sleep wouldn't come because his mind was taunting him, raging at him for being so gullible, so quick to lower his guard and fall victim to a person who was not who she had presented herself to be.

And he couldn't sleep because his heart was aching with the knowledge that all he'd believed he was going to have with Krista Kelly would never be. She didn't love him, but had used him for her own gain.

Why had she taken it so far? Been so incredibly cruel? She'd made love with him, told him that she loved him as much as he loved her, had accepted his proposal of marriage with what he now knew to be phoney tears of joy. She'd had all the details of the bizarre tale of what the Burkes and Maddie had done by then, so why had she continued on with the duplicity?

Unless…

Unless she really had fallen in love with him, wanted to be his wife, have babies with him and…no. No, if that was true then she would never have divulged the truth on the newscast of what had happened years before, exposed all the MacAllisters to the nightmare of reporters hounding them day and night.

But then again, Krista hadn't been the one to report the tale on the air—it had been that other guy, whatever his name was. Maybe he was the one who had discovered the truth somehow and been determined to further his career by breaking the story, not caring what grief it would cause.

Maybe Krista wasn't guilty of betrayal. No, she had to be because she'd introduced the man—Curtis—and by doing that, had endorsed and supported what he was about to do.

But Krista had obviously been upset when the newscast started, had fumbled over the words she was speaking in a voice that was trembling slightly. What did that mean? And if her goal had been to gain recognition as a reporter, why hadn't she been the one to relate the story to the citizens of Ventura?

His first thought on that, he now remembered, was that Krista would claim she was too emotionally involved with the MacAllisters to present the story herself. But that really didn't make sense. Why dilute her importance, allow the spotlight to be on that Curtis jerk, when the glory was hers to have?

"Ah, hell," Jesse said, dragging his hands through his hair. He was driving himself nuts going over and over this, creating questions he had no answers to, scrambling for something, anything, that would point toward Krista being innocent of what she was obviously guilty of.

He had to face the facts as they stood. He was a fool, a gullible, stupid fool. A part of him never wanted to see or speak to Krista Kelly again. Another aching, painful section of his being wondered how long it would take to stop loving her, stop torturing himself with the memories of all they had shared.

Krista Kelly, Jesse told himself, was an evil, conniving person who didn't care who she hurt as she accomplished her goal. She was not a sweet, caring and thoughtful woman who saw teddy bears in fluffy white clouds in the blue sky that was the exact shade of her beautiful, expressive eyes.

"Ah, Krista," Jesse said, then drew a shuddering breath.

He was so tired, felt as though he'd been beaten with a stick and wouldn't be able to move if someone yelled that the crummy motel was on fire.

He needed to sleep, he thought foggily, just escape from all this for a few hours in blissful slumber. Sleep. He had to sleep. Yes.

Jesse began to drift off, welcoming the dulling of his senses as he allowed the welcomed sleep to claim him. He was not aware that he spoke aloud one more time.

"Oh, my Krista, why couldn't you have been who I believed you to be? Why?"

Jesse's dreams turned into nightmares of being chased by a multitude of huge, white teddy bears, who jumped down from the sky and ran after him as he stumbled away. Menacing bears with the intention of catching him and smothering him under their massive forms until he was gone, simply no longer existed.

Chapter 17

Jesse entered Deedee and Ryan's backyard through the rear gate and made his way forward cautiously in the inky darkness. He finally emerged into the welcoming circle of light created by the beckoning glow from the windows of the house. He ran up the steps of the large deck, then across to the French doors and slipped inside.

"Jesse," Deedee said, rushing to greet him with a hug. "Oh, I'm so glad to see you. Talking to you occasionally on the phone during the past two weeks just hasn't been enough. How are you?"

"Surviving, I guess," he answered, allowing her to take his hand and lead him toward the living room. "I've just stayed holed up there in the motel and spent my days studying for the bar exam."

"Hey, Jesse," Ryan said, coming into the room. "Good to see you. Are you hungry?"

"No, I'm fine, thanks."

"Let's sit down," Ryan suggested. "We asked you to come over tonight because we need to talk."

Jesse nodded and sank onto the sofa. Ryan settled in his favorite recliner and Deedee chose an easy chair. Ryan propped his elbows on the arms of the recliner and made a steeple of his fingers.

"Okay," he said, frowning, "here it is, Jesse. I know from what you've said on the phone and from what Krista has told us that you're convinced she was the one to reveal the truth of what happened when you and Sarah were born, to use the story for her personal career gain."

"I—" Jesse began.

"No," Ryan said, raising one hand. "We're not going to get into a heavy debate about that tonight, because your mother and I believe Krista when she says she had nothing to do with it and was blackmailed into sitting on the anchor desk at the station when Curtis Cushman broke the story. We don't want to go round and round with you about that, because it's really between you and Krista.

"What we need to discuss this evening is the fact that the press is not backing off one iota as far as camping out at MacAllister homes. They're out front right now, which is why we told you to sneak in the back way. We've endured this type of attention before, but nothing this intense, nor for this long. It's taking a toll on all of us and it has to stop."

"Sarah is falling apart," Deedee interjected, "and the children don't want to leave the house in the morning to go to school because the reporters swarm around the car. I've been followed into the grocery store, for heaven's sake, badgered by questions about how I feel about finding out my baby was stolen at birth, and on and on. It's a horrendous situation, Jesse."

"I'm sorry," he said, shaking his head. "This is all my fault."

"No, it isn't," Ryan said, "but we're not going back over that old ground, either. What we're seeking is a solution to this dilemma. One of the questions they hurl at us whenever we emerge from the house is about where you are, and why they haven't seen you coming and going from your parents' home. They want to know if your absence means we're not getting along, haven't welcomed you into the family even though they somehow have learned you changed your name to Mac-Allister. Get the drift?"

"Yes."

"We can't go on like this, Jesse," Deedee said. "We have to regain the peace in our lives. All of us, including you. Little Jesse cried himself to sleep the other night because his best friend, Uncle Jesse, hasn't come to see him for such a long time.

"We think perhaps the best thing to do is to hold a press conference with the stipulation that it's a one-time event. Say we'll answer their questions in exchange for their promise to leave us alone after that."

Jesse narrowed his eyes. "Krista won't like that,

I'm sure. I imagine she'd want an exclusive interview with each of us. After all, it's her claim-to-fame story."

"Damn it, Jesse," Ryan said, nearly yelling, and causing Jesse to jerk in surprise at the loud outburst. "Cut it out. You won't consider for even one second that Krista might be a victim in this as much as the rest of us are."

"Jesse," Deedee said, "have you watched Krista delivering the news on television during the past two weeks?"

"No," he said sullenly.

"Well, if you had," Deedee said, "you'd see how exhausted she is because she isn't sleeping well. No amount of makeup can cover the dark circles under her eyes, nor the fact that she has lost weight. She's devastated, Jesse, because you believe she betrayed you. I had to tell her that you made me promise not to reveal to her where you are staying, so she hasn't even had the opportunity to explain to you what actually happened. She loves you so much."

Jesse shook his head.

"Ohhh, you are a MacAllister all right," Deedee said, throwing up her hands. "You're stubborn, so damnably stubborn."

"We're getting off the track here," Ryan said. "Jesse, would you be willing to take part in a press conference with me, your mother and Sarah, so we can hopefully put this to rest?"

"Yes, of course. I'll do whatever you want me to to end this nightmare," Jesse said. "I sure as hell don't want to discuss in public what happened all those years ago, but I will if it will satisfy the press and get them to move on to something else."

"Good," Ryan said, nodding. "Thank you for that. I'll put things in motion tomorrow to set up the press conference and get it over with as soon as possible."

"Fine," Jesse said.

"And right now," Deedee said, getting to her feet, "it's time for the ten o'clock news."

"I'll be on my way," Jesse said, starting to rise.

"Don't you move, young man," Deedee said, pointing a finger at him. "Don't even think about it."

Jesse sank back onto the sofa and stared at her with wide eyes. "Yes, ma'am," he said.

"Wise decision," Ryan said, chuckling.

Deedee turned on the television, gave Jesse another meaningful look, then settled back onto her chair. The usual logo and music for the news filled the screen, then the camera centered on Krista. Jesse's breath caught and he leaned forward, staring at her image.

"My God," he whispered.

"I told you," Deedee said. "She's exhausted, physically and emotionally spent."

"Good evening, Ventura," Krista said, producing a small smile. "I am here tonight to say goodbye to all of you, as this is my final broadcast for this station."

"What?" Deedee said. "I didn't know she—"

"Hush, honey," Ryan said. "Let's listen to what she has to say."

"Two weeks ago," Krista said, "despite my pleas to

not do so, Curtis Cushman, with the blessings of Milton Jones, the producer of the news, broke the story regarding the MacAllister family and what had happened to them many years ago.

"The MacAllisters' privacy, their lives, and for some of them their hopes and dreams, were destroyed because this station chose to put sensationalism before caring about the hearts, the emotions, of human beings when they reported the devastating facts of what took place when Deedee and Ryan MacAllister's twins were born.

"I can't be a party to that type of reporting. Not ever again. I stayed on here for two weeks under the terms of my contract because of circumstances outlined in a threatening manner by Milton Jones. Now, thankfully, those two weeks are behind me and I can walk away from the people at this station who have no souls."

Tears glistened in Krista's eyes and her voice trembled when she spoke again.

"Good night, Ventura," she said, "and goodbye."

The picture on the screen jiggled for a moment, as though the cameraman didn't know where to direct the lens, then a commercial for detergent came into focus, midway through a smiling homemaker's avid endorsement of the product.

"Wow," Ryan said. "What an incredible lady."

Only then did Jesse realize he had gotten to his feet, his gaze still riveted on the screen. The only thing he heard echoing in his mind was Krista's tear-filled voice and what she had said for all the citizens of Ventura to hear.

"She didn't do it," he said, his voice gritty. "She didn't betray me, didn't lie or deceive me, didn't break our bond, our trust, didn't destroy our love. She's innocent of any wrongdoing and I never gave her a chance to explain. I declared her guilty and turned my back on her. Oh, God, Krista, I'm so sorry."

"Doesn't do much good to tell *us* that," Deedee said, examining her fingernails. "We're not the ones whose heart you broke, Jesse MacAllister."

"Krista will never forgive me for what I did," he said.

"Never underestimate the power…" Ryan pointed one finger in the air.

"Of love," Jesse finished for his father. "It's not powerful enough to undo the damage I've done."

"So you're just going to quit without even trying to get Krista back?" Deedee said. "Shame on you. Are you a MacAllister or not?"

Jesse slipped his hand into the pocket of his slacks and grasped the key chain Robert had given him.

"Yes," he said, determination ringing in his voice. "I am a MacAllister, and MacAllisters don't give up without a fight. This is the most important battle I've fought in my entire life. Oh, man, I'm scared to death. What if Krista won't even listen to me?"

"Goodbye, Jesse," Deedee said.

"Right." He nodded jerkily. "I'm on my way to find her."

"Good luck," Ryan said.

"Right," Jesse repeated, then strode from the room.

"Oh, Ryan," Deedee sighed, when they heard the back door close behind him, "I hope Jesse gets a happy ending just like Teddy did. What do you think Krista's reaction will be?"

"Never underestimate the power—" Ryan boomed.

"Oh, put a cork in it," Deedee interrupted.

Ryan laughed, then grew serious the next moment.

"Well, sweetheart," he said, "before this night is over our son will know if he and Krista are to have a future together. All we can do is wait to hear how it turned out."

"Well, at least we can wait together," Deedee said, with love shining in her eyes.

Jesse drove above the speed limit to the television station, parked his car and went to stand in the shadows by the rear exit. His heart was thundering and a trickle of sweat ran down his chest.

During the drive there he'd attempted to rehearse what he would say to Krista, but hadn't been able to mentally string words together that even began to express how sorry he was for what he had done.

There was no reason on earth why Krista should forgive him. Oh, yes, he believed in Robert MacAllister's philosophy that a person should never underestimate the power of love, but if the love had been destroyed by an idiot like himself, there was no power left to cling to. This was hopeless.

Jesse once again reached into his pocket to clutch the key chain.

But he would try his best, he vowed. Oh, God, his entire future happiness was going to be determined when Krista stepped out of that door—the door that was now opening and spilling light into the darkness. The door that revealed Krista carrying a box that must contain her personal items from her office. There she was. Krista Kelly. His future wife?

Oh, Krista, please. Forgive me.

"Krista," Jesse said quietly, stepping forward.

"Ack!" she shrieked, spinning in the direction of his voice. "Jesse? You frightened me."

"I'm sorry," he said, closing the distance between them. "I didn't mean to scare you. Sorry. What a weak, do-nothing word that isn't big enough or strong enough to cover everything I've done wrong, all the injustices I… But, Krista, I don't know what else to say to you. I heard your broadcast tonight and now know the truth. The thing is I should have believed in you from the beginning."

"Yes," she said, lifting her chin, "you should have. Now if you'll excuse me, I'm very tired, this box is heavy and I'm going home." She turned and started away.

"Wait. Please."

Jesse rushed to stand in front of her and take the box from her arms. "At least let me carry this for you," he offered.

"Fine," she said, moving around him.

Jesse fell in step beside her as she headed toward the far end of the parking lot.

"I thought you had betrayed my trust in you," he said, his voice gritty with emotion. "It was like turning back the clock and learning the truth about Phyllis, Joe and Maddie, and what they did. I feared I had once again trusted and believed in the wrong person.

"Krista, I was so off base and there's no excuse for the way I treated you. All I know is that I love you with my whole heart, my mind, my very soul. You are my life. You are my wife. I am begging you to forgive me, to let us have a chance to follow the dreams, the plans we made together. I want to spend the rest of my years on this earth with you, have babies, grow old together. I don't deserve your forgiveness, I realize that," he added as they reached her car. "But I'm asking, begging for it. Please, Krista? I love you so much, so damn much. Have I destroyed your love for me so completely there's nothing left? Krista?"

She unlocked the car, opened the rear door, and Jesse slid the box onto the seat. She closed the door and met his gaze. The moon was shining brightly in the heavens and cast a silvery glow over them.

"You speak of forgiveness," she said, her voice trembling, "but when are you going to forgive what the Burkes and Maddie Clemens did all those years ago? It was terribly wrong, we all know that, but it was done out of a love so powerful it was greater than rational reasoning. Until you reach deep within yourself for forgiveness for them, you won't be complete, have enough of you to love me and our children the way we deserve to be loved."

Tears spilled onto Krista's cheeks and she swept them away with shaking fingertips.

"Oh, yes, Jesse, I forgive you, because I love you so much that I have no choice in the matter, not really. You are my life, too. My husband. Love *is* powerful enough to overcome the pain we sometimes cause the person of our heart. I want to spend the rest of my days with you, Jesse MacAllister, but I don't want to be in front of a television camera again. I've had quite enough of that. I want to write…stories, articles, all kinds of things. And, oh yes, yes. I want to be your wife, but only if you promise me that you will try with all that you are to forgive Maddie and the Burkes. They loved you, Jesse. It's time to let the anger go. I need, our children need, for you to come to us whole, at peace within yourself. Can you promise me you'll do everything within your grasp to do that?"

"I promise," Jesse said, making no attempt to hide the tears shimmering in his eyes. "Thank you for forgiving me. Thank you. Krista Kelly, will you marry me?"

Krista smiled. It was a beautiful smile, so soft and serene, so womanly, radiating love in its purest form.

"Yes," she said, and that was all she needed to say.

Jesse framed her face in his hands and kissed her gently, reverently, sealing their commitment to their future together.

Eight Months Later

A chill wind whipped across the small cemetery, shredding wilted flowers and scattering scraps of paper dropped by careless hands. Ominously dark clouds rolled across the gray sky with the threat of rain, and thunder rumbled in the distance.

Jesse stood staring at the three graves before him. Maddie Clemens had died several months ago and been buried beside Phyllis and Joe Burke, her dearest friends.

The Burke ranch had at last been sold and Jesse had signed the papers that afternoon, leaving just enough time to make this visit to the cemetery before driving to the next town to catch a plane back to Ventura.

"I came here," Jesse said, directing his words to the grave sites, "because there are things that need to be said, closure to be gained. What you did when I was born was so wrong there are hardly words to describe the depth of it.

"Yet I've come to realize that the power of your love for me was so great you honestly believed you were justified in doing what you did. I forgive you for your misguided judgment, and thank you for the love you bestowed upon me as I was growing up.

"The MacAllister family has forgiven you, and I, your son and theirs, forgive you, too. And Maddie? You were a fine, fine grandmother, just as Robert MacAllister was a terrific grandfather. Rest in peace, all of you. I…" Jesse stopped speaking as tears choked off his words.

"Shall I finish for you?" Krista said, slipping her arm through his.

He nodded.

"This baby," she said, looking at the graves as she splayed one hand on her rounded stomach, "was conceived in love and will be raised with love. Jesse and I want all three of you to know that we plan to name this child, our son, Burke Ryan MacAllister."

"Yes," Jesse whispered.

"Jesse," Krista said, smiling up at him as the first drops of rain began to fall, "let's go home. The future is waiting for us there. Oh, yes, my darling husband, it's time to go home.

* * * * *

If you enjoyed MACALLISTER'S RETURN,
you'll love Joan Elliott Pickart's next story
from Silhouette Special Edition,
coming to you in the fall of 2005.

Bonus Features:

Signature Select

BONUS FEATURES

MacAllister's Return

MacAllister
Family Tree

Throughout the years, Joan Elliott Pickart has delighted readers with her many books about the lives and loves of the MacAllister family and their close friends. MACALLISTER'S RETURN, which is the 19th story in the MacAllister family saga, introduces the long-lost son of Ryan and Deedee MacAllister.

THE MACALLISTER FAMILY TREE

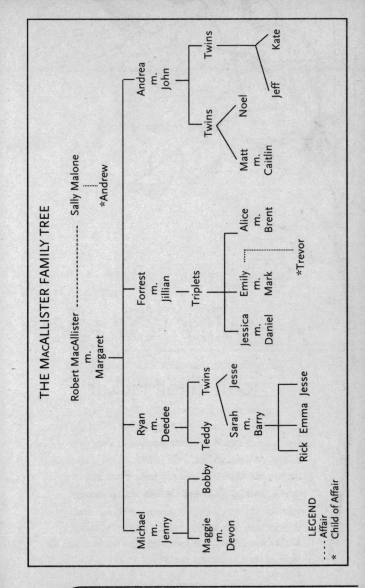

LEGEND
- - - - - Affair
* Child of Affair

Here's a sneak peek...

286

A FAMILY FOR JOEY
by
Joan Elliott Pickart

*In this adorable and emotional tale, Cedar Kennedy, a
gifted child psychologist, treats a troubled boy and
unexpectedly falls deeply in love with the child's uncle,
Mark Chandler. As little Joey heals from his hurt, can the
three of them become a family?* 📖

CHAPTER ONE

Cedar Kennedy glanced at her watch and frowned as she saw that her new client was late for his five o'clock appointment. Remembering that her secretary, Bethany, had left early, Cedar picked up the files she'd been updating from the day's busy schedule and went to the outer office, placing them in Bethany's in box.

She sat down in the chair behind the desk and flipped over the page in the leather-bound book to see what was on the agenda for tomorrow. As she closed the book, the office door opened and a man entered, shoving it closed behind him.

In one quick perusal Cedar cataloged the facts: He was tall, with broad shoulders that stretched the material of a faded plaid shirt to the maximum. His long legs were clad in dusty jeans, and he was wearing heavy work boots. His features—goodness gracious—were rugged and blatantly masculine, and his square jaw was covered in an obvious five-o'clock shadow, indicating that he was one of those men who would have to shave again if he planned a social evening.

He had thick, black hair that was badly in need of a trim, and extremely dark eyes that swept over the reception area, then met her gaze as he approached the desk.

This was, Cedar decided, one very earthy, handsome man. *Very* handsome. He was also late for his appointment and she fully intended to make it clear that being on time was of the utmost importance.

"Mr. Chandler?" Cedar said, getting to her feet.

"Yeah, I'm Mark Chandler," he answered.

Perfect voice, Cedar thought. Deep, sort of rumbly, befitting a man of his size and physique.

Mark Chandler glanced at the open doorway leading to the inner office and lowered his voice when he spoke again.

"I'm a little late for my appointment," he said. "Is this doc a real stickler about people being on time?" He looked at the name plate on the front of the desk. "I'd hate to start out on the wrong foot, Bethany. I'm a desperate man and I need this doc's help. Big time."

He swiped a large hand down the front of one thigh, then the other. "How does she feel about construction site dust? I didn't have a second to spare to go home to shower and change clothes."

Cedar snapped her head back up to meet Mark Chandler's gaze again as she realized she'd been watching the fascinating motion of that hand on those muscled thighs and… Oh, good grief, now he was dragging that hand through that thick hair in a gesture so incredibly male it was enough to make a woman weep.

"I…" she began, then stopped and cleared her throat as she heard the strange little squeak that used to be her voice.

"I've never talked to a shrink before," Mark continued. "Is she stuffy? Does she nod a lot and say 'mmm'? Man, I'm so out of my league being here, but I'm at the end of my rope. What's the best way to get on the good side of this Dr. Kennedy, make her forget I blew it by being late?"

"Mmm," Cedar said, because she just couldn't resist, and tossed a thoughtful frown in for good measure. "I personally don't think Dr. Kennedy is stuffy at all, Mr. Chandler. I'd suggest that you apologize for your tardiness and make it clear you'll be on time for your future appointments."

"Yeah, okay, I can handle that. Well, go for it. Tell the shrinky-dink that I'm here."

"The shrinky-dink?" Cedar said, her eyes widening. "Dr. Kennedy is a psychologist, Mr. Chandler."

"Whatever." Mark sighed. "Man, I'm beat. It was a long, rough day on the job. I'm tired, hungry, need a shower, so let's get this show on the road."

"By all means," Cedar said, coming around the desk. "Heaven forbid that you should be kept waiting now that you've graced us with your presence. Promptness is a virtue, Mr. Chandler. You'd do well to remember that."

"You had a long day, too, huh? I mean, you're not exactly Miss Sunshine, Bethany. You're a very attractive woman, but I'd bet you'd be even prettier if you smiled."

"Mmm," Cedar said, walking past him. "Follow me, please."

"Anywhere," Mark said, then cringed as she shot a glare at him over her shoulder.

Nice, nice, nice, he thought, his gaze sweeping over her as he trudged slowly behind. She had short, wavy blond hair, delicate features and sensational blue eyes. The navy slacks she was wearing with that pale blue sweater made it very clear that she had curves in all the right places. Oh, yeah, very nice. Except for the fact that she was a tad grumpy.

They entered a large, comfortably furnished office and Cedar extended one hand to the pair of easy chairs fronting the mahogany desk. Mark sank onto the closest chair and propped one ankle on his other knee.

Cedar stared at him for a long moment, then moved slowly behind the desk to settle onto the butter-soft, high-backed leather chair.

"Mr. Chandler," she said, folding her hands on top of the file on the desk and dipping her head slightly. "I'm Dr. Cedar Kennedy. Please be on time for your appointments in the future, and if that sounds stuffy that's just tough."

290

"Ohhh, hell," Mark said, closing his eyes for a moment, then looking directly at her again.

To find out what happens between Cedar and Mark, look for the continuation of this story in A FAMILY FOR JOEY by Joan Elliott Pickart, available in Silhouette Special Edition in the fall of 2005.

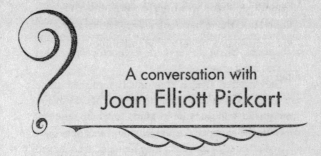

A conversation with
Joan Elliott Pickart

A two-time Romance Writers of America RITA® Award finalist, Joan Elliott Pickart is the author of over ninety-five books. Recently we spoke to Joan Elliott Pickart about her writing career, her family and her favorite pastime activities.

Describe your writing career.
I began writing short stories and very dramatic poems when I was a young girl. Years later, when I was a wife and mother, I sold over forty short stories and articles to magazines. In the early 1980s I took a course at a community college on writing the romance novel. Ten minutes after the class started I knew that was where I belonged and I sold my first romance novel a year later.

What inspired the story?
The character of Robert MacAllister had been a strong force in the MacAllister series from the very

beginning. I felt it was time to say goodbye to Robert and thank him for a job well done as a loving husband, father and grandfather.

Tell us about your family.
When my third daughter finished college I realized it was my turn to do what I wanted to do. So, after ten months of paperwork and red tape, I was able to travel to China and adopt Autumn when she was three months old. She's a happy, healthy, intelligent little sunshine girl and I'm so grateful that she's my daughter.

What are your favorite activities?
Like all writers I know, I am an avid reader. I also enjoy knitting and embroidery projects, working in the garden with Autumn, and we never miss a craft show on the town square.

What do you do for vacation?
Because Autumn is so young our vacations are centered on busy and fun activities. Last year we went to Disneyland with friends and had a super and exhausting time.

Describe your first romance.
I remember having a crush on a boy in fourth grade for no other reason than the fact that he had the same last name as I did.

Tell us about your partner.
I met Scott a zillion years ago on a blind date. We were married for twenty years, divorced, but remained friends. He is now back in my life as a very dear friend, and he thoroughly enjoys being a daddy to Autumn.

What are your favorite books and films?
I have read and reread every book by LaVyrle Spencer. I told her once that she was one of the few authors who could make me cry because her characters were so incredibly real. Like the multitudes, I was pouting when LaVyrle retired. Movies? I can be counted on to weep my way through *Sleepless in Seattle* no matter how many times I see it.

Any last words to readers?
No writer can have a successful career unless people read her books. I'm delighted to have this opportunity to thank everyone who has been so loyal to me for so long and written me such lovely letters saying they enjoy my work.

Getting to know the
CHARACTERS

Isn't it great when you read a book, and you've been so pulled into that world that you want more of the characters you've grown to love? Here are some more character tidbits to satisfy your curiosity.

Jesse Burke (MacAllister?):
He made a shocking discovery at his parents' funeral—one that sent him hell-bent on a quest for answers. Nothing had prepared him for such an upheaval, even though Jesse prided himself on knowing all the facts of every situation—or so he thought.

One event in Jesse's childhood had a powerful effect on him and foreshadowed his discovery at his parents' funeral. After he'd had a nightmare about being lost in a forest, he woke up and went to find his mother and father. Their bedroom was empty, so Jesse went to the kitchen, where he heard whispers. "We can never tell him. We just have to live with the guilt." Jesse knew in his heart that he was the topic of their discussion, but he couldn't listen anymore. This moment made him aware that people sometimes kept secrets.

Krista Kelly:

This beautiful television anchorwoman kept her heart under wraps, until Jesse Burke showed up in town. But love wasn't the only thing Krista craved in life.... When Krista was twelve she was convinced she was destined to be a world-famous movie star but would definitely need a more glamorous name. She informed her parents that she would answer only to the name of Floral Bouquet. After one week her father put his foot down and ended Ms. Bouquet's budding career.

Deedee MacAllister:

As mother bears go, there is none fiercer than Deedee MacAllister. And when Jesse arrived with a strange story of deception and true origins, Deedee was quick to claim Jesse as her own. But Deedee has other admirable qualities.... Although Deedee sold her bookstore and retired years ago she is still an avid reader. She reads five or six books at a time, all in reach throughout the house; in addition, she always has one in her purse. Her husband, Ryan, is amazed that she can keep all the stories straight in her mind.

Ryan MacAllister:

Protective to the core, Ryan wanted to keep his family safe. There was nothing he wouldn't do for his fellow MacAllisters. Ryan went through a very dark period in his life when his first wife was shot and killed causing him to quit the police force. But in time he knew he was meant to wear the uniform and returned to a life of protecting others. When Deedee stole his heart he knew how blessed he was to once again find love.

CHARACTER PROFILE BONUS FEATURE

Sarah MacAllister Barstow:
She had dreams where she sought something vital to her. When Jesse Burke declared himself her long-lost twin, her secret wish was answered and she welcomed him with open arms. Sarah's continual dreams of searching for an unknown something in a cornfield finally made sense when Jesse enters her life and she learned he was raised on a farm where corn was grown. Like Jesse, Sarah can't stand the sight of broccoli.

Teddy and Rosalie:
These two young lovers had a dilemma to solve. For their relationship to flourish, one had to leave his/her homeland. Both computer buffs, Teddy and Rosalie are a match made in heaven. They once purchased coveted tickets to an exclusive showing of "Computers of the Future" to surprise the other, only to discover they were receiving the same gift in return.

Robert MacAllister:
The great patriarch dreamt of joining his beloved Margaret in heaven, but he still had one lesson to teach.... As we bid a fond farewell to Robert, he would want his fans to know this: Robert never gave up on those he loved, even when they were behaving in a less than lovable manner. He would tell us to keep a candle burning in the window and the doorway to our hearts open to welcome those special someones home.

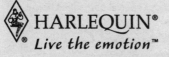

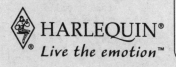

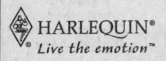

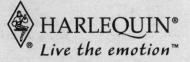

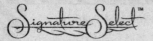
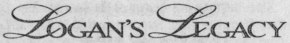

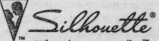

If you enjoyed what you just read,
then we've got an offer you can't resist!

Take 2 bestselling
love stories FREE!

Plus get a FREE surprise gift!

Clip this page and mail it to Silhouette Reader Service™

IN U.S.A.	IN CANADA
3010 Walden Ave.	P.O. Box 609
P.O. Box 1867	Fort Erie, Ontario
Buffalo, N.Y. 14240-1867	L2A 5X3

YES! Please send me 2 free Silhouette Special Edition® novels and my free surprise gift. After receiving them, if I don't wish to receive anymore, I can return the shipping statement marked cancel. If I don't cancel, I will receive 6 brand-new novels every month, before they're available in stores! In the U.S.A., bill me at the bargain price of $4.24 plus 25¢ shipping and handling per book and applicable sales tax, if any*. In Canada, bill me at the bargain price of $4.99 plus 25¢ shipping and handling per book and applicable taxes**. That's the complete price and a savings of at least 10% off the cover prices—what a great deal! I understand that accepting the 2 free books and gift places me under no obligation ever to buy any books. I can always return a shipment and cancel at any time. Even if I never buy another book from Silhouette, the 2 free books and gift are mine to keep forever.

235 SDN DZ9D
335 SDN DZ9E

Name		(PLEASE PRINT)	
Address		Apt.#	
City		State/Prov.	Zip/Postal Code

Not valid to current Silhouette Special Edition® subscribers.

Want to try two free books from another series?
Call 1-800-873-8635 or visit www.morefreebooks.com.

* Terms and prices subject to change without notice. Sales tax applicable in N.Y.
** Canadian residents will be charged applicable provincial taxes and GST.
  All orders subject to approval. Offer limited to one per household.
  ® are registered trademarks owned and used by the trademark owner or its licensee.

SPED04R   ©2004 Harlequin Enterprises Limited

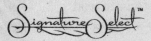

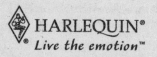